REMAIN SILENT

Newly married and navigating life with a toddler as well as her adopted adolescent son, Manon Bradshaw is happy to be working part-time in the cold cases department of the Cambridgeshire police force. Beneath the surface, however, she is struggling with the day-to-day realities of what she assumed would be domestic bliss: fights, fatigue, and going to couples' counselling alone. But when Manon is on a walk with her young son in a peaceful suburban neighbourhood and discovers the body of a Lithuanian immigrant hanging from a tree with a mysterious note attached, she knows her life is about to change. Suddenly she is back on the job full-force, trying to solve the suicide — or is it a murder? — in what may be the most dangerous and demanding case of her life.

SUSIE STEINER

◆

REMAIN SILENT

Complete and Unabridged

CHARNWOOD
Leicester

First published in Great Britain in 2020 by
The Borough Press
An imprint of HarperCollins*Publishers*
London

First Charnwood Edition
published 2020
by arrangement with
HarperCollins*Publishers*
London

*A catalogue record for this book is available
from the British Library.*

ISBN 978–1–4448–4610–2

Published by
Ulverscroft Limited
Anstey, Leicestershire

Set by Words & Graphics Ltd.
Anstey, Leicestershire
Printed and bound in Great Britain by
T. J. International Ltd., Padstow, Cornwall

This book is printed on acid-free paper

For Eve, with love and gratitude

'Every civilized people on the face of the earth must be fully aware that this country is the asylum of nations, and that it will defend the asylum to the last ounce of its treasure and last drop of its blood. There is no point whatever on which we are prouder and more resolute.'

The Times, 1853

DAY 1
MIDNIGHT

MATIS

His key in the door, he shoulders across the threshold, stumbles wildly up the stairs to the bathroom. He can't risk being beaten for soiling the carpet. His stomach is coiling and despite it being empty, he vomits into the toilet: acid bile. In a strange way, the retching comforts him.

Dimitri is at the bathroom's open doorway.

'Are you all right?' he asks.

Matis, kneeling by the toilet bowl, groans.

Dimitri approaches. 'Too much to drink?' he asks.

When Matis turns to look up at him, Dimitri says, 'My God, what happened to you?'

'Lukas is dead,' Matis sobs. 'I brought him here and now he's dead. I never saw such hatred, Dimitri. Why do they hate us so much?'

Dimitri shrugs, sadly.

'I hope he haunts them out of their beds at night,' says Matis.

'To be haunted, you must have a conscience,' says Dimitri.

'And they have none.'

Dimitri lifts him to his feet. 'Come, you need a drink.'

1

In the kitchen, while Dimitri locates vodka, Matis starts shaking.

Dimitri says, 'The police here, they will look into it properly. Not like back home.' He hands Matis the bottle. Matis swigs. Winces. It burns his sore stomach.

'It won't bring him back. This is my fault.'

★　★　★

In the bedroom, which contains four men sleeping on mattresses on the floor, Dimitri takes the empty place beside Matis, to comfort him. The mattress where Lukas used to whimper in the dark, until one of the men shouted *Užsičiaupk po velnių* — shut the fuck up.

'Do you need something to sleep?' Dimitri asks. 'That guy, the dealer who helped Saulius, he gave us pills.'

Matis shakes his head, rolls onto his back.

'Sleep,' Dimitri says. 'We must work tomorrow.'

If life were a force of will, Matis could wish himself dead. No such luck. His body, tired and broken, keeps going. He keeps on waking on the stinking mattress, soaked in the sweat of other men who had been in the same situation before him. *And what happened to them?*

★　★　★

When they are in the van at 4 a.m., it is a moment of reprieve — a moment to exhale. They have survived an ordeal, have dragged themselves from too-little sleep, got to the BP garage,

2

where migrants from across town are picked up for agricultural work, in time. They cannot be punished for missing the call, for being late. The next ordeal — catching enough chickens through the fog of their exhaustion, through the sting of the scratches on their hands reopening — would come later. Almost all the men fell straight to sleep in the van. Chin to chest. Forehead to window.

He was always asleep with this rag-tag of psychos, the weird intimacy of sharing a room. The snoring, someone talking in his sleep, the smells emitted by bodies at night, thick and human and perhaps repulsive, but also deeply, vulnerably personal. Lukas may have whimpered on his mattress at night, but Matis didn't. This had been his idea, and he had had to make it work, had had to make it look like it was working. Up to now, he'd had to survive, even though he didn't want to, to tell both himself and Lukas that their bind was temporary, a bump on the path to freedom. But with Lukas gone . . .

DAY 1
7.45 A.M.

MANON

'Wake me up now Mummy!' Teddy yells from the next room.

Manon gives Mark a shove and he rolls obediently out of bed.

She squints at her watch. 6.20 a.m. 'Fuck's sake,' she says, then turns over and descends back to delicious depths. The warmth of the duvet, the darkness of the room thanks to the blackout curtain lining, the numbness of her mind, broken by harsh winds of irritation: the feel of Mark and Teddy getting into the bed.

She would make all manner of pacts with Lucifer to be allowed fresh descent. Give me five minutes, three minutes, one minute. I will give you my soul.

There will be a moment of lovely cuddling, the velvety plush of Ted's cheek pads, his squidge-able limbs — forearms, upper arms padded with gentle fat, still of a toddler. She cherishes this remnant of babyhood. She's become a baby botherer in cafés, over-enunciating 'hallo!' into their cloudy eyes, while their mothers look on her with suspicion.

Ted pushes his fingers up her nose and says,

'Hello Defective Mummy!' because he doesn't know the word is detective. Or perhaps he does.

She can feel the crescendo of fidgetry begin: knees in the groin, kissing that becomes biting, until one of them submits to pre-dawn Weetabix.

★ ★ ★

Standing over her boy, she holds his tiny penis away from his body so the yellow arc of piss, warm and high, hits the hedge. She's wondering whether to ring Mark to tell him to nudge Fly, make sure he isn't oversleeping. He's in an important moment at school (GCSEs) and she permanently feels he's too lackadaisical, but then she argues with herself about allowing him to grow up and make his own mistakes. So much of her internal monologue these days revolves around where she is going wrong as a parent. To micromanage or to let go, that is the question.

The swings and slide were wet. Teddy went on them anyway. She was too comatose to object (*should she start taking iron, for the tiredness?*) despite knowing he would swing from happy and absorbed to freezing wet and miserable in a nanosecond.

She looks up. The sky is an ominous thumb smudge, the light low and the air damp. Classic British summer. The chestnut tree twenty yards away billows in the wind, its candelabra flowers bobbing wildly.

The air smells wet, fresh, with a trace of dog turd on its skirts.

She sniffs again, sensing something.

5

The wind is making things creak and knock.

She can hear a sound that is wrong. Wrong place, wrong context. She scans about, while Teddy concentrates on weeing.

There.

In the billowing tree that is twenty yards away.

She sees two black boots, high among the tree branches. She straightens, squinting to see better. Ankles, trousers. Swaying at head height. The creaking sound might be rope against branch.

She tucks Teddy back into his trousers, swivels him by the shoulders and lifts him. He is too big to be carried, they're always arguing about it, him standing in front of her — his block move — with arms in the air and her saying 'No, you can walk'. So he's bewildered at being lifted, but is certainly not about to argue. He is a dead weight; damp trousers, his legs banging against her body. But she is in flight not fight, holding his head down against her shoulder so he won't spot the legs, though it's unlikely he would notice.

Her boy is a strange combination of beady and myopic. If she has her head in one of the kitchen cupboards, eating an illicit biscuit, he can fix her with a steely gaze.

'What's that you got Mummy?'

'Nothing,' she'll say, over the rubble of a full mouth.

Yet if she were bleeding to death in the street, she has a feeling he'd stand over her, saying, 'Need a drink. I'm urgent.'

She is running away from the tree, carrying

Ted with one arm and digging into her pocket with the other for her phone to call it in.

First time she's ever run away from a body.

'Control, this is Officer Bradshaw 564, we have a deceased in Hinchingbrooke Country Park close to the car park. Repeat cadaver unattended in country park. Urgent attendance needed, send units. Cadaver is unattended in a public place. In a tree. Hanging from a tree.'

'Can you attend please, Detective Inspector?' says the control room.

'No, I am with a ch — a minor.' Manon is trying to use language Teddy cannot understand. Deceased. Cadaver. Not dead. Not body. 'I cannot attend, you need to send units.'

Despite her tone and use of jargon, Ted has sensed the rise in her vital signs, is prickling all over with transferred tension, and he lets out a wail — a combination of confusion and alarm. 'All right, Ted,' she says. 'It's all right. Mummy's all right and you're all right. Just a work call, that's all. Shall we go home and watch *Fireman Sam*?'

At home, once he's parked contentedly in front of the telly in dry clothes with a custard cream, Manon calls Davy.

'I'm at the scene,' says Davy.

'And?'

'Looks like another one from Wisbech.'

'Fuck's sake. I was with *Teddy*.'

'Is he okay?'

'Yeah, he's okay.'

7

DAY 1
9 A.M.

DAVY

They cannot cut him down until the scene photographer has got everything. And SOCO. They've cordoned a wide area — don't want members of the public rubbernecking the grey face or the snapped neck. And they would. They'd form a crowd, just like they did in medieval times at public executions. The public can't get enough of death in Davy's experience.

Pinned to the bottom of the victim's trousers, at shin height, is a piece of paper with some incomprehensible words written on it.

Mirusieji negali kalbėti

Davy is squinting at the letters, trying to decipher the handwriting accurately, then down at his phone as he types them into Google Translate. Google comes back with the answer:

The dead cannot speak

Standing so close to the trouser leg, Davy has been assailed by the stink of the cadaver — not decomposition, it's fresh. Happened last night, would be Davy's guess. It stinks because his bowels opened when he died and because he is an unwashed eighteen-year-old, or thereabouts. Young men kill themselves more frequently than anyone else, but that note puts the ball firmly in Davy's court. It's a threat or a confession. Either way, it smacks of murder as opposed to self-harm.

'What d'you think?' Harriet says.

'That note pinned to the body,' says Davy. 'Translates as 'the dead can't talk'. It's in Lithuanian.' He gives Harriet a pointed look.

She nods. 'You're thinking Wisbech?'

'Yup. Also, look at his hands.'

They both look at the cadaver's hands, which are suspended conveniently at head height. They are butcher's hands — thick fingers, curled, like a pair of well-worn gloves. Dark skinned. The backs of his hands are etched with multiple thin white lines.

'Think we need to check in with Operation Pheasant,' Davy says.

He doesn't want to confess, even to himself, how much he'd like to check in with Bridget on Operation Pheasant (as the Fenland Exploitation Team is known); the feelings this inspires in him. He is spoken for, after all. And not by Bridget.

'We can't let this go on,' Harriet says. 'This is the third. Makes us look like we've got no control. Any CCTV?'

Davy shakes his head. 'Not as far as I can see.'

'Were the victim's hands tied?'

'It doesn't appear so.'

'But if his hands weren't tied, did he try to

9

haul himself up the rope?'

'Derry Mackeith will tell us that when he does the PM.'

Davy can see Harriet thinking what he's thinking. Hard to get a man into a tree *with* his hands tied. Even harder to hang him *without* his hands tied. If he was drugged or unconscious, it would've been close to impossible to get him into a tree.

'We'll need to tell Derry to look out for fibres under the fingernails, burn marks to his palms from the rope, that kind of thing.'

'Yes,' says Davy, adding it to his mile-long mental list.

DAY 1
4 P.M.

MATIS

Twelve hours in the darkness of an industrial chicken shed made him forget himself. The stink, the noise, being scratched, being exhausted. Perhaps Lukas is best off out of it.

In the van back to the house, his head lolls against the seat rest and he dozes a blank sleep. When they are disgorged from the van, he looks at the house, sees the prospect of being alone with his thoughts, and starts to shake. He grasps Dimitri's arm.

'I can't go in. I feel sick,' he says.

'OK. We'll get a drink.'

He can see Dimitri is exhausted and would rather lie on his mattress, boots off. He is grateful to him for his companionship.

As they walk down the street, a car pulls up outside their house. Two men, both in dark suits, get out and go to the front door. Some kind of officialdom, Matis guesses. The communist regime had loved officialdom, Lukas's father told him. Matis admired Lukas's father enormously. Jűri was a thoughtful, gentle man, in contrast to Matis's own father. Jűri described languorous men in uniform, standing about pointlessly,

11

feeling important. 'Puffed up on their petty bureau-cracies. Four suited guys to take your ticket at the museum. Welcome to full employment!'

Matis and Dimitri take their bottle of vodka and drink it in the park. The air is soft, the temperature mild.

'Why don't you tell the police what you saw?' Dimitri asks. 'Let them take care of it?'

'Seriously,' Matis says. 'You trust the police?'

'It is different here.'

'Sure it is.'

Suspicion of authority is only a fraction of the reason why Matis won't talk.

'You must not say anything to the police,' Matis tells Dimitri. 'Promise me.'

Matis wakes to find himself laid out on the tarmac path, where he has fallen asleep. It is nearly dark. Someone has thrown coins at him. They have landed on the ground in front of his stomach. This kindness makes him cry.

DAVY

The ID card, or maybe it was a driver's licence — Davy can't tell because it's in Lithuanian — says the name: Lukas Balsys. A grainy photograph of a man who looks little more than a boy, though he was no less grey-faced when he was alive than after hanging.

'Davy Walker as I live and breathe. This is a nice surprise,' says Bridget as he walks into her Wisbech office, the ID card proffered for her to see.

Bridget is a senior officer on Operation Pheasant, whose offices are three rooms in a slope-ceilinged attic close to the town centre. 'Ah, OK,' says Bridget, looking at the card. She's got her hair in a complicated plait affair, two rows on either side of her head, rather like a schoolgirl. She's wearing a black cardigan over a patterned dress.

His attraction to Bridget is physical, primarily. Also the attraction of what he cannot have: the new and unknown and illicit. When all that is sanctioned is at home, there is a yearning for the unsanctioned. He realises it isn't deeper than that, and that his fiancée Juliet offers him

13

something real and complex, albeit cloaked in a somewhat pressurising commitment that he himself had wanted and brought on. It is Juliet, not Bridget, who puts up with his constant cancellations and late arrivals home because of work. The date nights postponed. It is Juliet who fights against the peevish feelings his unreliable shift pattern engenders. Bridget is a destructive impulse. Bridget is forbidden, hard to resist. Bridget is lively, bright-eyed. Her face hyper-mobile — with humour mostly. Also — and this is no small factor — Bridget is Up For It. How often does that come along? Davy can hear Manon's voice saying, 'Fucking never, if you're me.'

'Right,' Bridget says, after a search on her computer. 'We don't have Lukas Balsys on our books. But that's not unusual. Half these guys are not documented at all. He might be new. If I were you, I'd start at the HMO on Prospect Place. It's the Lithuanian hub, if you like. But beware of the house spokesman. Someone will be pushed in your face who speaks good English and he'll feed you a load of hokum about how happy they all are. Yes, yes, very heppy, very nice place.' She says this last bit in a thick Russian accent. 'You won't get a straight answer out of them. Take an interpreter. And try to shake off Edikas. They won't say a word with him in the room.'

'Righto,' he says, wondering if he could depart with something more flirty, but the subject matter of their conversation made this seem distasteful. Murder chat versus flanter (flirty banter). Murder chat wins. The attic room smells really nice — of

14

Bridget's floral perfume.

'By the way, Davy?' she says as he makes to leave. 'It's unusual that the note was in Lithuanian. Most of the guys who come over are Baltic Russians. Just thought it might help.'

'So, not from Lithuania then?' he asks, confused.

'Yes, from Lithuania, but Baltic Russians from Lithuania. There's loads of them, especially in Klaipeda, the town where they're usually from. They relocated there during the Soviet occupation.'

★ ★ ★

Davy pulls up outside a red-brick terraced house with plastic windows, front garden piled with rubbish that is escaping its bags. The house next door is immaculate.

'This must be driving them mad,' Davy says to the interpreter who is following him up the path. Davy gives him a glance, which is part grimace, intended to say 'it's going to be unpleasant in here'.

Initially, no one answers the door. They ring and knock again, Davy shouts 'Police!' through the letter box.

Eventually, a sleepy man in tracksuit bottoms and a T-shirt opens the door, leaves it open and walks away from them, back up the stairs, without speaking.

They stand awkwardly in the hallway until a rotund, bald man greets them from the back of the house, holding out his hand.

15

'Hello, I'm Edikas. How can I help you?' he says. In Russian.

Edikas arranges for Davy to talk to various residents. It is an awkward business as there is no seating — what would have been a lounge is set with mattresses, and the kitchen is a galley without a table. The house is dirty — smells of microwaved dinners, the kind made from meat of unknown provenance.

Davy stands at the doorway to one of the bedrooms with his notepad. His interviewee sits on a mattress, knees up, back to the wall. He doesn't make eye contact. Everyone denies knowing Lukas or anything about Lukas.

The interpreter looks uncomfortable as he translates. He can speak both Lithuanian and Russian, as most older Lithuanians can. He casts an anxious glance at Davy, then looks at his notepad and holds out his hands. Davy hands the interpreter his notepad.

Scared, the interpreter writes. The word is underlined. Then he writes, *Can you distract him?*

'A word out back, if you don't mind,' Davy says to Edikas.

'When you have finished, we talk,' Edikas replies, in English this time, folding his arms.

'What's this fella called?' Davy asks, bending to pet the dog. The dog bares its teeth, snarling.

'Skirta,' says Edikas. 'It mean devoted in my language.'

He is glancing into the bedroom where the interpreter is whispering to the interviewee. 'What are you saying to my friend?' Edikas demands loudly.

16

The man who had opened the door to them, the one in tracksuit bottoms, enters the kitchen and opens various cupboards. Edikas shouts at him in Russian, the man protests, but weakly. His face is ravaged with exhaustion. From the exchange, Davy guesses the man wanted food and Edikas told him he couldn't have any. The man trudges away again up the stairs.

'They never stop eating,' Edikas explains.

Davy steps into the bedroom where the interpreter is trying to get blood from a stone. It should be him leading the questioning, not the interpreter, so he intervenes.

'Did you know Lukas Balsys?' Davy asks.

The interpreter relays.

The migrant on the mattress shrugs.

'Is that yes or no?' Davy asks.

Another shrug.

'Would you like to come down to the station and talk to us there?'

Edikas enters. 'You cannot take him to police station unless he is under arrest. What can be for arresting? Nothing!'

'Do you know what happened to Lukas Balsys?' Davy asks, deciding to attempt an interview despite the obstacles.

Another languid shrug.

He writes on his pad. *Tell him we can protect him if he talks to us.* He shows this to the interpreter.

The interpreter writes, *I cannot tell him this without also telling the heavy.* And he nods at Edikas.

'Did Lukas have any things?' Davy asks

17

Edikas. 'That he left in the house?'

Edikas nods and points to one of the mattresses. It is covered in a sheet that was once white but has a brown, human-shaped stain taking up most of its surface. Beside the mattress is a bottle of vitamin pills, a leather belt, a pair of socks.

'What about his wallet, his phone?' Davy asks.

Edikas shrugs. 'That's all,' he says, nodding at the desultory collection of objects on the floor. Davy puts on a pair of gloves and places the objects into evidence bags.

He wants to get out. This isn't the way to break open this hub. It's a crime scene. It wants clearing out like a crime scene.

'We can go,' he says to the interpreter. He steps quickly around the mattresses and heads for the door.

Outside, Davy's phone vibrates.

When will you be home Dudu Bear?

He looks at his watch. It's only 4 p.m. and Juliet's asking. He texts back, irritably.

Late. Job's come in.

Can you give me an idea of time? Only it's really hard to sleep if I don't know when you're coming in.

You sleep. I'll go on the couch.

MANON

She has been bothered by the man in the tree — another thing to add to her sense that the country, nay the *world*, is going to the dogs. Bothered that Teddy got so close to seeing the hanging man. Bothered that Korea has fired another test missile. Bothered that her bin collection has gone fortnightly and that the streets around her home are rubbish-strewn. Funding shortfalls everywhere she looks. Detectives transfer or retire and don't get replaced. Police inspectorate warning of grave dangers to the service — poor response times, suspects not being apprehended, calls being downgraded. Calling 999? Yes madam, someone should be with you in the next couple of days.

Everything is so much worse than she ever imagined it could get. And middle age keeps on landing the blows.

'When I get out of bed in the morning,' Mark says, 'my whole body hurts for a moment or two.'

'Oh I know,' she says. 'Especially the feet.'

They are pale, with protruding bellies. Saggy-bottomed. In sharp contrast to their children, who amaze them with their shining, taut skin.

19

Lovely legs. When she holds Ted's face next to hers and looks in the mirror, it's like an age-related horror show. Like satin next to Viking-era hessian.

At forty-six, Manon has entered an age of crippling anxiety, a period of her life freighted with dread. Her furrowed brow, never un-furrowed, is a bother to Mark Talbot, she can tell (although he's no ray of sunshine); her *joie de vivre* abandoned at the coalface of worst-case-scenario planning. What if Teddy drowns or develops a tumour? What if the people she leaves him with are cruel to him? How will she know? Why won't he sit quietly with a book for an hour or two? *Et cetera, et cetera, et cetera* as the doomy King of Siam said in *The King and I*.

And marriage. Trying to keep that shit-show on the road. Not bothering to have the same old arguments because they are boring, but fearful of screwing it up because who else would have her, and also: The Children. Frowning at Mark Talbot while she heaves the bins out in the rain. *Because if you miss the bins, they'll stink to high heaven, they'll stink as bad as your rotting marriage.*

In fact, they are not married, she and Mark, but might as well be (all the tedium, none of the tax breaks); slogging through it like most couples. He is her constant companion, which is no small thing; conjoined in the forge of parenthood, which is 70 per cent delight at the emerging personalities of their children and 30 per cent resentful trudge. Meal preparation, dishwasher emptying, overflowing laundry baskets, Lego underfoot. Underneath, she wonders if there might be something darker brewing — how can one tell? Mark might have someone else. His online life might harbour appalling secrets. But these questions she asks only fleetingly because he is her constant companion and life without him would be a dismantling of unconscionable proportions. He is the conversation, the jokes, the affection, the loyalty, all her warmth. She cannot ask the darker questions because she loves him too much. It is better not to know, to settle down to another box set in a state of blissful and un-disruptive not-knowing. Human beings cannot bear too much reality.

The last couple of Januarys have seen a welter of break-ups among friends, Christmas being the straw that breaks the marital back. Mark Talbot secretly harbouring his midlife crisis, the extent of which she cannot fully ascertain. He looks malnourished, despite his pot belly, and unfit. He's developed a worrying Rennie habit. She watches him pee and worries about his prostate.

'You get to a point,' she explained to her oldest friend Bryony, 'where you realise his shit is never going to get better. His shit will always be your shit.'

'Yup. You should come on my school run. They're dropping like flies. Everyone in couples counselling, not all of it good.'

'I'm in couples counselling,' Manon replied. 'On my own.'

'Result,' said Bri.

'I know. I don't even have to listen to his side.'

'Isn't couples counselling on your own just . . . therapy?'

'Don't be absurd. I don't need therapy. All my

21

problems are because of Mark.'

'Course they are. Why won't he go?'

'Says it would just be me, wanging on,' Manon said.

It's not just the same old row about mental load, about who should be doing the utterly tedious bedtime routine while simultaneously preparing a nutritious dinner brimming with fresh veg, but also the deep chasm over The Anxiety of It All. Who is carrying The Anxiety of It All? Is it the person who is prone to anxiety? Or is it that person because one of you refuses to carry the anxiety and cunningly off-loads it onto the other one? She has her *suspicions*, which she keeps not very close to her (now shelf-like) chest. They barely touch each other these days, her and Mark. The bed is an icy canyon they cannot cross. Kissing is a thing of the past, unless it's with Ted. It's as if the physicality of looking after children, the lovely cheek-to-cheek of the bedtime story, the wrap of chubby little legs about the waist, has usurped the physicality of marriage.

Why does the mental load descend with such force? Is it late middle age? The anxiety has smothered her libido, once as bounding as a Labrador pup. It has smothered lightness. No more What the Fuck, Give it a Go, Devil May Care, C'mon Let's Have a Laugh *et cetera, et cetera*.

Where were all the full-blown feelings of her youth? Interrailing around Europe at seventeen, having regular epiphanies in Italian churches. Reading *Where Angels Fear to Tread* as she pulled into San Gimignano station, Tears for Fears through her headphones. The smell of Vidal Sassoon's *Wash & Go*, its green bottle perched in plastic soap dishes of campervan showers. God, everything was miraculous then. Music! Literature! Frescoes! She fancied everyone at seventeen, as opposed to no one at forty-six.

It was the absence of weariness. She could sit on a pew in some preposterously gold-leafed church and think seriously about Lucy Honeychurch, and Isabel Archer, and Gwendolen in *Daniel Deronda*, so fully engaged with them that they might have been interrailing together in some unwieldy, crinoline-wearing troupe. Why couldn't she live like that for ever? Why did one have to switch energy providers and set a mobile phone alert for bin day, only to find out you cannot set an alert because your phone storage is full, so you decide to pay for more storage (until you die), only to find you don't know your password. By the time you retrieve your password, you are sixty-five and howling into the abyss.

It's the children, she thinks. You can't jack in your marriage because of the children. You can't stick two fingers up to your job to go and tend orangutans in Borneo. You can't forget to go food shopping for, like, three weeks. You can't think fuck this, I fancy doing an MA in Classical Greek. You have to keep the sodding show on the sodding road. Weetabix at 6 a.m. whether you like it or not. Behind every meal is another meal. And can you imagine sitting across the table

23

from some loathsome Internet date (who hasn't half the charms of Mark Talbot, even on bin day) with your epic brow furrowed to the max, the Über-Furrow, and then looking at your watch and saying, 'Sorry, I can't get pissed and come to your place for a shag because I have to put the bins out tonight, otherwise the council won't come back for a fortnight.' Politicians so incompetent she can hardly bear to look.

No one replaces the lightbulbs, so they live in an ever-descending gloom.

It's either the children or it is Death. It might well be Death: that shadow of a notion that you might be more than halfway through and this is all you've got, this is all the powder in your keg. New experiences? You've had 'em. Except cancer, and that might well be the one remaining new experience left to try. Each holiday a repeat of a previous holiday: Eurocamp sites where the plastic houses were just a smidgen too close together so she could gaze on happier couples from her Verandah of Bitterness. Doing crosswords on her phone (storage allowing).

The great variable of it all after forty-five: when the reaper might call. Will it be fifty? Sixty-two? Will people shake their heads momentarily, saying, 'So young' before going back to their online food order? Or will it be ninety-two, blind, deaf and gaga? Once you're living after half time, it's a gamble — when death is going to take you and whether it might be your own fault for not 'eating clean'. Too many fags, not enough kale. Too much telly, not enough yoga. Sitting is the new smoking. Obesity is the new sitting. A scientist once told her the age of your death is set at your birth. If only we could *know*, we wouldn't have to spend so much time worrying about it. Imagine spending your life chowing down on kale, only to find you've got ninety years of it to get through? If someone could just inform you, at maybe thirty, that you've got until sixty-eight to do everything, love everyone, set your affairs in order, *have* your affairs. If only we could be taken less by surprise by death. People in the past who went quietly mad losing child after child, lived cheek by jowl with death, less utterly astonished by it. Perhaps if it surrounded you like that, like a terrible, dank lake, you would take less umbrage at its random cruelties.

Must research ISAs, renew contents insurance, remember Thursday is 'wear green to nursery day', and take in a panoply of exotic fruit. Which diet to follow as she hurtles towards matronly? Embark on daily seven-minute fitness? *Seven whole minutes though SO BORING!* Which new holiday idea might be the least Not Fun, and just as they decide on a place and a date after approximately three years on the Internet, they check in with TripAdvisor, which shits on all their dreams with close-up shots of moulding shower trays.

Bring back the high street travel agent. Get rid of estate agents, but bring back travel agents. Someone out there ought to be a purveyor of joy rather than a peddler of worry.

She thinks of the song 'Age of Aquarius', but substitutes Anxiety.

At the GP they tested her iron levels.

'I'm tired all the time. Like, I wake up tired,' she told the nurse.

'Forty-six-year-old women generally are tired because they're doing everything,' the nurse said, seemingly unable to summon much interest in her case.

★   ★   ★

She's been out of the office most of the day on some dull cold-case interviews that yielded close to nothing. Still, it was an outing. Manon squints into the brightness, wrapping her scarf around her neck. It's that time in the year when the coat has been dispensed with but, frankly, it's freezing, hence the scarf. Her mobile starts ringing before she's even at the end of the path. Bryony.

'All right?' says Manon.

'You on your way in?' asks Bri.

'Yup, why? D'you want a coffee?'

'No, McFuckface wants to see you.'

'Why?'

'Don't ask me.'

★   ★   ★

The new detective superintendent in charge of MCU and hence Manon's über-boss, above Harriet but below the commissioner (replacing the regrettably deceased and thoroughly discredited Gary Stanton) is, drumroll, Glenda McBain.

Glenda McBainofMyLife.

26

Glenda McBlameGame.

The promotion had taken place during Manon's maternity leave and according to pretty much everyone in the major crime unit, it was an over-promotion. What McBain lacked in policing acumen, she made up for in buzz words, trotting out references to social media, digital presence, and 'blue sky thinking' until the panic among the ageing interview panel was palpable. So the story doing the rounds in the canteen went, anyway. These senior officers, with their shiny buttons and epaulettes, were men of an age to smooth a physical newspaper across a kitchen table in order to keep abreast of current events. Word was that Glenda McPersonalGain had mentioned Facebook and Twitter, sticky content, and clickbait sufficient times to have them reaching for the Gaviscon. So terrified were they by her Internetty lexicon, that they ended up spluttering, 'Well, she seems to have it covered,' in relieved tones, hopeful they might never have to discuss it again.

Manon's first run-in with Glenda McBain was her return to work interview, it being never too soon to fall out with your new boss.

Manon was returning to cold cases three days per week — a very feasible pattern in a department that was not driven by round the clock 'live' investigations, their victims usually having been dead for decades, so another few weeks wasn't going to hurt. There was no middle-of-the-night responding, no sleepless first seventy-two hours like there was on MCU. Cold cases was the force's cultural backwater, thick with officer plankton, and Manon was more than happy to be swimming in it. Pottering in, coffee in hand, and logging on for a spot of Internet shopping was precisely what she had in mind when she thought of work-life balance. Admittedly, however, the work lacked a certain grip. Excitement couldn't be listed as part of her daily experience.

It made no discernible difference which days Manon worked, so she naturally chose Tuesday, Wednesday and Thursday. Long weekends a go-go, much of it spent in bed with Teddy, cuddling, kissing his face and reading *Dr Dog* on a loop. These mornings would be all the more delicious in contrast to the workday scramble; sleep-deprived if Teddy had been up in the night. Trying to shower/blow-dry her hair, feed and dress him, feed and dress herself, deal with the inevitable nearly-out-the-door poo he could muster at will.

Glenda McBain, however, had pretty randomly decided that Manon should work Monday, Wednesday and Friday. This, Manon was sure, was mindless sabotage from a boss she soon realised was . . . well, not the sharpest knife in the drawer. She might know Internet words, but Glenda McBain was, as Bri put it, 'thickety thick thick, stupidy stupidy'.

Subsequently, when Manon and Harriet were in Glenda's office discussing the complex mechanics of a case or some element of the Regulation of Investigatory Powers Act, she could see Glenda struggling to keep up: the tiny flicking of the eyeballs combined with physical delay. It was as if Manon could see Glenda's brain saying, 'Hold up lads! We're going to have to suspend arm and leg movements for a minute while we process this convo.'

Harriet knew it too, but was too institutionalised to use the full panoply of McFuckface monikers, in sharp contrast to Bryony, who was at the very vanguard of Glenda ribaldry.

'Something's happened. Something disastrous,' Bri had said recently, marching through Manon's front door, past her and into the kitchen, her beetle-like movements saying panic.

'Go on.'

'I called her . . . I called her — I can't.'

'Yes you can.'

'This was in a MEETING. And I blame you Manon, because you're always egging me on, encouraging me to be juvenile.'

'Come on, out with it.'

'I called her McFlurry. It was kind of quiet, and I corrected it mid-speak, so . . . '

Manon started laughing, so much she had to bend double.

'It's not funny.'

'Stop it, I'm doing a wee. Did you go for the full Det Chf Supt McFlurry? Or the more informal CE McFlurry?'

Bri frowned. 'CE?'

'Creme Egg.'

'Can I come and work on cold cases?'

'Only the finest minds on cold cases, Bri. Our best and finest minds.'

Manon had wondered what on earth Glenda was even *doing* in her back to work interview, it

29

being well below her pay grade.

'Can you manage the workload in three days a week?' Glenda demanded, all brusque and challengey, as if this is what powerful women can do. *Thank you, feminism.*

'It's cold cases,' Manon answered. 'I'm not heading up counter terrorism.'

Glenda, Manon reasoned, was meddling for the sake of meddling. Glenda was saying 'I want it pink' just because she could. Glenda fell into that group of people who seemed to believe that if they stretched their tentacles into the very far flung corners of existence — corners that didn't even concern them — they would Achieve Ultimate Control.

She agreed to McBain's preposterous working pattern, and then, a few weeks later, when McBain's laser gaze was focussed elsewhere, quietly shifted her working week to the way she wanted it.

★ ★ ★

On her way into HQ she wishes she had her M&S mackintosh, which she can picture in a rumpled heap on the floor beside the front door of their house. The coat hooks fell off the wall three weeks ago and they've been 'storing' their coats on the floor ever since. There is no prospect of anyone dealing with the coat hooks. It is beyond their skill set, and she's too embarrassed to get a handyman in for such a piddling job. Her sexual fantasies, such as they are, generally involve men performing minor

DIY while retaining their emotional equilibrium.

Knee twinges climbing the stairs to McBain's office. She glances behind her, to see if anyone's on the stairwell, so she can go up on one leg giving it maximum elderly hobble, but there are young uniformed coppers bringing up the rear, so she has to fake full mobility. She wonders what McBain wants. Is she going to lambast me for my footwear, or my use of stationery? Ask me to livetweet an arrest? Hashtag police! Open up!

'Ah, Manon, come in,' McBain says. 'I'm seconding you to team two, the Lithuanian job.'

Manon is about to protest about hours and her sacrosanct days at home with Teddy, but Glenda puts her hand up. 'You'll be SIO, but continue on your Monday, Wednesday and Friday shift pattern.'

Manon experiences a stab of heartburn at this.

'If developments occur on your days off, Davy can step up. He's more than capable. You might have to take the odd out-of-hours phone call. Is that a problem?'

Manon shakes her head. She's searching for the downside, literally rummaging about for a grievance in this scenario, but can't find one. She's been desperate for a sniff at this case, been turning it over in her mind, nearly called Davy with her list of investigative avenues he ought to go down, and now she gets to lord it about while still working three days a week. It's as if feminism has actually come through for her. There simply *must* be a downside, some horrific personal yet invisible cost that she must suck up while making a casserole and refreshing her patio pots. Is someone going to throw in the care of an octogenarian? Potty training a Retriever pup?

And yet all she can think is: *Back on the road with Davy Walker.*

'What about my cold case team?'

'Your team can carry on with their case load, update you when something shifts.'

I.e. never, Manon thinks.

'What about Harriet? Isn't she SIO on the Lithuanian job?'

'Yes. Harriet's taking some time off. Urn, I don't know how much she wants the office to know . . . but you're her friend, so. Harriet has discovered a lump on her breast. She's having a mastectomy this week.'

'Oh no!' Manon says, hand over her mouth.

Not feminism then.

At the door, Glenda says, 'Bit late to start today, and anyway Davy's still at the migrant house conducting interviews. Best you hit the ground running when you're next back in.'

* * *

Come evening, Manon storms into the kitchen where Mark is feeding Teddy, flings her keys onto the counter, and says, 'Guess what Griselda McFuckface did today?'

'I assume you mean Glenda McBain,' he says mildly.

'Oh right, you're her bezzie these days, are you?'

'What did she do to anger you, Oh Great One?'

'She wants me to lead a live murder investigation. The Lithuanian job.'

'And that's terrible because . . . '

'We've got no clean pants.'

'Sorry, what's the connection between pants and awfulness of being promoted, nay valued, by your boss?'

'Right, so we've got no clean pants,' she says, bending down her fingers with each point. 'The phone's been broken for weeks — we never fix anything. There isn't a single item of food with any nutritional value in our kitchen, and don't bring up tinned sweetcorn again; we are incapable of booking a decent holiday, we eat too many takeaways, our furniture is ugly. And there are no clean pants. So I can't think about complex investigations because, my darling perpetuator of the patriarchy, my mind is full of pants.'

'Don't think about the pants,' he says. 'Ignore the pants. Right, it's true what you say, but a) the only people who ring the landline are relatives and cold callers b) I love takeaways and so do you c) ignore the pants. You can reverse pants or put on swimwear d) we *are* good at booking shit holidays and e) who gives a fuck about ugly furniture? We sit on it, we don't look at it.'

'I do.'

'Well, stop.'

He doesn't, she notices, say, 'I'll do the pants.' (And even if he did, it wouldn't last more than a week.) Instead, he says, 'I think she's right. Heading up this case will be great for you.'

Mark sidles over to her, hands on her hips then up and under her top.

'How about, y'know . . . later,' he says, eyeing Teddy and winking at her. 'To celebrate. What d'you think?'

'Again?' she says. 'Seriously? Oh *fine*, Thai or Indian?'

In fact, he says he feels too sick to eat anything at all — practically unheard of for Mark.

'You look . . . yellow,' she tells him. 'Your eyes are the colour of urine.'

'You say the loveliest things.'

★ ★ ★

In bed that evening, as they are falling asleep, she says, 'I want you to get us some porn to watch. Liven things up a bit.'

'Righto,' Mark says.

'But nothing weird. Conventional stuff for people like us. Nothing . . . out there.'

'Middle-aged chubster porn,' says Mark.

'No, I don't want to see chubby people doing it. I can get that at home. No animals or anything alarming.'

'Middle-aged animal-free porn, got it,' says Mark.

'Is that a section in a porn shop?' she asks.

'Probably. Next to 'clergy'.'

'I wouldn't know where to get it, you see,' she says. 'Does John Lewis do porn?'

'If it did, it'd be exactly the sort of porn we'd like,' he says.

'Oh yes. John Lewis porn. That's exactly it. No surprising or unpleasant orifices. Nice table lamps in the background should the mind wander.'

DAY 2
8 A.M.

DAVY

The cordon has gone, SOCO and the scene photographer having got what they needed.

'How did they get him up there?' Manon asks, looking up into the tree. 'If it was murder, he must've cooperated. Pretty hard to get a fella up there if he doesn't want to. Not like they built a scaffold.'

'Ladder maybe. Could've kicked it away.'

'Any indentations suggesting the feet of a ladder?'

'Nope, but they might have scuffed the ground to cover it. What if they threatened him?' Davy says. 'Had a gun to his head?'

'I'd say, so shoot me. Rather be shot than hanged, any day. Can take an age to die if your neck doesn't break.'

'He might've been coerced into the tree,' says Davy.

'Tricky thing to do though, isn't it? I mean, if I were a serial killer, it wouldn't be my first choice of MO.'

'Serial killer?' says Davy, who had just now felt as if his murder was being taken away from him, not just by Mrs Big Boots clod-hopping all over

35

his scene, but by her suspicion it might in fact be suicide after all. And now she's bandying the words serial killer about?

'Well, this is the third hanging in as many months. They were all hung with the same rope. The rope is everything Davy. We need to be all over the rope.'

He wants to say, *Do you think I haven't thought of that? Do you think I'm not all over the rope?*

The two previous victims, one man and one woman, were deemed to have taken their own lives following an investigation by local officers. He reminds her of this.

'Why didn't they refer it up to us?' Manon asks.

'Thought they could handle it themselves,' Davy says.

'Could they though? Could be murder. We could be talking about our third victim in a serial homicide.'

'I think you're getting a bit over-excited.'

'I think we need to reopen those other two cases.'

'Good luck telling Wisbech plod that.'

'I'm not going to tell them,' Manon says, smiling at Davy. 'You are.'

She doesn't let up as they walk to the car. Did they leave notes, these other victims? Were there witnesses to the deaths? Were there statements about the deceased's states of mind in the run up to the deaths. CCTV? ANPR? Yes, yes, he wants to say, I'm on it. Give me a sodding chance, it's only day two. And he is so, so tired.

36

'You look tired,' she says.

'Thing is,' he says, 'you'd hang them to make it look like suicide, not murder.'

'Yes, but it didn't look like suicide, though. That note made sure it didn't. Something just doesn't fit about it. It's a suicidal method, not a murder method, and yet the note just knocks it out of the park. Also, if I were coerced into a tree, with whatever threats, I'd just keep climbing — out of reach.'

'There was a belt,' Davy says, 'next to his bed in the migrant house. A leather belt. If I wanted to top myself, I'd use my belt and the nearest bannister. No need to trek all the way to Hinchingbrooke.'

'Yes, it's very effortful,' she concedes.

Then she's back to her nagging. Locations of the bodies, how did they get to those locations, did they have help getting to those locations — they were quite remote, weren't they Davy? Naggedy nag nag. *It's only day two,* he wants to shout in her face. *Back, the fuck, off.*

'If we were on TV,' she says, the breath in her lungs pumped and lively, 'we'd be in an office with some kind of glass screen with a giant interactive map on it and I'd stroke my finger across it to triangulate the locations. And we'd be wearing tonal outfits, Davy.'

'Yeah, well, we're not on TV, so I can offer you a biro and an Ordnance Survey map.'

MANON

'Who's this fella we're going to see then?' she asks, while Davy pulls away from the kerb. They are going to Wisbech police station for the interview.

'Edikas. He's the fixer. He runs the migrants on behalf of Vasil the Barbarian, the gangmaster. Tells them what's what when they get off the bus. Vasil gets the cash. Bridget says salaries are paid into the migrants' bank accounts, so it looks like there's a paper trail, but their bank cards are taken off them when they arrive, so they don't have any access to the money. Vasil uses their accounts to launder his funds.'

'And why hasn't he been cleaned out by Op Pheasant?'

'No one will testify against him. Biggest problem Pheasant has is that the minute the migrants get away, they want nothing more to do with it. They hotfoot it back to Klaipeda and that's that. Wall of silence, Bridget says.'

'Oh, Bridget says, does she?' says Manon, gurning with Carry-On innuendo. Trying to nudge-nudge him, without causing an accident. 'How *is* Bridget?'

'She's fine,' he says, flushing.

'And what about Edikas's own situation. Wife? Kids?'

'Back in Klaipeda. He sends money back to them each month.'

'What's Klaipeda like?'

'Baltic sea port, Lithuania's third city. Lots of Russians, lots of jobs on the docks.'

'OK, so it looks to me like Edikas has the worst of all worlds. Doing all the dirty work for Vasil but not living in the lap of luxury like Vasil's lot. Where does Edikas live?'

'In a rental, but by himself.'

'Do we need an interpreter for this?'

'He says not. Says he speaks English just fine.'

'Hmmm, I've had that before. No interpreter, then you find there's lots of convenient misunderstanding when it comes to the detail. Lots of *no comprendo, DS Walker*.'

They drive in silence through the Fens for a time.

'And anyway,' she says, 'there are lots of ways of making it look like it isn't murder. Pills. Push 'em in a river, car accidents. Easy peasy. It's got an old-fashioned quality, hanging — makes me think of medieval times, or highway men at roadsides, or lynchings, the American Civil War, y'know? They hung slaves from the trees.'

'Yes, but this is Wisbech,' says Davy.

'Oh yes Davy,' Manon says, clasping an imaginary handbag mid-air. 'This is Wisbech, the last bastion of civilisation.'

She reaches out to turn on the radio. Immediately says, 'Oh fuck no, not him again, I

39

can't stand him,' as Shane Farquharson comes over the airwaves, his voice immediately recognisable — the everyman twang combined with stockbroker belt well-to-do. 'How can you listen to this awful crap, Davy?'

Out from the radio comes Farquharson's tell-it-like-it-is voice: 'Any normal and fair-minded person would have a perfect right to be concerned if a group of Lithuanian people suddenly moved in next door.'

'Not any normal people I know,' says Manon. 'What the fuck is he talking about? It's not fair-minded to be worried about someone's nationality! It's the opposite of fair-minded. It's Being a Big Bigot.'

'He's just a disrupter,' Davy says. 'None of it means anything.'

'Think it's worse than that,' Manon says.

Farquharson, whose primary job is media rent-a-gob, is of above average intelligence and articulate — he can express what his angry troupe are feeling, making sense of their futile fury, making their impotence seem momentarily like purpose. And though he has never won a seat in parliament, he dominates radio airwaves, a favourite of talk show phone-ins like the one currently polluting Davy and Manon's air. '*Urgh*, he's invited onto *Question Time* every single week,' Manon says. 'Just gives him a platform so he can feed more crazy to the base.'

Manon is aware she has descended into one of her diatribes and suspects Davy may have switched off, thinking instead about Big-Bosomed Bridget, while she pontificates about

40

anger and neglect in the air, meted out at polling stations. The misinformed holding sway. Anger in the pages of newspapers, anger on radio airwaves, anger that pushes to one side solid information. There are no facts any more. Instead, 'all the feels' and 'we've had enough of experts telling us what to think' and 'the elite have always run things, it's time for change' and drain the swamp and make Wisbech great again.

'Anyway,' Manon says, turning off the radio. 'How are the wedding preparations going?'

41

DAVY

He flushes, reminded of the adultery in his thoughts about Bridget.

Things have happened very quickly with Juliet because they were both so enthusiastic about the trappings of coupledom: the moving in together, the holidays, weekend walks, cushion choosing, casserole making, box set watching, less and less hot sex having; the whole insulation from loneliness a project in itself. This hunkering down, which in many respects is a closing off of the wider world, a narrowing of their circle down to two, but a sure-fire dependable two. Closing the curtains on the world's diverse riches — riches like Bridget and her snarky sense of humour and lively expression. While wanting to hunker very badly, Davy can feel the loss of his interactions — solo interactions — with the world at large. The way he used to say yes to every invitation in case he met someone, the way he would force himself to go to a thing alone, a force of will when every fibre of his being wanted to watch telly with a ready meal. He has been all too ready to give up the strains of moving through the world alone, but cannot help noticing the way he feels blunted by the seclusion he and Juliet are gathering about them like a thick wool blanket.

Not *all* his interests are contained behind the drawn living-room curtains, with the telly on and the heating a smidgen too high, comfy though it is. It is also boring.

No, he tells himself, Bridget can't be right for him because Juliet is The One, and Juliet has put her salt and pepper mills in the dental surgery starkness of his Sapley rental. And once you've pooled salt and pepper mills, there really is no going back. Also, Juliet has been soaking up the neglect and disappointment the job creates: the way investigations kick off at no notice, holidays postponed. She has greeted these disappointments with barely suppressed aggression. This complex interplay between them cannot (should not) be compared to the breezy clean sheet with someone where no guilt or recrimination has built up at all (aka Bridget).

MANON

'Do you know Lukas Balsys?' Manon asks after the long beep has sounded on the recording machine and she has informed it that she is in the room with Davy and Edikas, who has not been offered a brief because he is not under arrest. Yet.

'Yes,' Edikas says.

'What was your relationship with Lukas?'

'I find him work. Agricultural job.'

'He came over on the bus from Klaipeda, is that right?'

Edikas nods.

'For the tape please.'

'Yes.'

'Is it true you took away his passport and bank card when he first arrived?'

'No! Why would I do this? I have no need of Lithuanian passport. I have my own. I just help my peoples. When guys come from Lithuania, I help them. That is all.'

'Did you pay Lukas a wage?'

'Of course.'

'Can I see evidence of this wage?'

'Yes, we have document showing payroll. And

44

you can look in his bank account.'

'If he had his passport and bank cards, why were these not among his possessions? We retrieved only a belt, some vitamins.'

Edikas shrugs.

Manon allows a silence to linger. Time for everyone to ponder this situation. Silences reveal much, she finds, if only you refuse to take responsibility for them. When she was younger, she was a frantic silence-filler, feeling the onus was on her to make the moment smooth out, no matter how socially inept her companion. This led to plenty of absurd situations in which she deployed sexuality to fill in the gaps. Sit a younger Manon next to some chilly, pinched-lipped, public school boy type and she'd prostrate herself to make it go well. Gabbling away, hot-faced, to put at ease someone she didn't even like; often someone who palpably didn't like her. Sometimes she'd get into a relationship with them that lasted years.

No more. These days, she has got in the habit of mentally briefing herself before any social event. *Just hang back. Observe. Don't fill the gaps. Let other people do the running. It's not your responsibility.*

And the power of this, the way it releases her, still helps to this day. She has learned that awkwardness no more belongs to her than does the weather. She can observe it, like an interested bystander, rather than frantically trying to make it shift.

Not so Davy, who is a mass of easily-pricked embarrassment.

'Where were you on the evening of Monday May 14th, the night before last?' Manon asks.

'In my home,' Edikas says.

'With anyone?'

'No, just me. And Skirta, my dog.'

'When did you find out about Lukas's death?'

'Today. Yesterday was day off.'

'And what was your reaction to his death?'

Edikas shrugs, turns his mouth down. 'This was gloomy person. Very negatif. I'm not surprise he kill himself.'

'What makes you think he killed himself?' Manon asks, eyeballing him.

Edikas looks at her, shocked. 'I thought . . . I thought he heng hisself.'

'So?'

'It is not easy to hang another person.'

'You sound like you've tried it.'

Edikas doesn't respond.

'Who was Lukas closest to in the house?'

'Matis. He come from Klaipeda with Matis.'

'All right, we'd like to speak to Matis, then. Can you give us his number?' Manon asks.

Once again, Edikas turns his mouth down. Pats his pockets. 'I don't have my mobile phone.'

Manon nods, while sliding her own mobile phone under the table. While Davy supplies some questions about Matis's location, she locates Edikas's mobile number from an internal email and calls it.

Edikas starts ringing.

'That mobile phone, you mean?' Manon asks, smiling.

Unruffled, Edikas scrolls through his mobile

46

phone. 'No, I don't have Matis number.'

'Well, perhaps you could locate it for us. Or him. It's important we talk to him. Anything else about Lukas?' Manon asks.

'He was having sex with the neighbour. Mrs Tucker.'

* * *

'Right,' says Manon, clipping down her seat belt outside Wisbech police station. 'Mr and Mrs Tucker then.'

They drive in silence, Manon reminded of the pleasure of being with Davy Walker — so comfortable, they know each other too well for pleasantries, though she is worried, she thinks, glancing at his pale face. He looks shattered.

'D'you want to stop for a break?' she asks him. 'We could get a sandwich.'

He doesn't say anything but pulls up to park so they can walk to Greggs in Wisbech's pedestrianised shopping precinct.

Looking in the chiller cabinet, stomach growling, she peruses starchy baguettes filled with creamy mayonnaise-slathered chicken or tuna. *This is exactly what I need to stop eating* — a thought that makes her want it all the more. She takes a baguette as long as her forearm and an accompanying bag of ready salted crisps to the till. Because the combination is on offer in a 'meal deal'.

'What are you getting?' she asks Davy.

He is holding a sandwich (half the size of hers) and she takes it off him and pays for it along with her own, while he wanders outside. The smallness of his lunch compared to hers reminds her of the time she'd employed a nutritionist to assist her in the battle of the bulge.

'And do you eat the same as your partner at meals?' the nutritionist had asked.

'I'll say!' Manon had replied, appalled at the idea she should have less.

Back in the car, she says, 'So why wasn't Edikas at work as usual yesterday? Busy night murdering Lukas?'

'Might just be his day off,' Davy says, yawning.

'Time for him to do his Ocado shop and put a wash on, you mean? I don't think Edikas looks the type to take days off.'

★ ★ ★

They pull up outside two adjoined red-brick homes — identical, though the contrast couldn't be more arresting.

'These could be before and after photos,' she says to Davy.

'I know, poor bastards,' Davy says.

On one side, the Tuckers' side, the window frames are newly painted bright white. The lower bay window gleams. The path is creamy York stone slabs that look newly laid. Not a crack, not a weed. They are so clean Manon wonders if she should remove her shoes before walking up the path.

The front door is grey-blue with a stainless steel oversized door knob and matching house numbers. Window film with a tiny star design

48

frosts the front door's glass panels, where she can see a figure approaching to answer the bell. These are the sort to hoover their garden with one of those deafening leaf blowers. The sort to file a bill the minute it comes in. No 'storing' their coats on the floor for these two.

Next door, the lower windows have been closed up with particle board. The frames are rotting and grey. The rubbish in the front garden is so high that it reaches the sill of the bay window. The front door is uPVC with rippled glass. On the step is a collection of tottering beer cans.

The bags of rubbish that have been tossed out front have been raided by foxes so that debris — crisp packets, banana skins, fag ash, ready meal trays, teabags — spill over the path. It smells. Stinks, in fact, like the open back end of a bin truck.

As the front door opens, Manon and Davy raise their badges.

* * *

Both at home during the day, Manon thinks, stepping over the threshold into an immaculate hallway with pale beech laminate flooring. *Wonder how that's going.* The house smells of polish and Glade.

'Come through,' says Mrs Tucker. 'Can I make you a tea or coffee?'

'I'm all right, thanks,' Manon says, following her into a gleaming white gloss kitchen while Davy and Mr Tucker disappear into the front

49

lounge. 'No work today?'

'I work from home. Jim lost his job recently.' Mrs Tucker gives Manon a weary smile as if she is tolerating a great deal. 'A husband is for life but not for lunch! It's driving me mad, to be honest.'

'I can imagine.'

'He didn't much like his job, to be fair. But now . . .'

'What did he do, for work I mean?'

'Housing officer, Fenland Council. Cuts to local authority budgets are beyond savage at the moment, well, as I'm sure you know. They must be cutting police budgets.'

'They are, yes. It's a very thin blue line right now.'

They wait in silence for the kettle to boil.

'Right,' Mrs Tucker says, holding a laden tray, 'let's go through.'

In the lounge, Mr Tucker is telling Davy about his predicament. He has an intense look on his face, as if he can't unburden himself quickly enough.

'I put everything into this house, every penny I had. I wanted to leave it to the kids. We were going to be mortgage free in about ten years except since they moved in, it's worth nothing at all. Nothing! Who'd buy this off us with that going on next door? We can't fucking leave.' At the word 'fucking' he kicks the skirting close to where he stands.

'Jim!' says his wife. 'Calm down.'

'I won't calm down. Don't fucking tell me to fucking calm down!'

Mr Tucker clenches and unclenches his fists, his jaw protruding.

Manon glances at Davy, who is ashen, as if frightened. Perhaps he fears Mr Tucker might turn the fists outwards, there is that much pent-up aggression in the room.

Mr Tucker continues, not quite shouting, but spitting out the words, 'This house, it's like a stone around our necks. Who'd take this house off us? All that rubbish out front, the noise, the smell. They come in at all hours, banging about, arguing, fighting. The drinking! Everything was all right before that lot came. We've complained that many times to the fella in charge over there, Edikas or something, he doesn't pick up my calls any more. I'm at my wits' end, I really am.'

While Mr Tucker talks, Manon takes the couple in. Mrs Tucker wears a billowing shirt dress, black, and weighty black-rimmed spectacles. She has a look — makeup free, her hair short and practical, statement earrings. *Knows how to shop*, Manon thinks admiringly. Mr Tucker wears old jeans and a half-zip sweatshirt. He is not fat, but has the classic male shape — round belly, pipe-cleaner legs. He has lost his hair. On his wrist is a Fitbit, and Manon wonders if he is a man beset by resolutions: to be better. At which he fails.

Mrs Tucker, seemingly unable to take any more of her husband's tub thumping, leaves the room.

Manon says, 'It's all right, Mr Tucker. I can see what a difficult situation this is. Have you talked to the police or the council about what's happening? An antisocial behaviour order — '

51

'No one's listening,' Mr Tucker says, sitting at last. 'I'm powerless.'

Mrs Tucker re-enters and sits on the sofa next to her husband. She's sick to the back teeth of him, Manon thinks. He needs a job. He needs to go out each day to a job and come back tired in the evening and watch some telly. We all need that. Or perhaps he needs to rent, instead of own property. We used to be a nation of renters like the Germans; more mobile, less vulnerable to this kind of hurt.

'Lukas Balsys,' Manon says.

She watches the name settle between Mr and Mrs Tucker on the sofa; watches the discomfort that name causes the married couple. *What do you tell yourselves about Lukas Balsys?* she wonders. *Fucking hell, I thought my relationship was shaky. We're the Waltons compared with these two.*

'Yes,' says Mrs Tucker. 'What about him?'

'Are you aware that he has died?'

'Yes,' says Mrs Tucker. 'Very sad.'

'Did you know him well?' asks Manon.

Davy shifts — with discomfort, Manon thinks — in his seat.

Mrs Tucker looks at Mr Tucker, who doesn't return her gaze.

'Um . . . not well,' Mrs Tucker says, 'I wouldn't say *well*. He came here to fix some things — some plumbing. He was good at plumbing and we'd complained that many times to next door's landlord, Edikas was it?'

'He's not the landlord, but he is their boss.'

'Right, well I think he felt he owed us a favour.

52

Perhaps he thought we'd stop complaining. So he sent Lukas around to look at our boiler because the pilot light kept going out.'

Edikas, Manon recalls, hadn't put it so delicately.

'Banging the wife,' was how he'd described it. 'Everyone know she very into it. Very. Lukas could not force her, not that kind of man. Maybe Lukas kill himself for love. Anyway, we hear them through the wall.' Edikas gave a filthy chuckle at this, then a bad impression of female orgasm, 'Oh! Oh! Oh!' Then another phlegm-bubbling dirty laugh. 'They always complain, this neighbour, so I think, I send Lukas round — Lukas plumb her hole!' Edikas had shouted, laughing.

'Yes, all right. I get the picture,' Manon had said. 'That was fast work from the two of them.'

'Ask me, this wife would do it with anyone I send. Even Dimitri.'

'What's up with Dimitri?'

Edikas had screwed his face up and tapped his temple with a finger. 'Mental problems.'

Manon had looked at Davy, without having to say 'we should look into this Dimitri fella', because Davy was already writing it in his pad.

She looks now at Mrs Do-It-With-Anyone Tucker, sitting next to Mr Probably-Hasn't-Done-It-In-Years Tucker.

'Got any outhouses — shed or garage, that kind of thing?'

'A shed, in the garden,' says Mr Tucker.

'Mind if I take a look?'

She follows him out to a garden with an oval

53

lawn surrounded by flower beds, bisected by a washing line fashioned from blue plastic rope, the same kind that tightened around Lukas Balsys's neck.

Manon stands beneath the washing line. The pegs are rusted onto it. The coils at the house end, around a post, are webbed with mud or spiders' webs or algae, or whatever it is that welds things together, brownly, outdoors. Bits of the rope have faded to yellow. It doesn't fit with the immaculate nature of the rest of the house.

'Were you planning to replace this?' she asks, one hand hanging from the line.

'Oh,' says Mr Tucker, 'at one point we were. Can't see the point now. I'm not putting a penny into this house, not now. Been up donkey's years, that. It's not very clean to put clothes on.'

'So, did you buy the rope to replace it?'

She glances into the shed while Mr Tucker holds the door open. No spare coils of new blue rope.

'Not yet, no.'

The sky is impossibly bright, and they squint, though the day isn't warm. Neither of them makes to move inside.

'Look, sorry about in there,' he says. He seems calmer, sadder, away from his wife.

'You don't like immigrants,' she says to him.

'Is that a question?' His tone right up to punch level again. 'I couldn't hear a question. Do I like the migrants next door? No, I don't. Do I hate all migrants? No, though I think we could do with less of them. We're being flooded.'

'So you're anti-immigration?'

'Isn't everyone?'

'Certainly feels that way,' Manon says. 'If we can go in, I just have a couple more questions for you and your wife.' And she heads indoors.

★   ★   ★

'Can I ask where you were the night before last?' Manon says, sitting in the living room again. The Tuckers are on the sofa. Davy is taking notes in a corner chair.

'Here,' says Mrs Tucker. 'Trying to watch telly over the din.'

'The din?'

'Well there was a lot of disturbance next door. There was that anti-immigration gathering. I hesitate to call it a march because there weren't that many of them. One Wisbech, Dean's lot.'

'Dean?'

'Dean Singlehurst, he's their main guy. They came past here with their placards and banners, very noisy, and there was a kerfuffle with the people next door.'

'Kerfuffle?'

'Yes. There was the usual banging about next door, we're used to that. Then the marchers came up the street, chanting. There weren't that many of them — maybe two dozen — but they were trying to be loud about it.'

'Wait, the One Wisbech march came up a small cul-de-sac like Prospect Place?' Manon asks.

'Yes, we thought it was strange,' Mrs Tucker says.

55

'What sort of thing were they chanting?'

'Oh, you know, *English jobs for English people. Stop the flood. Foreigners go home.* They stopped outside here. We didn't see what actually happened — we had the shutters closed.'

'How did you see how many marchers there were then?'

'When they first started coming up the road, I went and opened the front door to see who it was. Shane Farquharson was with them, at the front. Then I came inside to the living room, where we couldn't see anything, but we could hear everything,' Mrs Tucker continues. 'Some marchers came up the path next door. Then there was shouting.'

'English or Lithuanian?'

'Both. We don't know if they went in or not, or if the migrants came out. The noise just receded eventually.'

'What could you hear being shouted in English?'

'Well, one of the marchers said, 'Wanna ask you something!' and then 'Oi! Oi!''

'What time was this?'

Mrs Tucker turns her mouth down. 'Ten, ten thirty? The news was on, not that we could hear it.'

'You didn't think of calling the police?'

Manon eyes up the tea tray to see if any biscuits are on offer. She is crestfallen to see an empty, crumbed saucer. Davy has snaffled the custard creams, damn him.

'There wasn't anything to call the police about. Just people gathering, a bit of shouting.

56

We didn't know about Lukas, of course.'

Manon glances at Davy, but he's way ahead of her, writing it all down. He stops, mid-scrawl, and says, 'So it's Jim Tucker? That's your full name?'

'Actually, it's Jerome Wilberforce Tucker.'

'Wow,' says Manon. 'Shall we just call you Wilberforce — keep it nice and informal?'

'You can call me Jim. I know it's a ridiculous name. My mother had . . . pretensions.'

'Ambitions,' interjects Mrs Tucker.

'Look, I'm called Manon, so I'm in no position to judge.'

'Not that that's ever stopped you,' mutters Davy. 'And your name?' he asks Mrs Tucker.

The best names, Manon is thinking, *have rhythm*. Maxim de Winter. Engelbert Humperdinck. Dante de Blasio. Fly is currently mooning over a girl at school called Temperance. 'I already love her,' Manon told him, 'for her name.' Perhaps she should change hers to Manon de Bradshaw.

'Elspeth. Elspeth Tucker.'

★ ★ ★

Outside, in the car, Davy is overcome.

'It's shit for him,' he says. 'What's he s'posed to do? He's paid for that house, blood sweat and tears, and now it's worth nothing because of *them*. I don't blame him, coming over all UKIP. I'd want shot of them, too.'

'Yes, but did he *do* anything, that's the question? Or her? There's no rope lying around.'

57

'And he's got an alibi. Both have.'

'Yeah, but their alibi is each other. So we have to view that with some scepticism. Lukas got around, didn't he? We need to chat to the residents next door.'

'Trouble is, they clam up if Edikas is about. Aren't you going to ask Mrs Tucker about humping our victim?'

'I will, but not yet. There's nothing that puts her in Hinchingbrooke on the night Lukas died, even if she had the strength to get him into a tree, which I doubt. We need to go back into the migrant house now that we have powers to search and seize — question everyone in isolation. It's part of the crime scene. Doesn't matter what Edikas wants, or his dog. Can you call in an interpreter? Also, we need to chat to these One Wisbech marchers. And we need to catch up with Demented Dimitri. Also, Davy?' She wonders if that's a tiny eye roll she sees, as he pulls away from the kerb. 'Have we tried to match the handwriting on the note? Might be something in the house that matches it. So that should be a priority in the search — anything with handwriting on it.'

MATIS

His path to the bedroom has been blocked by Edikas.

'The police want to talk to you,' Edikas says. 'I am not going to take heat from police for you.'

'I can't — ' Matis says.

'You can. You can talk to them without telling them anything. This is easy. You forgot this, you don't know that.'

Dimitri, who is increasingly man-marking Matis like a concerned nursery maid, has joined them, towering over squat, fat Edikas.

'Hey, he doesn't want to,' says Dimitri.

Edikas says, 'What's it got to do with you?'

'He's my friend.'

'*Urgh*, I've had enough of all this friendship bullshit. This was the problem with Lukas. *Useless!* You're here to work.'

'Leave him alone,' says Dimitri, almost shouting.

'It's all right,' soothes Matis. He notices Edikas fiddling in his pocket, and before he can react, Edikas's fist comes up and out, a heavy metal fitting over his knuckles as he punches Dimitri in the face.

'You come with me,' Edikas says, pushing a stunned Dimitri towards the bedroom. He orders the men who are lying about on mattresses to leave. Just before closing the door, Edikas puts his head out and whistles, and the dog comes bounding up the stairs and slinks into the bedroom.

Matis hears Dimitri shout *'Please! No!'*

Hears growling, snarling, a cry of pain, then Edikas whistles and says, *Enough*, calling the dog off.

The door opens. Edikas walks down the stairs, the dog trotting alongside him.

Matis enters the room to find Dimitri on the floor, clutching his leg. The trousers are torn and there is a gash on his calf, bleeding profusely.

DAVY

Armed with a warrant to search the migrant house, his officers can control what goes on in there and have removed Edikas from the scene. Consequently, the conversations with migrants take a more relaxed turn. Up to a point.

There was an argument, one of the residents tells Davy and Manon, between Mr Tucker and Lukas, on the afternoon before he died. Mr Tucker came looking for him.

'This argument, was it in English or Lithuanian?' asks Davy.

'Both. Mr Tucker shouting in English, Lukas shouting in Lithuanian.'

'What was Lukas saying?'

' "It's not my fault. This is your business, not my business." '

Davy is momentarily confused and wonders if the migrant is actually saying this to him, but his interpreter confirms these are Lukas's quotes.

'Any idea what Mr Tucker was saying?' asks Manon.

'Ne.'

'Was it about Mrs Tucker do you think?' Davy

asks, aware that he's going beyond facts and into conjecture.

The man nods.

'What sort of a person was Lukas Balsys?' Davy asks.

'Depressive. Very. Always looked sad. A little bit on the outside, you know? Pessimistic.'

Davy nods, feeling affinity with the dead man. *What a waste of a good depressive.* 'You think he killed himself?' Davy asks.

'Oh no. This was his nature. Nothing to kill himself over. I mean, he was quite cheerful about being sad. Matis said so.'

'Where is Matis?'

Shrugs. Every time he asks about Lukas's friend Matis, he gets a downturned mouth and a shrug. People say, *'Out maybe, he likes a drink.'*

When he asks each in turn what happened on the night Lukas died, there are furtive glances to one another, partial sentences, pinched lips. *They know, but they're not saying,* Davy thinks. Either they're protecting someone, or they're too frightened to talk.

'Was it unusual for Edikas to not be working yesterday?' Davy asks a chap who has given his name as Audrius.

'Yes, I never saw Edikas take a day off before.'

'And how was Lukas's relationship with Edikas? Did they argue?'

Audrius grimaces, as if short-tempered with Davy's stupidity. 'Edikas is not some kind of friendly uncle. He works us. He fights with all of us.'

62

* ★ ★

'They know, but they're not saying,' says Manon, heaving down into the passenger seat.

Davy is in the driver's seat, checking his emails on his BlackBerry. 'This is interesting,' he says. 'Previous incident involving Mr Tucker.'

'Oooh, really? What? Pushing someone up a tree?'

'Altercation with a motorist. Mr Tucker reckoned this motorist cut him up, so at the next traffic lights, he got out of his car and leered over the chap's windscreen and bashed on the bonnet with his hand.'

'Quite threatening,' says Manon. 'He's certainly got a temper. Never underestimate the anger of the overlooked white middle-aged man, Davy Walker, and I say that as someone who lives with one.'

'Has Mark been overlooked?'

'Not really, but lots of men who are very invested in their careers feel short changed when they get to middle age and things are no longer . . . going as well as they thought they would.'

'Whereas women?'

'Ah, you'll make me seem like a throwback. Women have other things to worry about, like being thin. Being thin and looking young, essentially.'

'Should we talk to the victim of the assault do you think?' *Not that he hasn't got enough to do.*

'Could do,' she says. 'Not sure it was an assault. I mean, having your bonnet thumped and having your head kicked in are not one and the same. Also, what do we learn? That Mr Tucker has a temper? I think we know that. Also, what does it tell us about Lukas's murder? I mean, his death is not a flare of rage kind of crime, is it? Someone took a rope to a tree with a plan.'

'Could've been an angry plan,' says Davy.

'Really? It's quite a ball-ache of an angry plan. My kind of angry plan would be to push him off a building or under a train. Grab the nearest kitchen knife . . . '

'But Tucker's motive is whopping. Out of everyone, his motive is *really* . . . being humiliated like that. And Lukas living next door, and the squalid migrant place wiping the value off his house. I mean, he had grounds and the temperament, from the looks of it.'

'Yeah, but that lot,' she says, nodding at the migrant house, 'they're proper scared. They're not scared of Tucker, are they? I think we need to work out some kind of protection set-up with Op Pheasant so they start talking.'

'Also,' says Davy, still reading his emails, 'the trace on Tucker's car has just come in, and it's negative.'

'Wait, which car?' asks Manon.

'The Beema.'

'Ah, that's Mrs Tucker's car. Mr Tucker drives a Nissan Micra.'

'OK, I'll put a trace on that as well.'

'Separate bank accounts too. And look how happy it's making them.'

'How do we track down Matis?' Davy asks.

'Maybe it's time to seize Edikas's mobile

phone. Also, let's see if that row between Lukas and Tucker escalated. Police could've been involved without a formal charge.'

'Why is Dimitri supposedly demented? Seems perfectly normal to me, in fact easier to communicate with than the others.'

'I think it's just that he's built like a double decker.'

DAY 3

DAVY

'Have you seen this?' DC Kim Delaney asks, in front of her computer screen. She leans back to give Davy a look. 'Facebook page. *One Wisbech* — the anti-immigration lot. This post, here,' she points at the screen. 'On the day Lukas's body was found, someone posted saying *It's time — time to get rid of the lawless vermin in our town!*'

'Charming,' says Davy. 'Who posted that?'

Kim squints at her screen. 'You need some reading specs,' adds Davy.

'Doesn't say. I'll get the tech team to trace the IP address, shouldn't be a problem. These crazies are usually super active online but kind of inert in real life. Or should I say IRL.' Kim snorts at her own joke.

'Except they weren't inert on the night of Lukas's death. Don't show Colin this site, he'll want to join.'

Colin Brierley, the team's civilian investigator and tech nerd, is the Ukipper in their midst. They tolerate his slightly uncertain brand of prejudice with mild annoyance tinged with affection. 'Bigots have feelings too,' Manon was

66

fond of warning them. Davy harbours a suspicion that Colin doesn't *really* hate foreigners, not deep down. He's just a man who hasn't found his tribe or his stride, and the wilderness in which he founders intersects with other marginalised white men of a certain age with whom Davy is starting to feel a certain affinity.

These men are equally wrong-footed by clever young women, clever young Muslims, clever young gay men — anyone who appears to have access to the crucial information they lack. Information about modernity, how to live, how to prosper, how it all *works*.

Colin is like the office pet; sometimes he blows off, ideologically speaking, and it smells revolting, but mostly he is just there, and if he weren't there you'd miss his rather stolid presence.

'Right,' says Davy. 'Briefing everyone.'

'Shouldn't we do this when Manon is in?' asks Kim. 'She *is* SIO.'

'Can't wait for that,' says Davy, aware that he is taking advantage of her working pattern. But he wants to press on, to take back some control for himself.

Take back control. Christ.

Forensics and SOCO have come back with DNA and fingerprints from the rope and around the scene, but for these to mean anything, the matches have to be on the database. Half the migrants in Wisbech aren't even documented, let alone listed on databases alongside fingerprints and DNA. Of course Lukas Balsys's DNA is everywhere, but that's to be expected.

67

To Davy's mind, there are several possible motives worth examining. One, Lukas was killed as a warning to other migrants not to snitch, to work harder, obey out of abject fear. Edikas is right in the frame on this count. Two, he was killed by other migrants in some kind of argument over money or drugs (he wants to pull local dealer Talcy Malc in for a grilling) or a girl. There was a culture of fighting in the houses of multiple occupation (HMOs) inhabited by migrants — a way of establishing the pecking order among hard nuts. Also, Bridget says, (*Oh, Bridget says does she?* he hears Manon say in his head) there is a higher than average level of mental health issues among the migrants, hence why they've got into this mess. Three, had Mr Tucker had enough of being cuckolded? Four, did Lukas get on the wrong side of the anti-immigration lot? Did he kill himself? Was he so ground down by the work, the hours, the lack of pay, the awful conditions, that he just wanted out? Davy is reluctant to go down this last road, not just because he wants a collar, but because he wants Lukas's mother to get the compensation he feels she deserves, compensation his own mother deserves by way of rent, for not deserting him age ten. Juliet, of course, doesn't know about *that* direct debit.

'Where are we with the rope?' he asks his team.

'Right,' says Kim, 'so we know it is polypropylene rope, blue in colour, which costs £12.77 for a big roll of the stuff. And we have Edikas buying a roll of it from Homebase on

Westlode Street in Spalding.'

'Why would he buy rope in Spalding?' Davy asks. 'When there's a B&Q five minutes from his house?'

'P'raps he was in Spalding on other business?' offers Kim. 'Or he prefers the Homebase shopping experience.'

'Well, which of us doesn't? I'm just wondering if he bought it in Spalding so that he wouldn't be caught, or remembered by the staff.'

'Actually, chap in Homebase remembers Edikas buying the rope because the dog was foaming at the mouth, and he remembers worrying that the dog was on a not very secure rope, and he said to Edikas, 'Hope the rope's for the dog', and Edikas kind of harrumphed like he didn't understand a word.'

'Good. OK, good, so Edikas bought the rope.'

'Yes, and thanks to that staff member's recall, we were able to look at the right date on their CCTV and we have got shop footage of Edikas making said purchase.'

'Good. And did we ask Edikas about buying the rope that hung three people?'

'Yes. He said some of the women wanted washing lines in their back yards, so he supplied washing line rope to three of the houses. I quote: 'How will I know they heng themselves viz vashing line? Zis is not my fault. Lithuanians are sad peoples.''

'Very good work, Kim, and excellent accent by the way,' says Davy. 'Who is going over the files for the other two hanging victims?' he asks, praying it isn't Tired Nigel, whose work is at best

69

slapdash, at worst incompetent.

Nigel raises his hand. *Of course,* thinks Davy.

'It's . . . well, I haven't finished reading the files yet,' Nigel says.

'Seriously?'

'They're quite big files,' says Tired/Incompetent Nigel.

Davy pauses. *I can't give it to Kim, otherwise Kim is doing everything because everything you give her, gets done. And done well. But if I leave it with Nigel, it'll never get done.*

'Perhaps Kim could help you out with it, Nigel,' Davy says.

'Yeah, great,' Nigel says, smiling broadly. Davy's biggest problem with Nigel is he has no problem being thought of as lazy and crap. No professional pride.

'Colin, I need you to trace Mr Tucker's car please on the night of Lukas's death. We're looking for travel from Wisbech to Hinching-brooke and back, obviously.'

'Righto,' says Colin.

'And I want you to check for CCTV around the other two hangings, maybe once Kim has looked at the case files and can give you location parameters.' He has written off Tired Nigel, they all have. He might as well be off the team. 'I'd also like you to Google Dean Singlehurst, Colin, see what he's been up to online. And get me an address for him, while you're about it.' He is surprised to see Manon walk into the room. 'What are you doing here?' he asks, prickling with embarrassment at being caught briefing the team.

70

'Couldn't stay away, so I bunged Ted at the childminder's. I think we need a meeting with Bridget from Op Pheasant asap. Can you call her in? And what are you doing holding a briefing?'

Davy flushes. 'I . . . I just wanted to keep things moving, that's all. I wasn't taking advantage of your day off — '

'It's not a 'day off', Davy, it's a day at the brutal coalface of childcare.'

The team has gone remarkably silent as they earwig this exchange.

'Right, well, I wasn't taking advantage of your working pattern.'

He hears Nigel say, '*Awkward!*' in a high-pitched whisper.

'Yeah, sure you weren't. You can fill me in while we wait for Bridget.'

MANON

They are in something called a 'break-out zone' — a shabby common room with a worn sofa and tub chairs. In the old days it would've been a smoking room and it still has that nicotine-yellow tinge.

Davy is fixated on Bridget when she is looking elsewhere, but the minute she looks back at him, he's eyes to the floor. She is wearing an impressively tight long-sleeved tee.

'Thanks for coming in, Bridget,' Manon says. 'The problem we're having is breaking open the Lithuanian hub.'

'Welcome to my world,' says Bridget.

'We need them to talk about the night Lukas died, but they're scared rigid.'

'Yes. This is our primary problem. They won't snitch on the gangmasters, and when we break open an HMO because we've got other evidence, they can't get out of the country fast enough. Makes prosecutions very difficult.'

'I'm not clear whether they're terrified of Edikas or of whoever killed Lukas,' Manon says.

'Might be one and the same,' Davy points out.

'Also,' says Bridget, 'Edikas may have used the

72

murder retrospectively to threaten them. You snitch, you're next, type thing. Even if he had nothing to do with it.'

'So what can we do?' Manon asks. 'Move them out of the HMO into safe accommodation?'

'Most won't go,' says Bridget. 'Even though they're effectively slaves, in terms of payment and conditions, they are there by choice. No one is locking them up. Often they have mental health issues, shady pasts, alcoholism. They think it's work, so they get on and do it, but don't get paid for it. They are locked up by the language barrier, by their mistrust of authority, their dependence on the gangmasters for their basic needs. They get petty cash to buy deodorant or a packet of crisps, but no wage.'

'What's your view of Edikas?' Manon asks. 'Could he murder?'

'Oh yes, in a heartbeat. Edikas is the hard nut to end all hard nuts. So cold he's almost reptilian.'

Davy sticks his tongue out while crossing his eyes, presumably some extremely lame impression of a lizard.

Bridget titters.

Christ, thinks Manon. If there's one thing she can't stand, it's sexual tension where she's not remotely involved. Like the pensioner she feels, she heaves herself up out of her chair, saying 'Get a room, you two. Oh, and Bridget? Is it always agricultural work, chicken catching, that kind of thing?'

'Mostly. That's where there's a labour shortage. Also picking fruit and veg. Vasil has a sideline in block patios. It's run by a guy called Jonas. Essentially, anything that's really hard graft, the Lithuanians are all over it.'

Manon's phone is going, unknown number. Her first thought is that something has happened to Teddy or Fly.

'Hello?'

'Manon Bradshaw?'

'Yes.' Nerves rising.

'This is Hinchingbrooke Hospital.' *Oh Christ, no, please no, don't let this be the moment.* 'We have admitted Mark Talbot with abdominal pain and he has requested that you come in. Is that OK?'

She feels a guilty relief that it's not one of the children.

'Yes, yes, I'll be right there.'

★　★　★

Having taken the ten-minute walk from HQ to the hospital at a run, her mind full of worst-case-scenario planning, she pants over the reception desk, only just huffing out the words, 'I'm here for Mark Talbot.'

'Just a moment please,' says the woman behind the desk, while typing and looking at her screen. 'Yes, fourth floor, oncology.'

Oncology, shit, shit shit.

In fourth floor oncology, the nurse, who had presumably rung her, knows who she is.

'He's resting comfortably. Follow me,' she says.

Trotting after the nurse down shining

linoleum-floored corridors, Manon's mind keeps step with Emily Dickinson:

Because I could not stop for Death —
He kindly stopped for me —
The Carriage held but just Ourselves —
And Immortality . . .

There he is, familiar in this strange setting, propped up and wrapped in sheets, eyes closed. He opens them to see her, smiles, takes her hand as she sits beside him.

'Thanks for giving me the fright of my life,' she says, her anger like popping candy on her tongue; little explosions of it. Why is he throwing her this curveball in the midst of her first murder job in years?

'Sorry,' he says.

'So what's going on?'

'I had the most terrible pain in my stomach,' he says. 'So I came in.'

'And?' she says.

'They're keeping me in to run some tests.'

'What does that mean?'

He gives a feeble shrug. God, this is like asking Fly how his day at school went. 'Fine' or 'Good' giving her no information whatsoever.

'Are you worried?' she asks him.

'A bit, yes,' he says. 'Are you?'

'Well I am *now*. Who do I talk to?'

'Don't bother them. They've got it in hand.'

This is no time to be apologetic, she thinks. He's always apologetic. Says things like, 'That's so kind', when someone is taking his credit card details. You have to push, in the NHS more than anywhere. She wants to manage him, the situation. Get control of it because her feelings are spinning like a whirligig. *Not this. Not now.*

'Stay calm,' he says, holding her hand.

'I can't,' she says. 'Not when it's you.'

She casts about the ward for someone, but it is empty, except for an orderly mopping. Eastern European probably. Kristine, Teddy's childminder, is Romanian.

'So when are you coming out?' she demands.

'Tomorrow, I guess.'

'You probably just ate a dodgy bhuna,' she says. 'Knowing you.'

★   ★   ★

Recently, she'd held Mark close and recalled their first dirty weekend away, while they were still hot for each other. 'What do you remember about that weekend?' she'd asked romantically, to which he replied, literally in a heartbeat, 'The pork pies.'

They don't call him Mr Romance.

At all.

What if he is taken away? The worst can happen.

People don't always get through things.

Who will she discuss everything with? Who will she talk to about what she had for lunch? 'It was under-seasoned to be honest.'

About how well the topside of beef turned out?

'It was my herby crust that made it,' she'd said.

76

'It was your herby crust was it?' he'd said, smiling at her ironically.

Who will have enough irony for her now?

She remains upright only by dint of the urge to bring her children home and hold them very close indeed.

Like an unexpected belch from the deep, she wonders, *Did they trace the rope?*

And, rather like someone drowning who grabs that rope, she reaches the dry land of the investigation and rests there.

In every case there is evidence that doesn't make sense, the element that threatens to unravel the whole. Even where there is doubt, they are trained to 'think murder', because if you assume the worst, you secure the evidence. With the Balsys murder it's how they got him into that tree. She wonders if there might have been some kind of ladder situation on the rear side, indentations missed by SOCO then erased by rain. She wonders if they brought apparatus, the murderers. Usually, perps are faced with the problem of the dead body: far weightier and more unwieldy than anyone expects. Not so in this: they left him where he died. No attempt at concealment in that sense.

But here was the problem of getting the live body to its execution. Problem: resistance of the victim. Advantage: agency of the victim. They could use their own muscle strength, under duress obviously. Unless . . . unless Lukas was unconscious, drugged or beaten. Impossible, surely? He would be a literal dead weight.

What she realises is there isn't one perp. There

are many. *They*. It is they, not him. A group, accomplices. A joint enterprise.

★ ★ ★

What if her own partnership is at an end? She has spent so long criticising Mark, this person she tells everything to, the person who is her lifeblood, the rug beneath her feet (and just as poorly treated), her walls, her roof, her warmth, and her seasons. She has wasted their short time together not appreciating him, and what if now he is to be taken away?

He is her fit, her equal, her better half. He is the stalwart presence that allows her to yearn for freedom; the one who loves her enough to put up with her, and who else would do that, even if she wanted them, which she never would because she only wants Mark Talbot? For ever and ever, amen.

Only tests, nothing is certain yet. Just get through the tests, wait and see, she tells herself.

Whoever would be comfortable enough to read with for hours at a time without talking (they would have, were it not for Teddy). Oh Teddy! Who will love Teddy like Mark loves Teddy? Who will look down on him with the benign yet brimming adoration that Mark displays and that only she sees? Teddy isn't even biologically his, but this has never made a difference to Mark. She should have had his babies, that a bit of his nature might live on. But a sixteen-year-old, a four-year-old and a two-year-old (had they gone again) and a partner dying of cancer (as it has become so quickly in her mind) — that would've been some package to deal with. Not to mention work, be it cold cases or a murder inquiry.

All their conversations about food, which were not really conversations at all but more like idle thoughts pushed outwards. Must they all be inwards now, like they used to be? What was it Joan Armatrading sang?

He is more than a lover, more than a friend. He is the recipient of her thoughts, the person she can say anything to, without fear of judgement. And she has spent so long finding fault with him, with them as a couple.

Only the other day, she'd nearly walked up to a complete stranger thinking it was Mark — in the way small children sometimes nonchalantly clasp the wrong adult's hand — she had walked up to this stranger-man and was on the brink of telling him, 'Time to clear the area, I've let an evil one go'. This is the kind of conversational gold she bestows on lucky, lucky Mark Talbot. Soon to be departed Mark Talbot. Who will she tell about her herby crust, her deadly emissions, about what they might watch on telly ('I think we ought to watch that documentary about migration called *Exodus*. Apparently it's excellent. Ooh, hang on, there's a *First Dates* on planner.')? Who will hear her smallest thoughts as if they are interesting? And he, he tells her the same things at least three or four times. She barely listens to the first rendition.

They text each other pictures of their double chins. These are love notes of sorts.

People get through things, only sometimes they don't.

★ ★ ★

'What's wrong?' she asks Fly, more aggressively than she intends.

'Nothing.'

'Why're you so quiet? Things OK at school?'

'I guess.'

'What does that mean?'

'Leave me alone.'

Fly is her adopted son, though the word adopted seems no longer relevant. The brother of a murder victim, he'd been eleven years old with nowhere to go when she'd taken him on as a stopgap that extended. He is the light of her life: thoughtful, empathic, intelligent, kind. Black, though the word seems no longer relevant. At sixteen, he now towers over her, is a hard worker at a school, which, like all ginormous state secondaries, has its rough element.

She monitors it and Fly constantly for signs of trouble. He is about to sit his GCSEs, and she has high hopes that finally the true depth of his worth will be visible to the world. As if GCSEs could achieve such a thing! But she has always felt the world at large — teachers, mainly — have been slow to catch on to her elder son's riches.

She follows him up the stairs, wondering if she should leave it be. He has to fight his own battles, after all.

'Anything you want to tell me about?' she asks, sitting on his bed.

'Nope.'

'Sure?'

'Yep.'

You have to come at it sideways with children. When they are little, like Ted, it is over toys or in the bath. With Fly, she often has to submit to some incredibly tedious tale about dodgeball or Greek mythology before the truth will out. The play's the thing . . .

'What are you reading?' she tries.

'*Madame Bovary.*'

'Oh yeah? I liked that one.'

'Yeah, same.'

'Is it for school?'

'No, the librarian recommended it to me, so I thought why not?'

He sits close beside her, leans in slightly. She puts her arm around him. He sniffs. He is crying.

'Oh lovey, tell me.'

'It's Sulaiman.'

'Right, what's he done?'

'He's . . . every time he sees me, he puts his foot out and trips me up.'

'You *what?*' she says, furious.

'It's super annoying.'

'Of course it is! Have you said anything to him?'

At nursery, Teddy is taught to say 'Stop it, I don't like it' as opposed to, say, biting back. But he is also taught to say 'sharing is caring', a line he can deliver with impressive venom while snatching a toy from another child's vice-like grip.

81

'No,' whispers Fly.

'Told a teacher?'

'No.'

'Want me to?'

'No!' He stands. 'Promise you won't.'

'Only if you promise you will.'

If she wants to appal Fly, she only has to a) meet him at school with her wheelie shopper, or b) bust out some of her finest dance moves in public. Or c) talk to his teachers.

'Why does he do it, d'you think?'

Fly shrugs. 'He's a bit rough. Thinks it's funny.'

Fly is rather reserved, she thinks. Sometimes kids want his attention and don't know how to get it.

'Does he laugh, after he's tripped you up,' she says, wanting to hurt Sulaiman very badly indeed.

He shrugs.

'That's horrible, Fly. You poor thing.'

He lifts his trouser legs, shows her bruises up to his knees.

'Jesus. We have to do something about this. Shall I talk to Sulaiman's mum?'

'No! Please, everyone overreacts when you get involved because of your job.'

'Mark then? Would you like Mark to deal with it?'

He shrugs again, which is tantamount to a yes. If Mark were here, he and Manon would workshop it for about an hour and she'd feel better about it.

She quietens the urge to travel out of the

house, track Sulaiman down and trip him up, saying 'How do you like it, you little shit?'

In fact, as far as she remembers, Sulaiman is a nice kid with nice parents. Teenage boys are tricky. Hard to read, everything under the surface.

Teddy stands in the doorway of Fly's room in his jammies. She scoops him up, squeezes him tight, which is what she'd like to do to Fly but can't.

The spectre of Fly leaving home for university hangs over them. She harbours a fantasy he might attend her alma mater, Cambridge, and live at home, while knowing this would only be a fraction of the university experience (cheaper though). She can't bear the thought of the house without children in it. The quietness. Just her and Mark and encroaching infirmity. Small dinners, elderly trips to the cinema (Ooh, there's a 6 p.m. showing! Bed by 9 p.m.!)

Perhaps she will foster. Take a kid from care, give them a home.

They had a wobble around Teddy being born, when Fly felt displaced. Replaced. By a biological white baby. But he misses his little cousin Sol, currently in some far-flung corner of the world with Manon's estranged sister (as far as she knows), and his affinity with small children soon took over. He is brilliant with kids, stooping, offering his hand to them, leading them off for a story. And little kids adore big kids, are amazed by them, as if they are an optical illusion, a unicorn version of themselves. The little kid inside the big kid makes contact with the big kid inside the little kid and magic happens.

Fly's parents, Maureen Dent (an Irish alcoholic, deceased) and Adewale Sane (a Nigerian of no fixed abode whose contact with Fly petered out), imbued their son with grace and patience. Intelligence. Fly's fantasies, at their peak just before Teddy's birth, that his father would rescue him from difficult feelings, had abated as the difficult feelings abated, and with evidence that Adewale Sane had little to offer other than an intense interest in money and a string of unsuitable girlfriends.

Fly used to call her Manon, using 'Mum' only occasionally and effortfully. But this, too, had ebbed away. He uses 'Mum' naturally now because that is who she is.

When she'd been at the end of her exhaustion-frayed rope with Teddy, Fly would lift him up, carry him to his high chair in the kitchen and feed him buttered toast soldiers (which he squished in his fist) and blueberries. Chatting away to the baby. Peekaboo. Round and round the garden (like a teddy bear). Wheels on the bus, his arms going 'round and round'. She lay on the sofa, eyes closed, listening to them, half an eye opening to check it wasn't going wrong. Sinking gratefully into the cushions.

She wished she'd had Fly as a baby, that she could have cradled him, lips to soft temples as he tugged on a bottle of milk like a tiny goat. She wished she could have kept him for longer, loved him for longer, because loving him is an expansion.

★ ★ ★

The silent house, late at night.

She finds herself sitting on the kitchen floor, her back against the units, the collar of her shirt damp with tears. Across the table are the remnants of Teddy's dinner and her and Fly's plates, the detritus that Mark would normally clear away late at night before coming to bed. She ought to have noticed that more, but she was too busy seeing the coats on the floor.

She leaves the mess and trudges up the stairs. Opens the door to Teddy's room where he lies on his back in bed, his mouth an oval. She climbs in with him, pushing her nose into his neck, which is lightly sweaty, smelling hamsterish.

She kisses his cheek. He frowns, rolls away from her. She spoons him, tight. Closes her eyes.

'I love you Teddy Bradshaw.'

★ ★ ★

She wakes over-heated by Teddy's furnace of a body. Rises groggily and goes to find Mark in their bed. *I wake and feel the fell of dark, not day.* You can always be out-miserabled by Gerard Manley Hopkins.

Then it returns to her, with all the violence of an ambush.

The bed's too big without you.

She lies on the cold sheets with the awful space beside her where he should be, where he has been all this time when she has been unloving, unkind.

85

DAY 4

MANON

They requested the pleasure of Dimitri's company at Wisbech cop shop but he declined to show, so they have returned to the migrant house to interview him.

There he is on a mattress on the far side of the room, all whopping seven feet of him, legs bent, back to the wall. The man is built like a Transit van. Giant headed. Shins like paddles. Manon wonders what he has to be frightened of. Surely he could lift Edikas off the floor with one hand. Speaking of shins, even at the doorway to this malodorous room, she can smell putrid flesh.

Dimitri has put a fabric stretch plaster over the wound on his calf, but it peels open on one corner. *That wound is wet*, Manon thinks, feeling nauseous. That's why the plaster won't stick.

'I'd put money on that being a dog bite,' Davy mutters to Manon.

'C'mon, let's go to the doctor's,' Manon says loudly into the room (via the interpreter). 'Get you sorted. I'd say a strong course of antibiotics was in order.'

Davy knows she's trying to bluster past

86

Dimitri's pissed-on-my-chips expression.

'Ne!' says Dimitri.

'It's infected,' says Manon.

Dimitri shrugs.

'Suit yourself,' says Manon. 'Good luck with the amputation. How was your relationship with Lukas?'

'We were the best of friends,' says Dimitri, his anger giving way to sadness.

'And do you know Matis?'

He nods.

'Where is he?' Manon asks. The three of them are still standing in the doorway, like wedding crashers, but she doesn't want to go nearer to Dimitri because that flesh wound really hums.

Dimitri shrugs. 'He shipped out. I don't know where.'

'Did he know what happened to Lukas?'

'Yes, but he wouldn't tell me. He kept saying it was all his fault. I don't know why he said this. It didn't make sense. He and Lukas were best friends, going right back to childhood. What happened to Lukas, it changed Matis, made him sick. This is a mystery to me, he didn't tell me. He said we cannot tell anyone or it will happen to us.'

BEFORE
KLAIPEDA, LITHUANIA

MATIS

'Look, I'll show you,' Matis said as Lukas arrived at the table with two pints of beer.

Matis showed the screen of his phone to Lukas. On it was an advert:

> Well paid jobs in UK
> £250–350 per week
> Food & accommodation provided
> Call —

'I called the number,' Matis said. 'The bus is leaving this Saturday.'

'I don't know,' Lukas was saying, turning his glass. They were in their local bar — pine tables and chairs in two rooms painted peach. They knew the waitresses. The beer was great. The food best avoided.

He needed Lukas on board that bus with him, to steady his nerves, to make this venture an exciting break with the past rather than a rattly days-long ordeal into the unknown.

Being motherless, it was assumed Matis would take a place at Lukas's family table on high days and holidays: Christmas lunch (when his father

88

was always drunk), Easter, birthdays. This kindness was performed without ceremony, the Balsys family barely remarking on the presence of their guest, and in this way they spared Matis humiliation and did not seek to congratulate themselves.

Mrs Balsys — Ludmilla — ladled home-cooked food onto Matis's plate silently. Beef goulash, dumplings, side salad of sliced beetroot. Squeezed him in at their table, which was barely big enough for four, let alone five. For Matis, it was a nutritious feast. His father never cooked and Matis felt, at Lukas's house, that he was packing away goodness for future use. Ludmilla had a brisk way about the house, which was always immaculate. She never stopped wiping surfaces, hoovering, washing curtains. Her capability was something he envied. His father maintained a level of squalor in their house, too busy nursing pints of Švyturys. Kitchen surfaces never wiped. Beds never made or changed. Their sheets always felt gritty.

At school, Matis and Lukas were not friends, having separate cohorts. Lukas was more bookish and did better at school. But even in their separation, whenever Matis was with Lukas, it was a homecoming of sorts, like being with family — a cousin or a brother, to whom he didn't have to explain himself or his home situation.

'Come on, we can't stay in Klaipeda. Even your sister has gone,' Matis said, taking a sip of beer. It was cold and crisp. He felt fortified by it, in the way his father probably did. Another reason to get out. Matis could feel himself developing a need for drink that he feared must be hereditary, or part of the national characteristic. Matis's mother had left more than a decade ago, unable to bear the degradation of his father's addiction.

For now, Matis was hell-bent on persuading Lukas: 'There is nothing here. Nothing to aim for. You work your butt off for 450 euros a month! For what? To line someone else's pocket. I want more. I want a better life, to know what else the world might have for me.'

In fact, money had never particularly interested Matis, though everyone around him was obsessed with it — all the parents of children who had gone to Denmark or Norway to earn better and send it back. Matis didn't fantasise about possessions or houses or cars. It was vistas he was after. He was familiar with the Matis that lived under the leaden thunk of the cranes in the dock: depressed Matis, stuck Matis, irritable with everyone around him, bored with himself. He made the common mistake of thinking relocation equalled reinvention, thinking his old self wouldn't follow him across Europe.

He wanted a new Matis: perhaps ruthless Matis in a sharp suit in a gleaming Western city. Or romantic Matis in the long shadows of a bucolic setting at harvest. Or in a small town where he might find culture or fall in love. Who knows? He wanted, above all, chances. Experience. An opportunity to play a part. A chance not to be defined by what came before; by his father, or transition, or the Soviets, or the Nazis.

In the UK, he would not drink. He would not trudge through snow to some menial job with no chance of moving up. He wouldn't live in a charmless Rybporte flat with a hard-faced wife, his life on a loop. In the UK, he'd be a different sort altogether. Perhaps he'd have a profession. Start a business. The UK was a nation of entrepreneurs. In Lithuania there were people with university degrees shifting containers on the dock. It was a nation of brothers — to achieve anything, you needed a friend in a high place. The UK, though, was a meritocracy, the land of Simon Cowell and Ed Sheeran. A place so rich that shopping was the national pastime; where you could *get somewhere*, and where his children might be professionals too.

'The problem is not where we are, but who we are,' said Lukas, miserable philosopher that he was. 'To change, you have to change inside.'

'No, the problem is *where* we are,' said Matis, as old Grigoriev sat at their table uninvited.

'Matis wants to go to England,' Lukas explained to Grigoriev.

'*Ach,*' Grigoriev said, 'who will look after your papa? How much longer can he work with his health? Then what, 300 euros a month to retire on, when his heating bills are 250? You must stay to look after him.'

'That's it?' said Matis, bubbling inside. 'That's all there is for me?'

'That's all there is for anyone,' said Grigoriev. 'And don't be thinking he's never done anything for you.' *Christ, he can read my mind*, thought Matis. 'Your papa never left you. He stayed. Not

91

like your mother, who you idealise so much. He might not be the most sensitive man, but he did not shirk his duty and nor should you.'

'And look how happy it made him,' Matis said.

'What's happiness got to do with it? Young people think happiness is owed to them. What we're talking about is duty. Our duty is, that while our parents take care of us when we are young, we must take care of them when they are old. This is what it is to be human.'

'But in between you need some life,' Matis said, nearly crying out with his sense of injustice. 'A life for yourself. You need to be allowed to make your own mistakes.'

The Internet had given Matis fresh horizons as well as a view on his own land. Lithuania: the third most unhappy country on earth, beaten to the top spot only by Chad and Syria.

'Well, I'm going,' said Matis, with false bravado. His insides were turning over themselves with fear. His need of Lukas was so great; his terror that he wouldn't accompany him close to crippling. With Lukas he could do it. Without Lukas, he might lose his nerve. 'When I'm rich and married to a beautiful English girl, don't think you can come and stay.' He gave Lukas a queasy smile.

Outside the bar, his emotions were in a high tussle, but he tried to keep things light. Matis said, 'Grigoriev only thinks of himself. If you risk nothing, Lukas, you gain nothing.' Then Matis had an idea: Lukas's father had been signed off with emphysema. He blamed the chemicals in the containers of fertiliser coming into Rybporte

92

from Belarus. 'Your father cannot earn now he's off sick. Your parents need money. We can get that for them. Imagine your mother's face when you send back half your pay cheque each month. Imagine her opening the envelope, how proud she'd be.'

Matis needed to fight for himself, for his freedom to leave. Much of his ambition sprang from a desire to leave his father behind, to mark out a difference between them as men, and yet he didn't know what that difference might be. He didn't know who he was, he only wanted the chance to find out. His chest felt tight at the strain of it all. Lithuanian men don't cry, they fight and they drink and often they kill themselves. He wanted the chance not to be Lithuanian.

'And what if the different thing you chase after is worse than what you've got?' Lukas asked him. 'What if *this* turns out to be as good as it gets?'

Matis couldn't explain it to Lukas because Lukas wasn't a similar type. Lukas was downcast. Couldn't look across the border because he was too busy staring gloomily at his shoes. Ask Lukas how he was and he'd say, 'I've known days when I've laughed more.' It was the reason they got on so well, this canyon of difference in their natures. The pessimism of one met by the optimism of the other and vice versa. If they were man and woman, they would marry.

When they left each other, Matis said, as lightly as he was able, 'The bus leaves at 8 a.m. Saturday, 8 a.m. — OK? Come on. You want to stay here all your life?'

'I like the misery I know,' said Lukas, shaking his head sadly as he walked away.

He knew that Lukas had a girlfriend, Janina, who might keep him in Klaipeda. But a girlfriend he was hot and cold about, which might allow him to leave. Matis felt sick with not knowing.

★ ★ ★

On Saturday morning, Matis left with a small rucksack on his back. He was hungry, but felt too nauseous with anxiety to eat anything. He stood on the road smoking a roll-up. Then he flushed with happiness as he saw Lukas walking towards him, also wearing a rucksack and smoking.

'Hey!' he said. 'You made it!'

He was so pleased to see Lukas, he wanted to shout with joy. Instead, he patted Lukas's shoulder, which was difficult because of his bag, so he ended up half-slapping the back of his neck.

A bus pulled up at the kerb and they boarded it. Not the shiny bus Matis had envisioned with television screens and air conditioning, but a yellowing coach with tobacco-infused seating, fogged windows, and a toilet door that didn't shut properly. Settled into their seats, Matis quickly fell asleep, comforted that the decision had been made and he had his best friend beside him. He was exhausted from his nerves and from the sleepless hours he'd passed the night before. Whatever the UK held, now that Lukas was with him, they could get through it together. With his best friend with him, he allowed himself some excitement about the future.

When he woke, he watched the last of Lithuania slip by through dirty windows. His mother would never find him in some English town. If she ever came looking. His leaving, he realised, closed the door on the hope that she'd return.

★ ★ ★

Forty-four hours later, the coach containing Matis and Lukas pulled up outside a small terraced house in a British town, location unknown. The houses seemed cramped to him, looking out of the coach window. And the roads cluttered with lamp posts and signs and too much civic furniture. *This is a crowded island,* he thought.

Neither of them could speak a word of English, so the road signs had been a mystery, much as they craned eagerly through drizzle at the blue panels with white roundabouts drawn on them. Their vulnerability was suddenly apparent to them both. At a service station stop, they couldn't ask for anything nor buy anything. No language. No pounds.

Matis told himself that once they arrived, he could shower and change clothes; maybe sleep horizontally for an hour before getting the lie of the land. Arrange his things on a night stand perhaps. His ankles were swollen from passing two nights in an upright position, and his hips ached. He was hungry still. They were given two cheese sandwiches on the journey. The bag of apples Matis had brought in his backpack had been chomped through while they were still in Lithuania. They were asked to fill out forms giving next-of-kin, addresses, etc, and this gave him confidence that there was some kind of official process in train.

Matis and Lukas were met by a man named Edikas, who was holding a snarling black dog on a rope. They were relieved that Edikas was Lithuanian, but their relief was short-lived. Edikas let them into the terraced house, showed them a room laid with several mattresses across the floor. The room smelled almost as bad as the coach.

Edikas told them he needed their passports 'for paperwork'. They handed them over. Also their bank cards, so that their salaries could be paid into their bank accounts. They handed over their cards willingly at the mention of pay.

The dog urinated over one of the mattresses.

The curtains were drawn, but in the half-light they noticed a man asleep in one corner of the room as they heard Edikas letting himself out.

Matis noticed the look on Lukas's face.

'It will be OK,' Matis told Lukas. 'We do some work. Then we get paid. When we are paid we can leave. Get our own place, learn English. OK? Lukas? It will be OK.'

Matis postponed his needs, as he'd been doing since the age of five: to clean himself up, to settle in, to eat. When his mother left, he told himself to wait until she came back. When she came back, there would be proper food and clean clothes.

She never came back.

Matis and Lukas took a mattress each, avoiding the one the dog had peed on. With his nose on a dirty pillow, Matis smelled the sweat of other men, stale and over-ripe. Yet he was soon asleep, a deep, blank, shutdown kind of sleep by which he escaped the uncertainty of his situation.

He was shaken awake by the man who had been asleep in the corner. Matis squinted at his watch. He'd slept for less than twenty minutes.

'Half an hour, we go,' he said in Lithuanian, holding up his phone as evidence of something. A text maybe.

'Where?' asked Matis.

The man shrugged.

They were loaded into a van, which was full of men. He could hear his own language being spoken again. Some Latvian, some Romanian. He tried to ask where they were going, but no one knew.

After an hour in the van, the men were unloaded on a track at the edge of a farm. They walked to a hangar, big enough to house several aircraft. Inside, it was dark, the air acrid with chicken shit and loud with the panicked warbling of birds.

Matis and Lukas tried to watch through the gloom as the men started to catch the chickens, as the birds flew up and pecked and puked and scratched and shat. They had to crate them ready for the abattoir. Eight hours in the rasping,

97

clucking, stinking dark. Feathers and claws. The stench, ammonia overlaid with gut-churning sweetness. Matis thought he wouldn't be able to stand up for much longer, that he might vomit.

As they filed out, one of the men, an old hand, saw Matis's shocked expression and seemed to take pleasure in it.

He said, 'The chickens are treated better than us. English like animals better than foreigners.'

★ ★ ★

He didn't know how many days passed because there were never more than two hours' sleep before the next van journey to the next chicken shed, where he was clawed and shat upon. A couple of times it was a field to pick vegetables, hacking at broccoli with a blunt knife, without gloves. But in that time he learned from the others that he would not be paid. That he was debt-bonded.

Matis learned that he owed the gangmaster, a Latvian named Vasil, £350 in work-finding fees, £40 per week rent and food (for that dump!), plus his travel over from Lithuania. So he would earn nothing for at least three weeks. Then there was the arbitrary docking of wages, the men told him, almost with glee at finding someone newly in their rickety boat — fines for defecating in a plastic bag in the van because there were no toilet stops; for being late to a shift; for drinking a can of beer at the filthy shared house. This last fine, the men said, was arbitrary — dependent on Edikas's mood. Sometimes beers were bought for them, drinking sanctioned. Other times, not.

In the week that followed his arrival, Matis was transported to enormous farms: industrial-scale operations housing a million chickens in a shed. Oh he grew to *hate* chickens: the smell of them, the sounds they made. His dreams were filled with the horrible watery cooing that rose in their throats like bubbles through a straw. During one nap, he dreamed police cars were coming to raid the house and to free them, but instead of sirens accompanying the blue lights, the police cars warbled like panicky birds and this sound merged with his own internal terror.

Soon, there would be an arbitrary rhythm to the work, also. Back-to-back shifts some weeks, but other weeks there was free time when there was a kind of languorous hanging about in the shared house. Some of the migrants played cards, and smoking was a key pastime.

Matis dared not look into Lukas's face and see his own culpability written there.

$\star$ $\star$ $\star$

The text had come in to be at the BP garage, the regular pick-up point, at 4 a.m. Edikas was in the room, making sure they were rousing themselves for work.

One of the men, Saulius, had fallen from a raised platform in the dark of the chicken shed yesterday. He lay moaning on his mattress while Edikas told everyone to hurry and get ready.

Edikas squatted next to the man. 'Where does it hurt, my friend?' he asked.

Saulius lay on his side, hunched over his painful chest with his arms crossed. He grunted, without opening his eyes.

Edikas raised himself from squatting to standing. Swung back his leg and his heavy work boot, and launched a powerful kick into the man's ribs.

'There?' he said, like it was a joke as Saulius cried in agony, neck back. 'You will work or you will be punished,' Edikas said, moving his leg back for another strike as Lukas crawled forward.

'OK, OK,' Lukas said, holding Edikas's ankle. 'He will be ready. I will make sure.'

Edikas saved a backwards kick for Lukas, sending him back onto his mattress, crying out. 'He better be,' Edikas said, 'or you'll get it too.'

When the pain had subsided enough for him to move, Lukas crawled to Saulius, administered vodka, and appealed to the others to help. Bandages were found, and these Lukas used to wrap Saulius's chest, which was a livid shade of red. They all knew he needed hospital treatment. Injuries like that took weeks to heal — weeks of bed rest and medical attention; X-rays, dressings, pain relief. Care.

'I have some painkillers,' said someone, and Lukas gave them to Saulius, washed down with vodka. Saulius began to visibly rally. He could shift position without crying out. Instead of lying in hospital, on intravenous morphine and sipping tea through a straw, this man would have to stand up for fourteen hours, trying to catch chickens.

100

'Come,' said Lukas, 'we will cover for you. I will catch your chickens,' while Matis thought *That's rich*, Lukas being the worst chicken catcher of them all.

Lukas helped Saulius down the stairs and out of the house.

★ ★ ★

During the short weeks since their arrival, language formed a ring around them, tight as steel. Violence took away their confidence, made them shake — a kind of shaking that was close to shivering; vibration at a cellular level, very inner. Matis felt jelly-like in his interactions with the world. He was never sure of anything, how to ask for something, where to find a doctor or a police officer, when he would next be beaten. The only thing that helped was smoking. His trust had gone. They were not on solid ground as they had been before violence entered their lives, and it was not as if Matis had experienced a cosseted childhood. When you are frightened, you behave not like a man, but like a panicky sheep. Home was not a place of relative safety, as it had been in Klaipeda.

'I don't feel well,' said Lukas. 'So tired.'

'Here, take this,' said Matis.

'What is it?'

'Vitamins. You have to take it. The food is crap and we're not getting enough sleep.'

They were frightened for themselves, for their bodies. What might give out? What if injury or sickness overtook them?

'We have to think of a way out,' said Matis. All his obligations towards Lukas pressed down on him.

★ ★ ★

As soon as Matis walked into the other house, his senses became excited. The smell of body spray, albeit covering up the dirt that existed in this place also. But the women's house had minor feminine touches that excited Matis, the way an apple would excite someone dying of starvation. A shelf with possessions arranged on it: a hairdryer, a pot of face cream. A decorative cushion on a mattress against a wall as if for lounging. Hanging on a doorknob, a floral print dress.

Matis had a weakness for such touches. He was the same when he visited the Balsys family home back in Klaipeda. The sight of a posy of — albeit plastic — flowers in a tiny vase on the dining table, put there by Lukas's mother, filled him with a renewed sense of his own neglect. There were no feminine touches in his house: no cloth on the table, no side lamps, no flowers. Only the masculine blindness to such niceties and why they matter, how much they bring.

He was so giddy around this kind of thing — a feminine smell, a patterned cloth — that Lukas said it made him a terrible judge of women. He was hungry for their sensibility, it didn't seem to matter to him what they were like.

Matis adored it when the girls at secondary school wanted to style his hair. He wished they

102

would style it more, put makeup on him, paint his nails, dress him as a girl so he could be in their world for longer. When Matis was seven, his father discovered he had dressed up as a girl at a friend's house. His father poured salt on the ground and made him kneel in it for ten minutes. Seven-year-olds' knees are always scabbed.

'Your turn,' said a hard-faced woman of about fifty with peroxided hair.

He sat on a chair in the freezing yard, surrounded by the shaved-off hair of his housemates. They all had lice, hence the shaving session, though this would do nothing to help the weals up his forearms from the bedbugs. The woman revved her clippers. Her name was Lina, she told him.

'Going away anywhere nice on holiday?' Lina said, in the jaunty way of hairdressers everywhere.

'I wish,' said Matis.

'Me too. Shall we pretend?'

'Yes, let's go to the Caribbean.'

'Where shall we stay?'

'The Marriott.'

'Sounds good. What shall we do?'

'Nothing but sleep and eat, eat more, sleep more. Lie in the sun.'

He closed his eyes, smiling at the fantasy. Matis wanted it so badly he could cry. When it was too late, he realised he *was* crying.

'I'm sorry,' he said, wiping his eyes.

'Don't worry about it,' she said, seeming unmoved.

It was the first time he'd been touched in years, by a woman whose hand rested gently on his shoulder and intermittently smoothed his head in between shaves. A woman old enough to be his mother.

He was overcome.

'What were you offered?' he asked her.

'Same as you. Job, place to live. A new start,' she said. 'Instead I got this.'

He was aware of her body, the heat of it. He wanted his hair to grow back so that she could cut it again.

His tiredness was like a sickness. Not only the lack of sleep, though this was crucifying. Also the muscle exhaustion from the hard manual work. Sleep was grasped needfully, the body desperate to shut down. The minute they were horizontal, they were unconscious. None of the old lulling in and lulling out. No gentle descent with thoughts wandering, libido activating as he went down. Instead, an immediate shutdown, followed by a brutal tug into wakefulness, too soon, with him clinging to sleep.

If he had been at home, he realised, he could've slept until noon in the safety of his own room.

BEFORE

MATIS

Three weeks had passed since they arrived in the UK, and still he earned nothing. Edikas told him he was in debt to the tune of hundreds of pounds. The look on the dog's face warned him not to argue.

Saulius with the broken ribs was in so much agony, he was given one day to sleep, but then had to rejoin the van out to the farms. Saulius started to drink heavily just to get through it. He looked waxy, a yellow pallor that gave him the appearance of a walking cadaver. Someone said they could get him some black market painkillers, Tramadol they said, but he'd have to pay. Lukas gave Saulius his petty cash — small sums doled out for toothpaste or shower gel — to help. 'You don't need to pay me back, my friend,' Lukas said. 'I'm not in the business of debt-bonding anyone.'

He seemed more cheerful, Lukas (it was all relative). Lying down next to Matis on his adjacent mattress, he lay the back of his hand on his forehead and said, 'I have realised that I love her. That she is the one.'

'Oh right,' said Matis. 'And does Janina feel

the same way about you?'

'Actually, she does,' said Lukas, with the broadest grin Matis had ever seen on his friend's face. His lips thinned by the grin, his features unused to being stretched in this particular direction. 'I have asked her to marry me and she has said yes. Life is good my friend. I just have to get out of this hell hole of a country.'

'I'll think of something,' Matis said. 'But if you love Janina so much, why are you banging the neighbour?'

Matis had watched Lukas spruce himself up before going next door — a shower, then selecting his least disgusting T-shirt from the dirty pile. Borrowing some deodorant from another migrant. Perhaps it took his mind off their situation, Matis reasoned. Nevertheless, it wasn't Lukas's style, to play around.

'That is nothing,' said Lukas, as if Matis were pedantic to bring it up.

'Doesn't Janina ask what you're doing over here?' Matis asked.

'She thinks I'm getting rich, making big money.'

'No wonder she wants to marry you. What about the husband, next door I mean?'

'She texts me when he's going to be out,' Lukas says. 'We have a code. She will say 'pilot light out again' and I will say 'on my way'. So that it looks like plumbing.'

Lukas said this as if it were the cleverest code ever. 'Yes,' said Matis. 'I worked out that it was plumbing-related.'

'Janina doesn't need to know, and it won't

hurt her,' Lukas said. 'It isn't the sex, actually, with Elspeth. It's the clean bed, it smells so good. She smells so good. The nice carpets. The bathroom where she lets me shower. Everything is new and clean over there. I feel like a human being for a short time. The kind of house I want for myself. For Janina.'

'Fair enough,' said Matis. 'I don't care what you do.'

This town, so the others told Matis, had been called Little Lithuania by the English newspapers, and he could see why. They had their own community here, and it protected him. Two shops on Norfolk Street — Pas Zemaiti and Marco Store — selling sausage and Vilkmergės beer. Lovely buxom Lithuanian girls with blue-grey eyes behind the counter who smiled and asked how they could help. All the food packets and tins from home. Inside, the shops even smelled like Klaipeda, he could be back there, just for a moment, and it meant the world to him. Also, these shops gave him confidence. People like him had made their homes here, set up businesses. It could be done.

Nevertheless he longed for home, pangs that were so painful they surprised him. He found himself looking at the moon and telling himself this was the same moon that shone down on Klaipeda. He missed the local lads — his friends, most of whom were training to be sea captains. They were so proud of this, so proud to one day be driving container ships in and out of Klaipeda port, the Baltic's only deep sea port. Yet Matis had been contemptuous of this dream of theirs

107

— the silly uniform, their excitement at the pretend 'status' of the job, though the salary was crummy and the prospects worse. They were being sold a pup by sea captain school. Matis had agreed with his drunken father, when he grew slurry-philosophical. 'What is the purpose of this life? You work to live but still you have to die. Why should we work for these other people? Basically we work to line their pockets!'

Matis was shocked to find he missed his father — in particular his father's disinterest in where he went or what he did. Viktor had always been too self-absorbed to really care about Matis, apart from keeping a close eye on his masculinity. That disinterest, which had felt so much like neglect when he had been a child, now seemed benign, redolent with its lack of exploitation. His father hadn't *run* him, as Edikas did, like a donkey or a clapped-out vehicle. The hatred Matis felt for his father was nothing to what he felt for Edikas. He could kill Edikas. He *ought* to kill him. This might be his solution.

Saulius was a different man on the Tramadol, practically euphoric to be experiencing moments without pain. Yet he still struggled to keep up with the relentless pace expected of the men.

Saulius became constipated — a side effect of his medication, according to Talcy Malc, the drug dealer who visited the house and listened to their symptoms like some creepy physician. Matis has no idea what Talcy or Malc might mean. He stored these words away, along with Pheasant, like little jewels in a waistcoat pocket, for future use. Saulius sat on the toilet, straining

108

away loudly, while Edikas called them from the open front door and the other men were hammering down the stairs in their work boots. And Saulius was drowsy. During breaks, when they would all nap on the floor, he went into deep sleeps from which Lukas struggled to rouse him.

Edikas was not best pleased with Lukas. His chicken catching was still woeful — half the average quantity, even when Matis strained to up his numbers — but also their natures were set in opposition. It seemed to Matis as if Lukas's very personality was a provocation to Edikas. His kindliness, his compassion were everything Edikas despised and wanted to stamp out among his workers. He was particularly annoyed by Lukas's constant efforts to look after Saulius. Edikas seemed of the view that Saulius had only himself to blame.

One unusually cheerful night when they were done with work, the beers were flowing, yet Edikas was stalking about grumpily in the hallways of their house, peering into bedrooms, checking on the men. He blocked Lukas's path, seeming further incensed that Lukas was smiling and holding an open beer. Matis was lying on his mattress, but he could see, through the doorway, that Edikas was pushing his face into Lukas's, close enough that his spittle landed there. Despite his exhaustion, Matis got up and went to the doorway, ready to defend his friend. Ready to give life to his fury.

'Your sweetheart,' Edikas said. 'Janina. I hear she is a pretty girl. Nice face.'

Lukas's eyes widened in horror. 'How do you — '

'My friends paid a visit to your mother in Klaipeda and who should be there in the kitchen? Janina. So lucky. If I were you, I would start to work harder on catching chickens and focus less on helping other men. Because my friends have canisters of acid, and it would be a shame to ruin such a pretty face.'

'No,' said Lukas, hurriedly. 'No, don't. I will do anything. Anything you ask, anything you want.'

'Here, we don't carry people. We don't carry sick and we don't carry lazy. Stop tending to Saulius like some mother hen. And work better, work harder.'

'Yes, yes, I will do both. I will do anything, just don't touch Janina or my mother,' Lukas said.

★ ★ ★

Later, Matis found Lukas sitting on the floor in the hall, shaking and crying. He had just been sick, Matis could smell it on his breath. 'I never knew such danger,' Lukas said. 'How did this happen to us?'

'I have to get us out,' Matis said. 'I got us into this mess. I have to get us out of it.' Not only had he failed to intervene when Edikas threatened his friend, he had no idea how to free them.

110

BEFORE

ELISE

Most of her friends were desperate to stop working. Getting a fella with a decent job and popping out a kid or two seemed like a way to do this, to absent yourself from the workplace. But not Elise.

Much of the work at the BP garage was boring. *One sixty please, any petrol?* Nevertheless, she liked it. She liked the nocturnal life — the spaced-out feeling of being awake before dawn, the yellow tinge to the light in the moments before sunrise, letting you know this was a planet you were living on, a species alone in the universe. The taste of a cigarette in a dry mouth, meant to be asleep. Getting out of bed at 3 a.m. was awful, but once you were dressed and out, you could experience it with curiosity. Most of all, she liked all the people passing through — the travellers, the strangers, the Lithuanians, the truckers. It was interesting to meet with such variety while sitting stock still. She learned a few words of Lithuanian so she could surprise them through the payment window by saying, 'Thanks, have a good day,' in their language. 'Ačiū, turite gerą dieną.'

111

They would raise their eyebrows at this, then smile or laugh, say something to their friends that she couldn't understand, and she would smile back. It was a connection, however slight. Isn't that what we're here for? Also, it made them fancy her, and she was all about being fancied.

She acknowledged this transitory melting pot was everything her dad hated, and that this might have something to do with her enthusiasm. Here at work, she was allowed to be interested and curious, to observe without the hating or rejecting that were required of her at home.

This morning, rough winds shoved the houses as she left at 3.30 a.m. for her shift; trees blowing about wildly, car alarms shrieking, bins turned over, an empty milk bottle rolling on a doorstep. To Elise, it seemed portentous, the weather. It blew her hair up around her face. She pulled her padded coat around her — her warmest winter coat, still used for night shifts even in May. Like a duvet against the night.

She liked the alone feeling walking along deserted streets, just her and the weather. The planet to herself. She would normally smoke a cigarette to wake herself up — a way of skipping breakfast in her battle to lose weight — but it was too windy.

Once she was in her seat at the till, a fan heater would warm her feet, creating a mini fug in her cabin. She served through a glass hatch, designed to protect her. The door to the shop locked against robbers. Change tumbling into

112

the little rounded tray, the metal worn down with use, at the base of the glass. The EEs — as her dad called the Eastern Europeans — wanting fags, chocolate. Their handlers wanting petrol. It was the manual labour pick-up point for EEs across the town. Men standing around, waiting for the vans that would drive them out.

There was one she liked particularly — had seen him regularly there for work at 4 a.m. He would smile at her, sometimes wink. And here he was now, buying a Galaxy, lots of eye contact, and when she slid his coins into the tray, his fingers lingered there, touching hers. He kept his there. And so did she. A touch. Eye contact. It was fucking electric.

When Dwayne came to join her on shift, she could take her break and go outside for a cigarette, and there he was, this EE fella with the electric fingers, smoking as well. He pursed his lips to blow her a kiss, smiled. *So cute.* So handsome, like a malnourished Harry Styles. He patted his chest, said, 'Matis,' then pointed at her.

'Elise,' she said, all shy.

It was all the language he had, she guessed. It was all the excitement she needed. Work, from that moment, felt like a hot date — what to wear (padded coat covering it all, so what was the point?); hair, makeup. Sometimes sexy-secretary glasses and an up-do, to radically change her look, show him how many sides she had.

And the smiles, the touching. The winking and the blown kisses, burgeoned like buds in spring. Became their language. They had an understanding. She was sure of it, yet if so sure, why was she

113

asserting the evidence in her mind like this, telling herself it was real?

She observed him, her EE boy band member with his intense eyes dark as currants; watched him stamping his feet in a huddle of them, his clothes too thin. Laughing with them sometimes. He didn't look all that well, but this made him cuter — in need of rescuing perhaps. She waited for his eye contact and his smiles, which shot through her like a voltage. Going to the garage became all she thought about.

'I'll do earlies again this week,' she told the manager, so urgently he looked at her in surprise. 'Can't sleep anyway,' she explained. 'Might as well make some money out of it.'

Was it sleep deprivation, turning her head? The foggy, woolly feeling that enveloped her early, libidinous self? She was happy when she saw him, that's all she knew. Her life had a point of light and it was him, across the dark of a petrol station forecourt at 4 a.m.

They began meeting to smoke, provided Dwayne was there to cover her breaks. A habit, unsaid — everything was unsaid, of course. Everything was looking and smiling, electricity and bodily lust. It was, at the most basic level, honest. Not based on hating anyone (unlike her dad's relationships), not based on need, except perhaps the need to mate. Not based on language.

'I just love him,' she confided to Amber, her friend from school.

'You don't know him,' Amber said, pulling down on the straighteners while Elise's hair steamed.

114

'Who knows anyone?' Elise asked.

'They talk, that's how they get to know people.'

'Maybe that's overrated. Maybe it's more honest to see what you like and taste it.'

'You've been reading too much *Fifty Shades*,' said Amber.

★ ★ ★

She was in her bedroom at her dressing table, pulling up the front of her strapless dress, wiggling side to side to get it higher. It was gaining a not-very-secure purchase on her bosom. She sprayed on some of her new perfume — L'eau by Jimmy Choo, bought for her by her dad. The £60 bottle, too. He liked to spoil her, he said. When he wasn't pushing her around, the odd kick when he'd had a few cans of Wife Beater. Spoiling her, kicking her, spoiling her, kicking her. That's how he operated. She was used to it.

Her scrawny Harry Styles had invited her out, Norfolk Street (the Vilnius of Little Lithuania). He didn't say what they'd be doing. Just hanging maybe. *And the rest.*

Maybe her strapless dress, or what was *in* her strapless dress, would turn him on, because she was sick of the English blokes, the Darrens and Garys and their empty heads. They had no *culture.* Elise had more to her than that, didn't find foreignness a turn-off. In fact, she found it interesting — would've liked to try their foods and get to know the culture, because at least it

115

was *different*. She'd been in their shops and it was so interesting in there, all the packets looked new to her and intriguing. Not like picking up a Fray Bentos at the Co-op. In fact, it was probably exactly like picking up a Fray Bentos in the Co-op, but *seemed* more exotic. Like the way certain French bakeries seemed posh over here, when in France they were viewed like Greggs.

Since their fag breaks had become a 'thing', she'd started fantasising that Matis would become hers. She'd teach him English. Yet all the while, his shaved head and hard face would be a turn-on. Her own bit of rough. She thought this, even though whenever she walked down the stairs towards the front door, her dad shouted, 'No talking to any EEs, right Elise?' while he was hunched over his awful Facebook page, turning himself on with hatred.

EEs. Eastern Europeans. He made her 'like' his posts: about immigrants destroying the culture, about loss of British identity and sovereignty, about the UK being overrun. 'That's it 'Lise,' he'd say. 'More likes, more the word gets spread.'

Outside the front door, phone to her ear: 'Come on Amber, let's get jiggy with the Baltics.'

She knew her dad would be pleased if she got together with Wayne, the sparky whose dad was his pal. They did their One Wisbech stuff together. But she couldn't stand Wayne. He had no curiosity, no zest for life. He didn't want to travel or try new foods. He was the type to be scared of eating squid, let alone squid in *garlic*. She thought Wayne was thick, even though he

116

had a decent job and that was pretty rare round here.

She and Amber met with a group of the Lithuanian lads in Norfolk Street, but the conversation dried up pretty fast. Once they'd smoked about ten fags, there was nothing left to do. Someone said there was a disco on at a community centre, the Rosmini. So they trudged there in a group.

The disco ball in the ceiling sent polka dots of light down the walls, then around and around, it could almost make you seasick. Purple and pink. Teeth shone bright — Elise had had hers whitened, it was a thing, like the people on reality shows. What they didn't tell you is whitening makes your teeth kill when you eat anything hot or cold. Katy Perry singing 'California Gurls'. Elise loved the purple wig Katy Perry wore in that video. She'd love to look like Katy Perry; watched vlogs to get her makeup close.

Elise was dancing with Matis, though he kept scratching his arms like a weirdo. They smiled at each other. Elise didn't lose her quarry, kept her dancing in his orbit; her arms above her head, moving so her boobs shifted inside her bustier. The rub of the fabric against her skin turning her on, as well as his gaze.

A slow dance led to them kissing against the wall, the lights stroking their bodies with dots that smudged and rotated. He tasted of beer and cigarettes and something rougher underneath, unwashed, like building site rubble. She led him by the hand outside. They walked for a while hand in hand back to Norfolk Street and into a shop doorway where it was dark and a bit private. She'd let him have sex with her here, she didn't care, wanted to take her chance. Shake things up, see where it took her, away from her dad hopefully. But the boy stopped before they got that far. They sat for a while. Then she got up, stood in front of him and held out her hand.

She led him to the shop, the EE shop her father would call it. Pas Zemaiti. She waved her hand at the shelves and said, 'You show me, what should I try?'

He frowned at her, could not understand.

'You like?' he said, and she thought they might be his only words.

'I like,' she said, laughing. She wanted him to notice that she could be pretty, vivacious, lively. Sometimes she felt a bit pudgy, in her trackies and T-shirt, but not tonight. Tonight she felt ripe.

He chose for her a beer, something called Vilkmerges — 'for womans' he said — and some snacks. They sat on a step outside a record shop eating and drinking, not talking because — what with? — but being in each other's orbit.

'You like it here?' she said, pointing downwards at the pavement. 'I don't mean the pavement obviously, I mean England.'

He shrugged, then made his flat hand seesaw. So-so, he seemed to be saying.

'You want to learn English?' she said. Pointing to herself, she said, 'I teach you English?'

He shrugged again, looking queasy.

She wanted to sign the following:

I (pointing at self)

Heart (hands forming a heart shape)

118

You (pointing at him)

But she didn't because she knew it was silly. And if he wouldn't take her English lessons, it was unlikely he'd take her heart.

Sitting in their doorway, they were eating a thin sausage, like a Peperami, each with an end in their mouth, nibbling until they kissed in the middle. He was easy to be with, Elise thought. As if they'd been together for years. When he laughed it was so cute, chuckling like a little boy. He had dimples and those serious dark, dark eyes.

Until *she* came along.

Hard-faced, bottle blonde, she stood before them like post-transformation Olivia Newton John in *Grease*, only twenty years older. *Tell me aboudit, stud.*

Matis scrambled to his feet like a maidservant, saying 'Lina.' As if he'd been caught doing something he shouldn't. What was she, his mother? They spoke to each other in their language, the one that excluded Elise. She didn't know what was going on, couldn't believe it — after everything she'd allowed him to do in that shop doorway — Matis just trotted after the sourfaced old cow with barely a backward glance.

Elise could've gone with anyone after that, she was so pissed off. First bloke that came along. She didn't care, hoped it'd get back to Matis and he'd feel gutted that he'd missed out on his chance with her. She looked down the brick shops of Norfolk Street. The double yellow lines on the road. It was more of an alley than a proper street. An alley that went nowhere. Suddenly she didn't want to go with anyone. She wanted to go home and get out of her stupid dress, put on her trackies and a hoodie and cuddle her giant teddy on her bed. Maybe write in her diary.

She'd never go to the Rosmini Centre again.

★ ★ ★

It was a long trudge home, feeling the disappointment churn in her stomach. The way Matis tossed her away like rubbish, after she'd thrown herself at him. She kept picturing herself giggling, stroking him, trying to make herself adorable.

She let herself in, forgetting there were mascara tear-tracks down her cheeks.

Her father was still at the kitchen table, though no longer hunched over his Hatebook page. Now he was surrounded by his cronies, and she rolled her eyes when she was just inside the front door, hanging up her denim jacket on the hooks, then wishing her strapless dress wasn't so revealing. She put her denim jacket back on. They'd be talking about foreigners, winding themselves up as usual. About how Britain used to be great but had lost its way.

There were four of them standing about in the kitchen holding beers when she walked in. She could smell the alcohol on them. Couple of them in their twenties, hanging out with an old fucker like her dad and his mate Gary Evans, who had named his son Evan Evans. Thought it was funny, after the Neville Neville football chant. *I mean I ask you,* Elise said in her head.

'The fuck 'appened to you girl?' her father said.

'Nothing,' she whispered. She wanted a cup of tea to take up with her, so she could get proper snuggly in her room with her slippers shaped like bunnies.

'Why you been cryin' then?' her father said.

'I haven't,' she said, wiping her cheeks with her palm, turning her back to them so they couldn't see.

'Come 'ere,' her father said.

She approached him and he reached an arm out, grabbed her and pulled her onto his lap. 'What's a matter w' you then?' he said, looking up at her. 'Bad evening?'

'Could say that.'

'Who upset you sweet cheeks?'

'A boy.'

'What boy?'

'Doesn't matter.'

'It bloody does, what boy?'

'No it doesn't.' She struggled out of his lap because the kettle had boiled. 'Anyone want a cup of tea?'

'We've had a right result here tonight,' her dad said.

'Oh yeah?' she said, without turning from her tea making.

'Yeah, Shane Farquharson, *the* Shane Farquharson, has only come out and endorsed One Wisbech on national radio.'

'Actually it was local radio,' ventured Gary.

121

'Yeah, but it'll get picked up. 'S'massive. He's got proper influence, says we're making good points, valid points, about being overrun, becoming Little Lithuania. We're gonna go global after this, Elise. 'S'gonna be massive.'

'Very connected, is Farquharson,' fawned Gary.

'Oh right, well done,' she said, taking her tea out of the room. He'd always idolised Shane fucking Farquharson. Idiot.

Maybe it happened because I'm so fat, she thought, looking down at the undulations of her cleavage and then her belly. *Maybe if I lost weight, like a couple of stone, he'd see me at a disco and do a double take.* Like, woah, who is she?

★   ★   ★

You've got to choose life, that's what Elise thought, trudging to the garage at 3.30 a.m., but without the joyful bounce she'd had of late. Her disappointment in Matis hung heavy on her. It'd definitely knocked the shine off him, though not entirely. She'd still applied her makeup this morning with a view to seeing him, but more in the defensive way you did when you knew you were going to see an ex.

You've got to try new things, take a risk, try a new person, a new culture, she told herself. The conservative tendency, her father's turned-up nose at new foods, new smells, his fear of germs on public transport, which was actually a fear of foreigners — that kind of thinking could trap

122

you. There's a fork in the road and you could choose which way to go — open or closed. She told herself this, but it felt less robust than usual.

She could understand her father's anxiety. In many ways, she shared it. When she'd booked an exotic holiday in the past, for example (funds courtesy of her eBay entrepreneurism, joined by Amber who'd had a redundo payout) she'd become beset by nervousness about drinking the water, eating salad, getting robbed, disease from mosquitoes — to the point where she became an obsessional visitor to the TripAdvisor talk boards, a veritable hive of communal anxiety. *Are there stray dogs on the beach? Is it a five-star resort?* But when she arrived, those fears melted away because what she found was just human beings, mostly kind, beautiful new landscapes, interesting morsels to try. It was nothing to be afraid of, and her heart had opened up at how beautiful the world was and how much there was to see. How good it was to be alive.

She wasn't like her dad. She had broader horizons than most of her cohort. She was often surprised, when she met disappointment, how quickly she rallied, how soon her mind began strategising for another try, as if it was just too active to wallow.

No, she wasn't like her dad. Dean Singlehurst was a painter and decorator who never dealt well with disappointment, for example when Elise's mother — a woman whose desire for attention was the candle that burned all the oxygen in their home — went off with someone else. Why he was surprised was beyond Elise. She was forever throwing herself at men. Her father, as if wilful in his stupidity, viewed her mother's preening as an asset to him. 'Keeps herself nice,' he'd say.

Dean Singlehurst's disappointments became all too regular when EE tradesmen began quoting several thousand pounds underneath him on jobs, working from 8 a.m. to 6 p.m., painting by the light of a bare bulb in winter and not repairing to the greasy spoon for an hour and a half at midday but instead squatting on the floor with a Tupperware of dumplings or cabbage from home. They would work weekends and bank holidays to get the job finished. And to a good standard, too.

Elise's dad saw those jobs as his own. Until he stopped getting them. He would quote, trying to put the homeowner off employing whichever Pole or Romanian was undercutting him, but he would never hear back about the work. Elise suspected it put his customers off, to hear him badmouthing the competition.

'You don't want to trust that lot,' he'd say, but the price always won the argument.

Perhaps Elise got it from her mother, the free movement of her emotions. That would be romanticising her. Her mother was a narcissist for whom Elise's needs were an inconvenience too far. 'She's been a nightmare,' her mother would say, dropping her back at her dad's. Eventually, after one too many arrangements unkept, Elise had to cut contact. Her mother, never one for birthdays or parents' evenings, seemed relieved.

* * *

'S'like it never happened, Elise thought bitterly, looking through the scratched foggy glass of her garage cabin. That's how little their fumble in the shop doorway meant to him. He looked exhausted. Hollow-eyed. Kept yawning. Still good-looking though.

She wished the podge wasn't clinging to her like a suit right now. It hung in swags under her chin and below her arms.

He's got some worries, she thought, pushing his change into the tray but not leaving her hand there to touch his. *He looks bad.*

'Are you all right?' she asked, frowning through the glass.

He shrugged, neither a yes nor a no. Yawned again. Rubbed his neck as if he were in pain.

'Do you need my help?' she asked, but he turned and joined the group at the doors to the van.

125

MATIS

All the men in the room jerked off at night.

Matis was no longer perturbed by the shaking turned backs, the rustling, the urgent breaths. He had his own Rolodex of fantasies he reached for to help him get off. Almost all of them involved Oksana.

Oksana was his one true love, the one he yearned for. She was older than him and not at all beautiful, but she had this self-contained quality about her. She knew what she liked and wanted and didn't have to explain it to anyone. It was as if she had all the confidence he lacked.

She barely tolerated him, that's what really lit the spark for Matis. He had to pursue her for a date, or bump into her fortuitously, which he managed by hanging about for hours in the Akropolis shopping centre, next to the ice rink. She never sought him out or promised him anything. On her birthday, when he had prepared gifts and a card and planned a meal, she said, 'I'm going out with my friends.' She was often an hour or more late to meet with him, didn't possess a mobile phone (or so she told him), so couldn't be tracked down. It made him

126

yearn in a way he had never experienced before, as if his ultimate satisfaction was just around the corner. She moved to America without informing him.

He only found out when he bumped into a friend of hers on the street; had to hide his extreme shock — that he could have collapsed there and then on the pavement. Her behaviour was in keeping with all her previous behaviours, and yet he couldn't believe it. He had filled in all her gaps with his ardour so that he was convinced it was only a matter of time until they made a life together.

'Did she . . . leave an address?' he asked Oksana's friend.

'Not for you,' she said, laughing as she walked away.

Oksana made it clear to him, had he been able to read the signs, that she didn't love him, though in bed once she said, 'I think about our wedding.'

She made it clear that he was only sex or a diversion. She didn't even treat him with kindness. This is what he got off on, on his stinking mattress.

The women who had shown him kindness or love — and there had been a couple — turned *him* into an Oksana. It was very hard, he found, to love someone who was willing to love you back.

ELISE

The following morning, after Dwayne had come on shift, Elise stood with some of the Lithuanian guys including Matis in the darkness at the side of the garage, the smoking zone, which was littered with butts. There was an outside ashtray — a letter box affair that had been screwed to the wall when the smoking ban came into force — but it had long since overflowed, bringing the tarmac back into use.

'Do you need my help?' she asked.

'Need job,' said Matis.

'Right, what kind of job?' she said.

They mimed brushes up and down, paint the fence, and hammering. Painting. Domestic repairs.

'OK, so shall we do some flyers for you on my computer?'

They looked at her dumbfounded.

'Oh for God's sake,' she said, typing into her phone for Google Translate.

They read, nodded enthusiastically.

'Right,' she said, 'where though? Can't go to mine. Rosmini Centre?'

There followed a long argument in Lithuanian

between Lukas and Matis. Elise was about to say, 'Oh look, come back to me when you've sorted it out, OK?' when a meaty chap shouted at them and they trotted off to get into the van.

You've got to choose life, she thought, when some part of her questioned why she was forgiving him so soon. You've got to choose something over nothing.

MATIS

'How can we arrange to meet her when we are always working?' Lukas asked. 'We have to sleep. Already, I am not well.'

'We can go to Rosmini in the evening,' Matis said. 'We are not catching chickens then.'

'And get up at 4 a.m.? I cannot,' said Lukas, and Matis thought he might cry. 'It is too much.'

'Then I will go, for both of us.'

'And if Edikas finds out?'

'How will Edikas find out?'

'How did he find out about Janina? I can't risk it. If anything happens to her . . . '

'OK, OK. Stop being such an old woman. I will go for both of us. I have no one they can harm. If Edikas's heavies go for my father, I will be happy. If he comes around you can say to him that I have gone to the shop or I'm in the bathroom.'

Lukas bent double in a coughing fit, into his handkerchief. He held his chest and looked at the handkerchief which was dark, with phlegm or blood, Matis couldn't tell in the darkness. 'My heart . . . ' Lukas said. 'I'm not well

130

enough to take this.'

At that moment, Edikas discovered their huddle, and told them to get into the van.

131

ELISE

She sat at her dressing table, getting ready to go back to the Rosmini Centre. Behind her, her laptop was stowed in her backpack on the bed, ready to show them the flyers she'd mocked up on Word. Nothing fancy, just basic information with their mobile numbers.

She frowned. What was the point of giving their mobile numbers when they couldn't speak English? She'd have to give her own, although this would make her their agent, negotiating jobs on their behalf, supplying quotes and suchlike. Taking calls about painting or renovation jobs — jobs her father wasn't even up for. She wondered what would happen if her father found her pimping for Eastern European decorators. She'd have to keep it on the down low, and anyway, it'd only be until they could speak well enough to take the calls themselves. They'd have to get going on learning English.

Despite the dangers of this endeavour, she thought they'd make a great team. Her efficiency, her sheer drive and her personable style on the phone, coupled with their excellent grafting. She could tell they were the kind to be up and out early and to get the job done. Good quality, while she greeted clients with, 'Yes madam, how can we help you today? Absolutely, no problem. And would you like any furniture disposed of at the same time?'

She planned to print the flyers at the centre on the mono laser they had there for CVs.

Whenever she saw Matis, warmth spread through her. Excitement and also comfort. He had in his smile a kind of paternal kindness and also sexuality. She was attracted to him, oh yes, that was an understatement, but she wanted his protection also. He gave her this feeling of home, of comfort and yet he was other: maleness and foreignness, that she yearned for.

She couldn't stand to choose from the type of guys who gathered in her kitchen. All that sameness.

Despite Elise's feeling that everything was in their favour — their joint enterprise brim full of potential — nevertheless she was uncertain. She sensed Matis wasn't keen. He might not want her taking his calls or running his work for him. He might not want her at all.

Lumatis Painting and Decorating. That's what she'd called it. Or would *Lumatis Interiors* be better?

Better than Matkas, which sounded like some kind of industrial insulation panel or a pre-made potato accompaniment.

Looking at herself in the mirror, she liked how she'd done her makeup (not too much, she'd been toning it down lately) but then she wondered why she bothered. Matis probably

133

wouldn't give her a second look. He was probably still fixated on that peroxided old bag.

She stepped into the garden for a cigarette, looking up at the twilight sky which was violet, supernaturally luminous.

The air was sweet scented with burgeoning growth. She breathed deeply, reminded what a dirty habit smoking is, especially when she'd just showered, applied body cream, straightened her hair and done her makeup. And now she was in a cloud of stinking smoke, which would cling to her hair and coat. Make her breath smell. But on the plus side, smoking helped keep her weight down. And it killed time, literally. If she left now, she'd be early.

She'd just finish this fag, then walk to Rosmini. Life was good: rich and full of possibility. She was impatient to push things on with Matis. Urgency too, from the For Sale sign at the garden gate, her father saying, 'We're moving up in the world 'Lise. Shane says he's got a cottage on his land and I can 'ave it for below market rent. Things with money are tight. Anyway, it'd be an honour to work more closely with Shane . . . '

She was nodding, making all the right noises, as if praising this fragile idea of his, while thinking *I'm not going. No way am I following you and your suitcase full of bitterness to Shane Farquharson's place.*

What Elise felt her dad couldn't see was that he'd been unlucky. And she thought if he could only see the powerful role of luck, he might feel less aggrieved, less as if there was a conspiracy against him.

134

He was unlucky in his work. He was a sensitive sort, and working in a trade didn't leave much room for sensitivity. Customers were often disdainful towards him, treating him without respect. There was a certain kind of rich person who thought they could talk down to 'the lower orders'. This was a measure of a person — how they spoke to people working for them. How they treated waiters, cleaners, handymen. She suspected this was another draw of Farquharson: he seemed posh, but he spoke to men like her dad on a level. As if they were equal, which financially they weren't of course. But she had to admit Farquharson didn't talk down to the meatheads who followed him.

Elise acknowledged she'd been unlucky with her mother, but she viewed this as bad luck rather than a conspiracy against her, and in some ways she saw this event as connected to her entrepreneurial spirit. She had drive. She didn't expect anyone else to get stuff done for her. Her mother had certainly never done much for her.

Her father was unlucky in his friends, who didn't comfort or diffuse him, as she wished they would, but instead endorsed him with a kind of limp cronyism. They were willing to go round and round and round with phony political discussions, which never amounted to more than 'they've ruined everything', like dirty water round a plug. Her dad tended to go for the sort of friends who followed rather than challenged, but Elise thought this was less egotism on his part than insecurity. He couldn't quite hold his own. He needed bolstering. Who knew what he would've made of himself if he'd had learning, had gone to uni or had been in a job where he'd been sensitively treated, had friends who gave him thoughtful support rather than mindlessly egging him on. If he'd had the chance to be creative and to prosper, or just do well in a job, he'd be a different sort altogether.

She ground on her fag butt with her shoe. She didn't have to hide *this* dirty habit. Her father was fine with smoking, but God help her if he found out she was consorting with EEs.

★ ★ ★

'Nature loves a distant gene pool,' Amber had told her, when she had a temping job in the College of West Anglia's science department. 'That's why mixed race babies are so beautiful. Also why the royals are not the brightest.'

That's where her dad and his cronies had it so wrong. The plankton in her father's pond could barely procreate from the looks of them, whereas every molecule in her body yearned for Matis.

At the table in Rosmini, she said, 'Shall we begin?'

Matis shrugged.

'What is your name?' she asked, slowly. Enunciating.

'*Mano vardas* Matis,' he said, yawning.

'No,' she said. 'My name is Matis.'

'My name is Lukas,' said the chap next to him. He was eager, sitting forward. He had brought a pencil and notepad with him. A-star pupil, though he looked half-dead. *You couldn't help*

136

liking Lukas, she thought, looking at him fondly.

'Very good,' she said. 'And how are you today Lukas?'

He turned his mouth down. 'So-so,' he said, wavering his flat hand. Then descended into a coughing fit.

Matis and Elise laughed, but it wasn't mean. It was born of affection, she thought.

'We need job,' said Matis.

'Yes, so I have made you these,' she said, opening the lid of her laptop.

★   ★   ★

When the fliers were done and she'd packed her laptop into her backpack, she walked out of the Rosmini Centre. Lukas and Matis stayed behind at the table, said they had something to talk about. Argue about, more like.

The air was still sweet, the sky black. The pavement glistened under her feet. She was so happy she could jump home. And she noticed she hadn't felt happy in a really long time.

If they married, she thought, walking along Queens Road, *they could hire the Rosmini hall as the place where they fell in love.* Capacity 100.

At the end of the street, she heard a shout. 'Hey!'

She turned and saw Matis jogging after her.

Once he was alongside her, and before she'd thought it through, she'd got her mouth on his and she was consuming him, ever so hungry, ever so urgent. They moved to a shop doorway.

137

Elise wanted him so badly. She didn't know it yet, but a magical spark, the work of a species inhabiting a planet — that essential work of continuing itself — that spark ignited in her belly. A Lithuanian sperm met an English egg — their best selves. Nature loved a distant gene pool. Oh she felt it, the moment of magic, only she mistook biology for love.

They slid down onto the floor, still in the shop doorway. Lit cigarettes, now that they were spent.

'I like go university,' he said.

'Oh right, to study what?'

She got her phone out, knowing Google Translate would be heavily involved in the conversation.

'Engineering maybe, architecture.' He said the 'ch' as in chair, reading the word off her phone. 'But . . . ' he rubbed his fingers together, indicating money or lack of it.

She pictured him, her handsome Lithuanian architect in the house he'd designed for them. Her head was light, her body both tingling and flooded.

'I could support you through college,' she said. 'I've got savings, more than anyone knows. I set up this company, Easy eBay?' Everything in her life was EE, she realised. 'First it was my dad, he wanted to sell some old fishing equipment but couldn't work eBay so I did it for him.' This tumbled out of her, Google Translate abandoned, despite her awareness that he couldn't understand the half of it. 'Then he says to his mates, 'Oh Elise'll do it for you, she's a whizz on

138

the 'puter.' Then I started taking a cut. Now I sell for everyone in Wisbech pretty much, out of Dad's garage. I've got ten thousand pounds saved up. Hey, we could add it as a service to Lumatis Interiors — decorate your home, get rid of your dodgy old furniture. Everyone has a clear-out when they decorate, don't they?'

She thought there could be no stopping them, together — their entrepreneurial spirit. Her drive, his skill.

'Ten thousand English pound?' he said. Interesting that he'd understood *that* part. His eyes were wide, and she wondered if he was looking at her in a different way. 'Why you pay me university?'

'Cos I like you,' she said, smiling.

He smiled, but didn't say it back to her.

Language barrier, back again.

MATIS

The ominous drone of a hornet trapped inside the house, as hopeless and angry as the men.

He was looking for Lukas, putting his head around the doors of various rooms where people were sleeping on mattresses or standing and eating in the kitchen. On the upstairs landing, he could hear sobbing from inside the bathroom.

'Lukas?' he said, his head against the locked door.

'Go away,' said Lukas.

'Let me in.'

You're not the only one struggling, he thought. Matis had noticed the change in himself since coming to this country. He was knotted up from the minute he woke and remembered where he was. At home, he would wake — often at midday on the weekend — with a crushing sense of ennui. *Another day in this shit-hole.* What a pleasure that would be now, when the knot began at the base of him, its strands in the slackness of his face — without joy. He struggled to find anything funny. How could anything be funny when he might be kicked with steel-capped boots or bitten by a dog at any minute?

140

How on earth could light and fun exist when he was captive with nothing to call his own and when there was no end to it in sight?

It had taken coming here for him to realise he was a homebody. A conservative homebody. Why had he just leaped in? It was Lukas who had been cautious, nervous about what lay ahead.

'What's wrong?' Matis said, when the door was unlocked.

'What's wrong?' said Lukas. He slid down the wall to sit on the tiled floor, knees up. His eyes were red raw. 'How can you ask what's wrong?'

Matis perched on the side of the bath. Strips of toilet roll lay on the floor where it had been used to dry hands.

'I hate my life,' Lukas said. 'I wish I was back at home. I wish I was with Janina.'

'I know. We can get out of here, get out of this. It's not impossible. That girl, the one at the petrol station. She will help us get other work.'

Lukas was shaking his head. 'Edikas told me he knows where my mother lives. He knows about Janina. I cannot risk anything happening to them because I made a stupid decision.'

* * *

They were on the mattresses, in their room.

Saulius was looking better, more alert. Lukas was changing the dressings on his chest.

'You are the only human being in this house,' Saulius said to Lukas.

'Rest, my friend,' said Lukas. 'Did you take a painkiller?'

141

Saulius shook his head, started to cough and strain for breath. His gasps sounded as if he was drowning. Then he lay back, entirely still, eyes open to the ceiling.

A soul had left the room. Lukas saying, *'Saulius! Saulius! Hold on, hold on.'*

Prayers were being muttered, Catholic incantations under the breath, as if this might assuage Saulius's suffering, at last.

★ ★ ★

Weals along Matis's forearms and lower legs itched furiously. The bedbugs shaded the door frame in the bedroom. They were being moved to the women's house, ostensibly while the bedbugs were 'dealt with' by Edikas, but they knew it was for the removal of Saulius's body.

Matis was surprised they would put men and women in the same house, but Lina, the woman who had shaved his hair, shrugged. 'What will they take away? My virtue? I don't care if the house is shared. Women-only houses are a nightmare anyway. This is better.'

All of them were chastened to a new level by Saulius's death. They could die here and there would be no funeral, no telling mothers, no repatriation of the body. It would be as if they had never existed at all.

The only person crying was Lukas.

'How did we let this happen?' he said. 'We are complicit in this, we stood by and watched!'

142

DAY 4

MANON

She nearly takes Dimitri's hand, which is the size of a dinner plate, while he waits on the trolley in A&E, then remembers this isn't Mark she's waiting with. Mark is four floors up in oncology.

Dimitri had continued to refuse medical help until he passed out. In the absence of Edikas, a migrant handler called Dominykas had phoned for an ambulance.

She is spending far too much time in Hinchingbrooke Hospital, has grown fond of its blue striated linoleum, its bustling corridors, queues for the pharmacy and in the canteen. Hospitals are vibrant places — the epicentre of humanity, written on the myriad faces walking in and out.

'Am I go die, like Saulius?' Dimitri asks.

'No, you're not going to die. Antibiotics should sort you out,' Manon says. 'Who was Saulius?'

'In house. He die in house. He hurting catched chickens. No hospital him. He die.'

'And Edikas knew about Saulius's death?' Manon says. She is already digging out her mobile phone.

143

Dimitri is nodding with his eyes closed. 'He take body.'

'Will you excuse me just a moment?' says Manon, rising and making her way out of the department while phoning Davy to bring him up to speed on Saulius.

'That's enough to arrest Edikas,' she says, 'for preventing lawful burial at the very least, if not manslaughter. Enough to give us search and seize at his property. We need the paperwork relating to payroll and mobile phones. He must have them.'

'Edikas has gone to ground,' says Davy. 'No answer on his mobile number. None of the migrants know where Edikas is. In fact, they haven't seen him since yesterday morning, which they say is very unusual.'

'Think you'd better pay him a visit,' says Manon. 'With a battering ram. Hang on, something's coming in on my phone. Speak to you shortly.'

A text. From Bryony.

BREAKING: Witch Doctor gel is amazing on arse spots. Seriously, they should rebrand it Arse Gel. B

What makes you think this has any relevance to me? M

Educated guess. B

When she returns to Dimitri, he is being seen to by a doctor who appears to be about twelve.

There was a time when Manon would have fancied said doctor. Now she identifies more with his mother. The doctor is fortunate to be wearing a face mask while dealing with Dimitri's putrid leg.

The relief on Dimitri's face at being seen to is palpable.

'Very good man, very kind,' Dimitri says, his arm laid out with a drip attached. 'Lukas. Not like most. Most of the guys who comes here not educated. Rough guys, like Edikas. In Klaipeda they work in dockyard, very drink. Lukas was different. He want get out. I hear him talk with Matis. He say he need break Edikas house get passport. He save petty cash for bus — she is not expensive, maybe hundred pound.

'Lukas help Saulius. He find painkillers, he give his cash to Saulius because he don't want him have pain. This is good man.'

145

DAVY

Davy is outside Edikas's house — a modest mid-terrace, not unlike the migrant house, but without the piled rubbish and rot. He has rung the bell several times.

On the phone Manon says, 'He's probably shipped back to Lithuania. That'd be my guess. Felt the heat turning up from us and decided to make a run for it. Damn. We should've arrested him days ago.'

'We didn't know about Saulius days ago,' Davy says.

'You have my permission to gain entry,' she says.

Tired Nigel is in the car, seemingly minutes from taking a nap.

Davy tenses the muscles in his leg, aims the heel of his foot and kicks the door in. It yields easily.

Inside, the house is fastidiously tidy, the remote neatly lined up on the coffee table in the lounge, before a vast television. It isn't a posh house, but it's homely and well kept, unlike the migrants' quarters. But then, Edikas wasn't sharing with anyone.

Davy checks upstairs first. There's plenty of

146

evidence he's shipped out. No toothbrush by the sink, empty hangers in the wardrobe. Gaps and spaces where possessions used to sit. Davy is single crew (well, not quite — Napping Nigel is a force to be reckoned with, out in the car), and he works his way methodically through Edikas's things, noting in the search log anything he'll be taking as evidence.

He finds a drawer full of mobile phones which might yield much, particularly if one of them belonged to Lukas Balsys. The trace on his number, supplied by Ludmilla, has drawn a blank — which it would if the phone was turned off, as these are.

On the upstairs landing, he looks up at the ceiling and sees a square hatch that must lead to an attic. Davy goes on the hunt for a ladder. Glancing through the lounge windows, he sees that Tired Nigel still has his head tipped back in the driver's seat and eyes closed.

Davy finds a ladder in a utility cupboard that also contains a mop and an ironing board.

The attic is very warm and dark. The air thick with dust. Boxes of papers and files, which he knows they will want a very close look at. He switches on the torch on his phone.

In the corner, under the eaves, is a bin liner, which Davy opens. It is full of money, rolled into bundles and kept there with elastic bands.

★　★　★

'There's loads of paperwork in there,' he says to Nigel through the window of the car. 'Can you give me a hand bringing it down?'

Back inside, he approaches a closed door that can only lead to the kitchen. Davy pushes the door, but it is halted just a sliver ajar by a dead weight. He peers through the gap and sees the dog, stretched out on the floor and stiff as a board. Nearby is a half-eaten bowl of dog food.

MANON

'Don't come over all *Pet Rescue*,' she says, standing over the dead dog. 'Would've been destroyed anyway. That thing was the very definition of the dangerous dogs act.'

'She was used like that, wasn't her fault,' Davy says.

She thinks he looks devastated. Why is he devastated over a dog who was used to attack migrants?

'Let's worry about the humans being used, OK?'

She loves dogs, just like she loves babies. Except their mouths. Where babies' mouths are soft and gummily vulnerable, dogs' mouths make her recoil. The teeth. The wolf-like length of the jaw. The slobber and the smell. Dogs' mouths remind you they are wild. You cannot kiss them on the lips, whereas babies . . .

Edikas, never a man for sentiment, killed his dog before his departure. A confession? A joke — you'll never catch me! Or a big fuck you — that would be Manon's guess.

Or a man busy packing who used what he had to hand? Rat poison probably.

149

She knows Glenda McTrainAgain will over-react to the dog. Will take it as evidence that Interpol can take it from here and never mind the other suspects. But Edikas is a roughneck. He'd kill a dog if he was going on holiday for a fortnight, as soon as make provision for it. If he'd had some goldfish, he'd have flushed them down the toilet.

Or has *she* become monomaniacal? Is she wrong to think it *isn't* Edikas? Keeping an open mind, she finds, is hard to do. She is awash with unconscious bias. Remaining open to Mark living, to Fly surviving secondary school without going off the rails, to who their perp might be. Open minds search for their fixed point, an end to the oscillation. They long not to have to remain open at all. The only way to have a truly open mind is not to care. And she cares so much about everything. This is why the Holmes database was invented — a police IT system to collate and store evidence so that officers' open minds were not involved in the equation. Holmes told you to follow every lead. Holmes didn't care about your hunches. Trace. Eliminate.

Perhaps she is wrong, and Glenda McBain is right, after all.

★   ★   ★

When Teddy was smaller, she fantasised about hospitalisation. Something non-life-threatening, which involved enforced bed rest and being sequestered away from the family for maybe two weeks. Being served hospital crumble and

150

custard in bed, watching Netflix. Shrugging helplessly at Mark while he held the fort. *What can I do? These bunions won't heal themselves.*

But past a certain age in life and hospitals hold the promise of a more permanent kind of bed rest.

'So, what have they said?' she asks Mark.

'I can come home,' he says. 'I've had blood tests, a CT scan, and an MRI. Results can be anything from a few days to two weeks.'

'Oh God,' she says.

'I know.'

'You do still look yellow. Can they do anything about that?'

'Apparently not. Only try to find out what's causing it.'

'Tummy pain?'

'Bit better, just feel sick.'

'Who do I talk to about getting you out of here?'

'No one. I've got my discharge papers.'

She climbs in beside Mark, on his little uppy-downy bed with the buttons.

Holds him. Breathes him. While he is still there. She starts to cry. He is everything she wants. Not the perfection of a Cosmo relationship — all sex and 'communications' — but just his existence.

'Hey!' he says as her tears leak into his neck. 'I'm not dead yet.'

'You mustn't leave me,' she says. 'I can't bear it.'

She's horrified by her nit-picking in the face of separation. How could she have been so critical, so unsatisfied when he was here — reliably, stoically here. Best of friends.

'Think the NHS could save a fortune just by turning the thermostat down a notch,' she says.

'And opening some windows. I long for fresh air,' he says. 'I'm so scared,' he adds and she raises her head to look at him because it is unlike him to say anything emotional.

'Me too,' she says. 'We just have to have to face what we've got. No positive thinking.'

'Urgh,' he says, 'I hate positive thinking. Just a way of bullying people, making them feel the bad stuff is their fault.'

'I don't want to live without you,' she says. 'I only want to live with you.'

Cheek to cheek, the smell of him (albeit a bit ripe) is home, her safe space. She vows she will never take him for granted again.

'When they say 'little scratch' for a cannula or whatever, it never is a little scratch. It really hurts,' he says.

She notices people who have no one to go home to, no prospect of being looked after, who must make their own cups of tea. The fear must be so intense, the vulnerability.

She resolves to cook for an elderly neighbour who's alone (if she can find one) even though cooking was never her strong suit.

She pulls the curtain around his bed and watches as he gets out of bed, his gown open at the back. He is stooped, elderly seeming, his hair matted. He appears weak and wobbly as he tries to pull his trousers on.

'D'you need a hand?' she asks.

'I'm not at that stage yet,' he says.

'I'll drop you home, but then I have to nip into the office, is that OK?'

'Of course,' he says.

★ ★ ★

Barely a sip on her Americano and McBain 'wants a word'.

'Everything all right?' asks Manon, closing the door to Glenda's office.

McBain says, 'How's the Lithuanian?'

'Still dead I'm afraid.'

'Is it looking tidy?'

'I'd say it's pretty much the opposite of tidy at this moment,' Manon says. 'There are, ooh, three suspects in the frame right now.'

'Oh dear.'

'Why?'

'Well, it'd be good to clean up the Lithuanian problem before Wisbech goes to the polls. It's driving a lot of clickbait online. Lots of misinformation out there. Shane Farquharson's all over it.'

Here we go, McBain and her Internet Words. Manon cannot understand the current frisson about fake news. In her experience, newspapers have been getting it wrong and printing it anyway since time immemorial. And she, the daughter of a newspaperman, whose eyes lit up at the prospect of 'a great story'. She can, however, see an increasing problem with media 'balance', where swivel-eyed maniacs are asked for their views, seemingly to balance rational

153

thought or evidence from bona fide experts. Her father always told his trainees: if one side says it's raining and the other says it's dry, it's not your job to quote both. It's your job to look out of the window and find out the truth.

' "Clean up the Lithuanian problem"?' she says. 'Seriously?'

'It's not in our interests for this area to become even more divided. Things are very uncomfortable indeed on the streets of Wisbech right now. Atmosphere is . . . febrile. Local policing is stretched.'

She thinks of Morrissey. *Panic on the streets of Wisbech* . . .

'I think it's for Operation Pheasant to clean up the Lithuanian problem. We're only finding out who killed Lukas Balsys, if indeed he was killed.'

'You think it might be suicide?' says Glenda, looking brighter.

'It's possible. Except for the note.'

'Things are very tense,' says McBain, as if she's head of MI5 or something. 'You've seen the *Daily Mail*?'

Oh yes, she had seen the *Daily Mail*, seeing as the link was doing the rounds at the speed of light.

McBain had written a piece for the *Fenland Citizen* about the problem of policing 'a divided society'. To be fair to her, it was merely setting out the reality, but the *Daily Mail* had picked it up, taken her quotes out of context and run the screaming headline **Migrants Making our Town Lawless, says Top Cop**.

Top Cop, thinks Manon. *Top fucking Cop*.

154

'You're the top cop,' she says now.

'Hardly. Look, a collar on the Lithuanian murder, I can't emphasise enough how helpful it would be right now.'

'Oh you've emphasised it enough,' Manon says. 'Look, you'll have a collar when we know who did it.'

'Which is when?'

Manon shrugs. No way is she giving in to this kind of pressure. If McBain's put her foot in it, McBain will have to get her foot out of it.

Nevertheless, back at her desk she feels jumpy, the kind of inner fizz that would've seen her jogging outside for a cigarette in younger days, when she wasn't so scared of cancer. She wonders if Mark has collapsed at home. It used to be nice to stand outside, especially when the seasons were changing. Gave her a chance to sniff the air, take stock. Stop. A moment. Smoking wasn't all bad. Bigots have feelings too. Things are complicated.

She picks up her mobile from her desk.

'You all right?' she says.

'I've seen better days,' says Mark. He sounds weary.

'What do you need? What can I get you?'

'Nothing. Although I have a slight yearning for a black cherry yoghurt. Probably couldn't keep it down though. How's your day?'

'*Urgh*, fine. I'll try and source you a yoghurt. Do you need me to come home and look after you?'

'No, you're all right. I'll try to sleep.'

McBain was right. The streets *were* tense in

155

Wisbech. Fights in pubs escalating into brawls that involved knives and often a Lithuanian or Latvian getting slashed. Graffiti worsening. Vans carrying Britain First knuckleheads were coming in on a Saturday night, stirring it up. There was talk of a special force being drafted in to calm the situation — army boots, khaki fatigues.

A business, pledging support to One Wisbech, vowed not to employ any EEs.

'Is that even legal, to refuse a job according to nationality?' Manon asked Davy, who shrugged.

The business owner got plenty of publicity — an interview on local BBC news (heady glamour), a profile in the *Fenland Citizen*, which is just what he wanted.

Yet he couldn't fill his jobs with English workers. Hours too long, tasks too menial. There was strikingly little coverage of this, just a niche piece in the *Guardian*, which she'd read aloud to Mark. Both of them shaking their heads, worried.

'Shall we move?' she asked him. 'Get the kids out before World War III breaks out?'

'Where to?'

'Dunno, Sweden? Australia?'

'Too cold and too hot. I like the seasons,' he said. 'Also, I'm not keen to leave the NHS right now.'

When she re-engages with the office-present, she is confronted with Davy, looking at her anxiously. 'Are you all right?' he asks. 'Everything with Mark — I heard . . . '

She wants to say, 'Oh, we'll get through it,' with a blase hand wave, but instead finds herself adopting an expression that shouts *I'm on the very edge* and saying, 'Don't be kind to me Davy. Just . . . really, don't be kind to me.'

But he is stooping over her with excess kindness, saying, 'D'you want to go and get a cup of tea together?' And she walks with him through the double doors, and before she's even at the bottom of the stairs, she's close to shouting at him (the stairwell not helping the volume) with more aggression than she intends: 'I cannot bear to lose him Davy. I can't contemplate it. So you'll have to put up with me being brittle and . . . on the edge.'

'Unlike normal, you mean?' he says, smiling at her ever so kindly. He rubs her upper arm.

'Yes, unlike normal,' she says, folding into his embrace.

'Righto,' he says. 'Just — I'm here, if you need me. That's all.'

'You're all right, Davy Walker,' she says, wiping her nose on his jacket shoulder. 'You're a good sort.'

DAY 5

MANON

'Any public order offences involving Tucker?' she asks Davy.

'No. Well, there are incidents involving him, like the driving altercation, but nothing that went on record. He hasn't got previous.'

'Hmmm. It's Mrs Tucker who pushes his buttons.'

'There was a PC in attendance to the house on a call of domestic unrest.'

'Let's get that PC in here pronto. Who made the call?'

'She did.'

She goes out to the car park to get some air, which is soft, a fine mist of rain held there like a net. Sweet smell of summer oxygen, rain and plants and lushness. No better country for the seasons.

An hour later, the PC is standing before her in an office she has requisitioned to make herself appear more important than she is. Nothing she likes more than lording it over the junior ranks.

He has introduced himself as Officer 329. She recognises him. She'd been at some kind of investiture at Shotley — a graduation of new

158

recruits — because some other DI was off on his jollies.

Officer 329's parents had loomed in, stooping, beady-eyed, and said in thick Glaswegian accents, 'He's a baby bobby. A baby bobby! Just a wee thing.' And she'd seen him wince, a little close of the eyes. She'd thought, *One day you'll give your eye teeth for five more minutes with these two fools. Everything you have, just to see them again.* 'A wee baby bobby,' they kept saying, tears in their eyes, their pride.

Their son looks about fifteen.

'Come on, Officer 329. You must have a name.'

'Brian,' he said. 'Brian McCoole, ma'am.'

'I'm not ma'am. I'm Manon.'

She notices him glancing out of this glass box of an office, to the main MCU room. He'll be excited to be here, will've told all his colleagues that he's wanted in the murder squad.

'We want your help with an investigation, Brian,' she says, and watches his eyes widen like it's Christmas morning. Freckles over his nose, pale orange eyelashes.

'Aye ma'am.'

'You were called out to Prospect Place a couple of weeks ago, to an altercation, domestic, is that right?'

'Aye.'

'Can you tell me what you found at that address?'

He has his notebook in his hand and is reading from it.

'So there was a Mr and Mrs Tucker. Mr

159

Tucker was in the downstairs toilet, bangin' and hollerin' to be let out. Mrs Tucker was in the kitchen dabbing at her face with a tissue. She had a split lip. A foreign fella was holding the toilet door shut to keep Mr Tucker in.'

'Foreign fella — can you describe him?'

'He didn't speak much English. Short cropped hair — shaved, like — blue-grey eyes, kind of darkish skinned. Flat back of the head. Said his name was Lukas with a k.'

'And what did you do?'

'Talked to Mr Tucker through the toilet door. Asked him to calm down. Told him if he calmed down we could let him out, talk it through.'

'Very good,' she says, and he glows, orangely. 'And then?'

'He stopped banging and shouting. Went down to crying, sobbing really.'

'Was he saying anything?'

'No, just 'oh God' and *argh*.'

'And when he came out?' She nearly says 'oot' in Officer McCoole's Scots brogue.

'He sort of scuttled out, pushed past the migrant fella and out the front door. Didn't make eye contact with anyone. I went after him, to talk to him, because I was concerned he'd head back to the house later and the situation would resume. I ran down the road yelling 'Sir? Sir!' And then he stopped and turned. He was hunched, fists clenched, breathing through his nostrils like a bull. Thought he was gonnae lamp me to be honest ma'am.'

'And what did he say?'

'He said, 'You're after *me*. *Me*! But you won't

160

do anything about *them*. They've ruined my life but you're not interested.''

'And then?'

'I told him if he wanted to make a complaint I'd take all the details, look into things for him, but he said 'Oh what's the point? You're not going to *do* anything, are you?' And he carried on walking then. I went back to take a statement from Mrs Tucker, but she wanted to leave it, didn't want to make an official complaint against her husband. I was concerned for her injuries, which were quite nasty. She was shaking. I think it was the shock. I told her to get in touch if things got worse again.'

'Well, you did everything right Brian. Everything. Your training has paid off. I'll need that notebook, OK?'

★ ★ ★

'For my money, Mr Tucker has the strongest motive,' she tells the room. God it's fabulous to be back at work, no one asking for a drink or a poo, though glancing at Tired Nigel, he could do with both. 'But as you know, we don't start with motive, do we? We start with evidence. The rope is the strongest place to start.' The feeling of control, the feeling her myriad problems are sequestered to one side. The feeling of moving through the world alone without loneliness. Yes, work is wonderful.

'We've been through the rope,' says Kim Delaney.

'Oh right, have we? When?'

161

'Davy held a briefing yesterday, when you were . . . ' says Kim.

At the hospital, Manon thinks. She nods, reaches for the back of the nearest chair for support and covers her hurt with a smile. 'Oh . . . right. Great. And where is the rope pointing then?'

'Nowhere,' says Kim. 'This type of rope is very easy to come by. Edikas supplied it to several of the HMOs for washing lines.'

'OK,' says Manon. 'And victimology?'

Davy says, 'Lukas was the depressive type. Miserable about his situation here, generally pessimistic by nature, even when he was living in Klaipeda. Doom balloon was the general consensus.'

'He's sounding like my kinda fella,' says Manon. It's this kind of tone that usually leads to her offending someone. 'Are you saying suicidal? Or just your common or garden Eeyore?'

'The other migrants say that by nature he was a bit of a downer, but that this was normal for him.'

Manon nods. 'It rather keeps suicide in the frame though, doesn't it?'

'There is one missing bit of the puzzle,' Davy ventures.

'Go on.'

'His best friend Matis. Chap he came over with from Klaipeda. He's gone AWOL along with another migrant — a woman called Lina. Although we don't know if they've hotfooted it together. Literally no one seems to know Matis's whereabouts. He might hold the key.'

162

'Operation Pheasant got anything on Matis?'

'Nope,' says Davy.

'And what about the handwriting — did the search of the migrant house throw up anything that matched?'

'There wasn't anything with writing on it in the house, full stop,' says Davy.

'Right, I want an update as soon as anything comes in,' she says, eyeballing Davy with a look that she hopes says *And don't try to brief in my absence.* 'And I mean anything.'

⋆   ⋆   ⋆

Manon engages in some office-style time wasting. Reading unimportant emails, even responding to some. Sample, from Colin Brierley:

Manon, have you left cheese in the fridge? If so, it is imperative you remove it immediately. Cheese is malodorous and retaining it on the premises runs contrary to Cambs constabulary regulations.

Carefully worded response:

Get a fucking life Colin.

Despite being pedant-in-chief, Colin Brierley was sloppy with language, which was a hill Manon was willing to die on.

'No skin off my back,' he'd say.

'It's nose,' Manon would mutter.

'Sorry?'

163

'It's the skin off your nose, not your back.'

The more he made these errors, the testier she became. When asked about a gadget he'd recently purchased, he said, 'Doesn't live up to the hike.'

'Hype, Colin.'

Colin always threw out these statements nonchalantly, with a certain jaunty aplomb.

One time, and it must've come after a run of mangled phrases, Colin said his weekend in Broadstairs had been 'a bit of a damp squid' and Manon had flung around with evident fury, 'SQUIB, it's squib Colin. For fuck's sake. Squib, got it? Stop murdering the language.'

* * *

Somehow, the day slips away from her, chatting while standing beside someone's desk (she can't even recall who, or what about, telly probably or the shocking state of the British summer, 'I've genuinely had enough.'). She calls Mark about five times, to check his vital signs.

She wrestles with the printer, which is predictably jammed; walks three miles to the canteen to get a coffee. Maybe five minutes* (*45 minutes) on the *Daily Mail*'s showbiz sidebar of shame. At last, she is back at her desk, settling down to read the files on the other two hanging migrants, who didn't leave notes at all. Let's face it, if she leaves this backgrounding to Tired Nigel, they'll be here all year. Should she manage Tired Nigel out of his job? She has neither the energy nor the heart. He has twins.

Let him be incompetent on Her Majesty's pay. Incompetent people have mortgages too.

The first victim, a Latvian woman named Dzilva, was a steaming alcoholic in an abusive relationship. Body was covered in bruises; plenty of evidence she hung herself, including CCTV footage of her walking to her lonely tree alone. Even her mother, back in Valmiera, Latvia, said, 'She just wanted it to be over. The struggle of life. She wanted out.' According to the case file.

Dzilva had been at the university of applied sciences in Valmiera. In the UK, she washed dishes until 2 a.m. at the back of a not very clean restaurant. A restaurant that had been awarded a hygiene rating of zero.

From science to a sink full of Fairy. Christ, thought Manon, *I'd want out, too.*

The second case was a Lithuanian man in a similar situation to Lukas Balsys: debt-bonded, couldn't see a way out. He was injured while working but given no time to recuperate. Rather like Saulius. Perhaps chronic pain drove him to end it all. Despite the balance of probability being that he killed himself, a note from Op Pheasant says, 'Both hangings used by illegal gangmasters retrospectively as threat to migrants.'

So Wisbech plod had been right. Suicides, unrelated either to each other or to Lukas hanging from a tree in Hinchingbrooke.

She still can't work out the significance of that crime scene location. Why on earth drive him an hour away to Hinchingbrooke Country Park? Why choose somewhere vaguely urban, when there was a proliferation of countryside all around?

165

It seems unlikely Lukas Balsys knew the lay of the land sufficiently to get himself there. And if you were going to do yourself in, surely you'd trudge miserably to your nearest climbable tree or accessible rooftop. Who could be bothered with a scenic Fenland drive?

If it was Mr Tucker, driving all that way only risked his quarry fighting back en route. There were no ligature marks on Lukas's wrists according to the PM — he hadn't been tied up. He was scratched from catching chickens, and somewhat malnourished, with an untreated chest infection, so said forensic pathologist Derry Mackeith.

'Some shocking cavities in his teeth,' Derry told Manon. 'His breath would've been ripe. Prolonged toothache could make you kill yourself.'

She thought of Elspeth Tucker having sex with him, underneath that revolting breath. Perhaps turning her head to the side and breathing through her mouth.

But the note, how did the note happen?

If it was Jim Tucker, who is quite possibly not the brightest bulb in the chandelier, he might've handed over paper and pen.

Edikas? Edikas would've understood the note and removed it, realising it was incriminating. There were definitely no flies on Edikas.

Why couldn't that note have been more incriminating? Why not go the whole hog and say, 'Take a close look at X, Y or Z'?

She thinks it must be a language thing.

She looks up to see Davy standing by her desk.

166

'I'm not reopening the other two hanging cases,' she says to him. 'There isn't evidence of homicide.'

'Um . . . ' he says.

'What?'

'It's Mr Tucker.'

'What about Mr Tucker?'

'Well, first off, you know how the trace on his Nissan came up negative?'

'Yup.'

'Well, I went back over it and there were four misreads in that trace, so I printed them off. Look at this one.'

He shows her an image of a partial number plate, the end of it obscured by a flash of light.

'I take it this is the first half of Tucker's number plate.'

'It is, yes.'

'Right, well let's arrest him, then. He's a veritable Titanic of motive, and his car drove to Hinchingbrooke.'

'Yes, slight problem,' says Davy. 'He's dead. Fire at the house. She got out. He didn't make it. I think we need to get down there.'

★ ★ ★

In Davy's car, she texts Fly.

Can you get Teddy for me? I have to go out on job, Mark too sick.

Fly can be more than a little tardy about responding. Perhaps she should call instead of

167

texting, but as she has this thought, her phone whirrs.

Yep, no worries.

My God, she thinks, *this darling boy.*

Thank you darling boy. Love you x

Simultaneously, Manon is saying to Davy, 'Mrs Tucker has certainly got the knack for it. First her lover, now her husband.'
'That's a bit harsh.'
She is texting Mark:

Have to go out on a job so home a bit later. Fly getting Ted. You OK? Anything you need?

Am fine. Enjoy yourself. Anything juicy?

Tell you later xx

'Housing officer, commits murder then can't live with himself,' she says to Davy.
'We don't know it was him driving the car. Could've been stolen,' he says.

★ ★ ★

Prospect Place is filled with blue lights: three fire engines and an ambulance. The Tuckers' once-immaculate house is charred black, smoke

168

still rising, but the sound is of dripping water after a thorough dousing. Fire crews have their hoses off.

'We have to keep a close eye,' says the fire chief, 'make sure it doesn't reignite. We're evacuating the neighbouring properties.'

'Where's Mrs Tucker?' Manon asks.

He nods towards the ambulance, where the back doors are splayed. 'She's very lucky we could get to her,' the fireman says. 'Bedroom in the attic. She was out for the count. We found him down-stairs, next to a canister of petrol. My guess is he took pills, then torched the place. The smoke would've assailed him pretty quickly, then the pills, then the flames. But Derry will tell you more.'

'Why not just kill himself?' Manon asks, partly to herself.

'Perhaps he wanted to take his wife with him,' says the fireman. 'Destroying the house is a pretty big statement.'

'Yes,' Manon says, 'the house tormented him.'

She approaches the ambulance, peers in to see Elspeth Tucker on the bed, head tipped back and eyes closed while a paramedic bandages her arm.

'Mrs Tucker,' Manon says, climbing in.

'We think she's been drugged,' says the paramedic. 'Very lucky the fire crews could get to her in time. They had to carry her down. We need to admit her to hospital to check her fully.'

'Can I have a word first?'

'You can try, but I doubt you'll get much of a response,' says the paramedic.

'Mrs Tucker?' says Manon. 'Elspeth? Can you hear me?'

She doesn't open her eyes.

Manon looks at the paramedic. 'She'll be all right, won't she?' she whispers.

The paramedic shrugs. 'I'd say so, yes,' he says.

DAY 6

MANON

She's putting Ted in with the childminder far too often, but she can't stay away from the office. Besides, Kristine lives only a couple of blocks from Manon's home and is the most laid-back woman on earth. It is too tempting for words.

'Hi Kristine, could you take Ted today?'

'Yes of course. Odette is here. We are making rock cakes together.'

Odette is the most gorgeous toddler Manon has ever seen, and Teddy is in love with her, so, win-win.

'Rock cakes with Odette today, Ted,' she tells him, as if she's arranged it as a special treat.

'Odette,' he says, dreamily, and they proceed to have a massive battle over what he's going to wear.

'You can't do cookery dressed as Spiderman,' she says, as if dealing with a rational human, 'it's the most flammable outfit ever.' Perhaps she's being paranoid, having just seen the effects of fire up close.

Davy is going to Klaipeda on victimology, so someone has to steer the ship. Mark is at home seemingly permanently taking a nap but still

171

eating nothing and still looking yellow. She longs for him to say 'I'll look after Ted,' but it is far too much to ask of him in his weakened state. You needed the energy levels of an Olympic athlete to look after Ted for a day. Not to mention Dalai-Lama-level patience, possessed only by Kristine.

★ ★ ★

'What time's your flight?' she asks Davy.

'Not 'til this afternoon,' he says. 'What are you doing here?'

'Too much to do. Tucker's death yesterday took us off the phone work, and you're away to Klaipeda, so I figured I was needed. All set for a few days alone with Bridget?'

''S'just work,' he says. 'There's nothing . . .'

'Yeah right. I'm not minded to open an investigation into Jim Tucker's death, are you?' she says. 'Fire crews seem pretty certain he torched the place. Mrs Tucker is sleeping off a heavy dose of barbiturates in hospital, by all accounts.'

★ ★ ★

They have cracked open the backs of the mobile phones found at Edikas's place, taken out the SIM cards, and matched the numbers so they know which is Lukas Balsys's.

Colin the tech nerd has downloaded the contents for Manon. Google Translate should get her far enough, but if not, an interpreter can be called in.

172

Davy has wheeled a chair beside her at her desk.

'Let's go into texts received,' she says. 'Oh *Christ!*'

She's recoiling from the image of a woman's distorted face; skin bubbled and stretched, eyes unable to open, neck deformed, the strands of tissue like molten wax. Like a victim of war, like someone rescued too late from a burning building. In the criminal justice system, they call these 'life changing injuries' in a masterstroke of understatement.

The text underneath the photo reads, once she has translated it, *This is because of you.* From Janina.

'This has got to be Edikas's work,' Manon ventures. 'Wouldn't you say?'

'Maybe Lukas killed himself because of what happened to his girlfriend,' suggests Davy.

'Then why the note?' asks Manon. 'Why not say, 'sorry Janina' or 'it's all my fault' or 'forgive me'? You need to find out what the Lithuanian police are doing about this when you're in Klaipeda. You'll need to visit Janina, wherever she is.'

'Doesn't this kind of put Edikas *out* of the frame?' Davy asks. 'I mean, if you've acid-attacked the girlfriend, why would you need to kill Lukas? Seems like overdoing it.'

'Edikas might be an overdoing it kind of guy. Or maybe Lukas refused to play ball even after this. Or a message to the other migrants. Fear is very contagious.'

★ ★ ★

173

That afternoon she gave a statement to the press about Mr Tucker's death and, with this in mind, had nipped home to change into her favourite navy dress, in which she thought she looked both svelte and professional. Why did the internal image of oneself halt at around thirty-six, while time marched cruelly on? She applied makeup. Badly, as per.

'You look nice,' Mark said, as she was leaving.

Come evening, they are watching the regional news together. She is horrified to see herself in HD.

'Who is that exhausted-looking old hag?' she shrieks at Mark.

'That's no hag, that's my wife,' he says.

She told the cameras they were not treating Jerome Tucker's death as suspicious.

'How did he die?' asked a reporter.

'In a house fire,' she replied. 'There is no evidence of third party involvement in Mr Tucker's death. The murder investigation remains open into the death of Lukas Balsys. We are not ruling anything in or out at this stage.'

'Christ, I need to lose weight,' she says to Mark, rewinding the news so she can scrutinise the fat deposit below her bra strap, just under her arm, visible to the east of the podium.

'No you don't, you look great,' says Mark. 'Not sure you've told the press anything.'

'That was the aim,' she says.

On the television, another reporter shouted, 'Is it true Mrs Tucker was involved with one of the migrants?'

'Where's your information from, Tiny?'

Manon asked the *Daily Mirror* reporter, who she knew of old. His name was Tony, but everyone called him Tiny because he was absolutely massive.

'We ask that you respect Mrs Tucker's privacy at this difficult time,' she added.

'Your chief said migrants were making Wisbech lawless — ' Tiny again.

'No she didn't, if you'd care to read her original piece for the *Fenland Citizen*. You'll have to refer those questions to her.'

'Oooh, landing McBain in it,' says Mark.

'No I'm not. Oh God, look, I'm about to waddle off the podium . . .'

'One more thing,' said TV Manon. 'We are opening an investigation into the death of another migrant, Saulius Butiene. There is evidence that Mr Butiene died at the migrant house in Prospect Place and that his body was unlawfully removed from that address. Anyone with information, anyone who saw suspicious activity at Prospect Place around ten days ago, should contact the police immediately.'

'Least my buttons didn't come undone,' she says to Mark.

'Small mercies,' says Mark.

They hold hands these days, on the sofa.

'What d'you fancy for dinner?'

He grimaces. 'I can't face anything.'

'Another black cherry yoghurt?' she offers.

'Maybe that.'

'I shall bring it to you on a tray.'

175

DAY 6
KLAIPEDA

DAVY

The Michaelson Hotel doesn't do evening meals so Davy and Bridget walk to Theatre Square, a cobbled nineteenth-century affair, where there are restaurants, and choose Forto Dvaras, a Lithuanian eatery with tables outside under white linen umbrellas.

He is surprised by how nice Klaipeda is (pristine streets); surprised at how European it feels — and chic — when he'd expected something more Soviet and Baltic-depressing. It feels affluent, more like Belgium than Belarus. What on earth made Lukas come to Wisbech when it's so nice here? Mind you, Lukas won't hail from this smart tourist centre. He'll be from a rougher part altogether, and they have a Lithuanian interpreter taking them there tomorrow. Another reason for mild indigestion. After an extremely heavy meal, they head back to the hotel and turn in (separately) by 10 p.m.

★ ★ ★

Having breakfast with Bridget is a bit much. What he wanted was a strong black coffee by himself while his vital signs returned to normal. He likes the look of the cottage cheese lazy dumplings (Lithuanian speciality). A man at the next table, who has 'business trip' written all over him, says 'When I first moved to Switzerland, you could only get two types of cheese,' and shakes his head seemingly in disbelief.

'So, Davy Walker,' Bridget says, elbows on the table. Her hair looks nice — soft just-woken-up hair.

The piped music is too loud — a kind of folksy classical which surely no one can like — and he feels wreathed in sleep, deprived of rest. He'd been awake at 4 a.m. worrying: about visiting Mrs Balsys (a death knock in a rough area, oh woe), about Juliet, and being away from home. The hotel air has dried him out even more than the plane. He realises it's 'When the Saints Go Marching In', on manic violins.

'So, Bridget,' he replies wearily. 'Not looking forward to today.'

'No. Poor woman,' she says.

'Have you got kids?'

'Two.'

Bloody hell, he thinks. *You're coming on a bit strong for a married mother of two.*

'So I'm going to leave the death knock to you if that's OK,' Bridget says. 'Can't trust myself to keep it together.'

'Didn't know you had a family,' Davy says.

'Why would you?' she says. 'Me and the fella . . . we're not in a good place. TMI, sorry.'

'Why not?' he asks, because he wants to know.

'It's not that we don't get on,' she continues.

'Or that we're not fond of each other. It's just we're not really intimate any more.'

He nods, wondering if that's what's up ahead for him and Juliet.

He has ordered, not the dumplings, but an omelette with vegetables, and it arrives on a vast plate, looking as if it has been made with a minimum of ten eggs.

'Crikey,' he says.

'You just get in the habit of not doing it,' Bridget continues.

'Just popping to my room,' Davy says, as his bowels shift, urgently grabbing his white key card off the tablecloth and rising. 'Back in a minute.'

DAY 6
HUNTINGDON

MANON

'I need parameters for the search for Saulius's body, and I don't have any. I can't have POLSA searching the whole of Wisbech and outlying areas.'

'No, you can't,' says McBain, and Manon can see horrified financial calculations going on behind her eyes. 'None of the migrants know where they took him?'

'No. We have to hope the dog walkers of Wisbech have their eyes peeled.'

'What about a trace on Saulius's phone? Might still be in his pocket,' McBain suggests.

'Given that he died ten days ago, that phone will be as dead as he is.'

'Still, worth a try.'

★ ★ ★

Reluctantly, she puts in an application to trace Saulius's number, but without much hope. When the call data analyst rings her with the results, he says, 'So, you were right, that phone's dead.'

'Thought so,' she says, wanting to end the call because this was so obviously a waste of her time.

179

'But, the good news is, we were able to get the last GPS location for it, and it's an interesting one.'

'Send it over,' she says.

★   ★   ★

The last GPS signal from Saulius's phone has placed it in the semi-rural North Brink area just outside Wisbech.

She has driven out of Wisbech along the B198 to see if anything in the vicinity smacks of burial site. It's a smart place dotted with well-to-do detached properties, and she is struck by how much home improvement is going on. There is barely a house without a skip, a ladder, or a bit of scaffolding outside. She decides to do some light house-to-house work. 'Having work done madam? Lovely. Can you tell me the nationality of your workmen? Irish? Right, sorry to trouble you.'

At the entrance to one property — a gorgeous detached Georgian house, the kind that might be used as a location for a Jane Austen TV adaptation to denote 'fallen on hard times' but is in fact ludicrously delightful — she notices bags of sand.

She rings the doorbell.

'Just had this laid?' she asks the owner, one Vincent Guthrie, as they both stand on a pristine block-paved front drive.

'Yes, about ten days ago. Rather pleased with it,' says Vincent, rocking onto the balls of his feet, his hands in his corduroy trouser pockets.

180

'And who laid this for you?'

'Chap I dealt with was called Yonas,' says Mr Guthrie.

'And where was he from, do you know?'

Mr Guthrie turns his mouth down. 'Latvia, maybe Lithuania?'

'Thanks very much,' says Manon, wanting to make for her car at a run, but forcing herself to make a dignified exit.

On the phone to McBain, she says, 'Right, so the last connection made by Saulius's phone places it in North Brink. Phone might have died before continuing on somewhere else, or might have been destroyed, but, and this is a big but, there's been building work in the area at the same time as the disposal of Saulius's body. A driveway laid by Lithuanians or Latvians. Bridget from Op Pheasant said Vasil has a sideline in block paving. Nice fresh tray of concrete might be the perfect place to deposit the body.'

'Mmm, I don't know Manon,' says McBain. 'That's a lot of dots you're connecting. If there's nothing under that drive, I'll be paying for a replacement, as well as Davy's bar bill in Klaipeda.'

'But Saulius might be under that paving.'

'Or he might be somewhere else entirely.'

DAY 7
KLAIPEDA

DAVY

Lithuanian police have supplied them with an interpreter/guide called Sergei who drives them to the housing estate behind the industrial port, an area named Rybporte.

The dock is bordered with giant yellow cranes, twice the height of the surrounding buildings — the sound of clanking ringing out. Red, green and yellow containers line the wharf.

A few meters back from the dock is a Fifties' estate, Soviet-built — low-rise buildings rendered with salmon-coloured plaster that is flaking, balconies that look like they might fall, yet the place is fastidiously tended. Neighbours chat, weeding their gardens or exercising their dogs.

''S'quite nice,' Davy says. He'd expected a place that reeked of deprivation.

They enter a building — a dark, concrete stairwell, walls painted gloss peach. It smells clean. It *is* clean. On the windowed landings are posies of plastic flowers.

'In England, this would stink of piss,' Bridget says.

Jüri and Ludmilla Balsys open the door, and there is some awkward mingling in the hallway until they are led into a comfortable lounge, immaculate, as if the cleaner's just been, which she has. Ludmilla is a cleaner at the local school. Net curtains at the window, brown chenille sofa, huge and comfortable-looking, a vast television, and a computer in one corner.

'We Skype our daughter in Norway,' Ludmilla explains via the interpreter when she sees Davy take in the laptop. Her red eyes and lined face tell Davy she already knows about Lukas. 'She sends back money, our daughter. Lukas went to UK to send us money — he wanted to help since Jüri has been signed off work.' And she starts to cry.

'We are investigating what happened to your son,' Davy says. 'We want to get to the truth.'

He wonders how they feel about official personnel like him and Bridget. Sergei the interpreter had told them that when he was a child, he once said something negative about the USSR at school and this got back to the KGB via the woodwork teacher. He was questioned about it. He learned to play his cards very close to his chest as a child.

But the least Davy can offer Ludmilla is the feeling that something is being done, that someone cares. Jüri, they learn, used to work on the docks, moving containers of fertiliser which came in from Belarus. He thinks the chemicals affected his health.

The pink carpet is striped from the Hoover's passage.

Ludmilla brings a tray — gold, set with doilies, sweet meats and tea.

'We bought this flat fifteen years ago. Lukas helped to do it up. Such a good boy. When will he . . . come home?'

'We cannot repatriate his body until the investigation is concluded,' Davy answers.

Davy asks to use the toilet and has a little nosey. The kitchen is immaculate, floral vinyl wallpaper, wood-effect units, a little gas oven. The decor is dated — has a touch of Communist set-piece about it. A small table set for two. Off the hall is a tiny bedroom, the bed smaller than a double. *How on earth did they fit four in here?* he wonders.

The not unpleasant sound of the thunking cranes in the dock is carried on the May air, along with the scent of the lilacs in bloom in the gardens. Perhaps this place would feel bleak in winter when it's minus twenty and covered in snow.

Davy shows Ludmilla and Jüri pictures of Lina. 'We think she might have gone off with Matis,' he explains.

But they don't know who she is. Downturned mouth. 'Matis was never good with women.'

'How d'you mean?' asks Davy, wondering if he has a domestic violence situation brewing back in the UK.

'He is unreliable,' Ludmilla says, rapidly translated by Sergei. 'Doesn't know how to form good relationships. But Matis is a good boy. This is his mother's fault. I knew him from a young boy. I love him like a son.' And she is assailed by a sob. 'Not like Lukas,' she continues. 'Like a nephew. Matis had a hard life. His mother left

184

and his father drinks a lot. This is true of lots of Lithuanians. It is the national disease.'

'Where might we find Matis's father?' Davy asks.

'In the bar,' says Jüri.

DAY 7
NORTH BRINK, WISBECH

MANON

The Fenland skies are blue with very 3-D clouds that look as if they've boiled up into its vast expanse.

She'd cross-reffed Jonas-pronounced-Yonas with Op Pheasant. 'Yes, he's Vasil's foreman on the patio-laying side,' they told her. The magistrates have executed a warrant over the phone to look under Vince Guthrie's drive.

'I'm afraid we have to dig it up,' she says to him at his front door, watching a crime scene van pull up at the end of the driveway.

'Over my dead body,' says Mr Guthrie.

'Actually, we have reason to believe it's over someone else's dead body. That's the problem.'

Watching full-scale destruction at her behest, while her phone pings with anxious texts from McBain saying 'Anything yet?' and 'Guthrie has been on to Police Legal Services for compensation ALREADY. Let me know the minute you find something' is the very definition of stress. If there is no body under there, she'll have some serious fences to mend/paving to lay. The waiting is close to agony. The din of jackhammers, white suits crawling over the site. They go slowly so as not to destroy evidence. If there is any. And it's all on her.

She becomes as bad as McBain. 'Anything yet?' she keeps asking SOCO.

'Give us time,' says one of them, tartly.

'You won't be getting any offers of tea from Mr Guthrie,' she says, noticing him watching proceedings from his front bay window. His expression is pure 'about to ring my lawyer'. She daren't ask to use his toilet, despite being desperate.

After what feels like an eternity, she hears a shout from one of the paper suits. 'Boss? Over here.'

She picks her way through the rubble to where they are working.

'Oh thank *fuck*,' she says, at the sight of upturned boots in the concrete. She takes a photo and texts it to McBain with the words, 'Saulius's final resting place', to which McBain responds with a series of celebratory emojis.

Vince Guthrie's driveway had been mid-lay on the night Edikas removed Saulius's body from the migrant house in Prospect Place. An inviting tray of fresh concrete in which to lay Saulius (and his phone, which is concreted into his track pants) under cover of darkness, and in a semi-rural location to boot. The phone must've transmitted shortly before being buried.

'Where are you?' Davy asks her over the phone, as she's getting into her car.

'Digging up Saulius,' she tells him. 'He's under a drive in North Brink.'

'Wow,' says Davy. 'That's a result. Well done.'

'Thanks. How's it going over there?'

'Not bad. Terrible to see the parents. They are destroyed.'

'Did you tell them about the compensation?'

'Shit, no. I forgot. I'll have to go back tomorrow.'

'Any contacts for Matis?'

'Yes, we're about to go and see his father.'

'Get a mobile number for him, will you? McBain wants us to trace it.'

'Righto, will do. How did you find Saulius?'

'McBain suggested tracing his phone. There was a GPS location for it in North Brink, where I discovered recent building work by a Lithuanian crew. Tell you what Davy, I was cacking it that we weren't going to find anything.'

'Still, it's great. Don't forget it's great,' Davy says. 'Otherwise he'd be under a driveway for all eternity.'

'Yes, I wonder how many other Lithuanians are under Vasil's block paving . . . '

Manon wants to sign off with *miss you*, but that would be weird, so instead she says, 'Anyway, speak to you later, yup bye, bye.'

DAVY

Around the corner from the Balsys's flat is a bar with a small wooden terrace adorned by rope rigging. Inside, the rigging motif continues on the walls. There is a ship's wheel and netting, in case the theme wasn't clear. The boating scheme seems silly to Davy, the dock being so heavily industrialised.

They find Viktor in the corner wearing a black shell suit with narrow green stripes down the arms and legs, and a silver link chain necklace.

Viktor is visibly half-cut. Davy looks at his watch. 11.30 a.m.

'Let's offer to buy him some drinks,' he says to the interpreter.

Viktor is voluble to say the least, and even in a language he doesn't speak, Davy can tell he is slurring his words. He can't wait to pontificate, about politics, art, economics. Viktor is a Baltic Russian.

'There is no hunger in Russia. There is hunger here,' he says, while Davy thinks *No hunger in Russia, really?* 'People complain about repression, about KGB, but these are what made Russia great!'

From Jüri's knowledge of where Viktor would be and in what state, Davy can see that Lukas and Matis's families are intertwined in the community of Rybporte. If not friends, then tolerant of one another under the thunking cranes of the dock.

'I wanted to be a poet, a musician,' says Viktor. 'But life forced me to be a welder. Money lets you live freely. Money means you don't have to worry about the next day.'

Viktor was glad Matis had left to work abroad. 'You want your children to have better lives,' he said. 'This is a country of brothers.'

Davy frowns at the interpreter, who explains that a country of brothers means a society where nepotism holds sway. To get a decent job, you need friends in high places.

'The most important thing,' Viktor pronounces, while another beer is set before him, 'is to avoid war. If you can avoid war, you can survive.'

He used to serve in the Soviet army, the interpreter explains.

★ ★ ★

They leave Viktor and swing by the Lithuanian police station, where Davy finds himself in the office of a fat man leaning back in his chair while the interpreter translates. Davy has asked what they are doing to track down Janina's acid attackers.

'Ach,' says the fat man, bobbing backwards on his chair. 'It is not so easy to trace these people.'

190

Davy doesn't need the interpreter to translate the laissez-faire attitude. The wave of the hand, the downturned mouth. A magazine lies on his desk, rolled open at the page he's reading. 'They got away on mopeds. No witnesses.'

Davy says, 'We have a lot of paperwork relating to Edikas Petrov — enough to secure a conviction if he were extradited.' He feels positively hyperactive next to the reclining man weighed down by his paunch.

'But where is he?' the police officer says, almost as if he is in panto. 'We don't know! His wife and children are gone also. The neighbours don't know where.'

Davy's fury has no place to go. He has no authority here. There is nothing he can do to chivvy this man. On the way out, he takes in the yellow gloss walls, the khaki metal filing cabinets, pictures on the wall of some dignitary in official robes. They pass an interview room where someone is being very audibly beaten up.

DAY 8
KLAIPEDA

DAVY

The plinky plonky hotel music is oppressive. He's surprised it doesn't drive the staff to homicide.

'Have you seen this?' Davy asks Bridget, who is braving the cottage cheese dumplings for breakfast. 'Lithuanians are the world's heaviest drinkers.'

'You'd think the Russian Federation would give them a run for their money,' says Bridget.

He's been looking around Google. 'That's got to contribute to their depression.'

'The men drink, the women clean,' says Bridget. 'As usual, we get the best deal.'

'Actually, I'd rather be a cleaner than a drunk,' says Davy.

'What about a cleaner married to a drunk?'

'Maybe not that.'

'Sweet Lord, isn't this the theme tune to 'Allo 'Allo!?' Bridget asks.

'There's no excuse for it,' says Davy.

'How many times have you nutted yourself on the shabby-chic wooden beam in your room?' asks Bridget.

'Only a couple of times actually. First thing in

the morning I forget it's there,' Davy replies.

'Same, nearly knocked myself unconscious. There's an interior designer somewhere, laughing into his polo neck.'

★ ★ ★

Back at the Rybporte estate, they spot a group of youths fishing through bins for bottles to claim the recycling deposit. The housing blocks are low — twenty-seven flats in a block, nine to a floor — which goes some way to maintaining the pleasant ambiance. The flats came into private ownership in the Nineties, following independence, Sergei the interpreter tells them. The owner-occupiers take good care of their individual flats, but there is no money for upkeep of the buildings. Hence the flaking plaster and crumbling balconies.

'Are you aware of what happened to Janina?' Davy asks Ludmilla and Jüri.

This prompts fresh tears from Ludmilla. 'It is so terrible,' she says. 'Such a lovely girl. A beautiful girl. She and Lukas were engaged. We don't know why this happened to her.'

'We need to speak to her. Where is she?'

'She lives in hospital. She cannot eat or speak, now. The injuries . . . ' Ludmilla gestures weakly at her own face, and after translating this Sergei, mimics the movement.

Oh God, Davy thinks.

He is gearing up to tell them about the Criminal Injuries Compensation due — £6k or thereabouts, not an insubstantial sum in this

193

economy. He feels terrible for thinking money can pay them back for a dead son, but money can compensate many things, or so Davy feels at this point in his life. He once interviewed a cruise ship mortician, a busy man — the death rate on cruise ships being persistent to say the least. The mortician said he repeated the same phone call to relatives. *I'm sorry Reg passed away last night, peacefully in his sleep. This must be a terrible shock. You have a couple of options now. We can repatriate his body at a cost of £1,995.*

Yes, oh yes, we want Reg home. Doesn't matter what it costs. We'll want to give him a proper send off.

Or there is another option. We can bury at sea for £150.

Silence.

Would you like some time to think?

Well . . . now you mention it — Reg always loved the sea . . .

Ludmilla waves away talk of money, though Jüri listens intently.

★   ★   ★

They find Janina in a chair facing a broad window. She is dressed in mint green trousers and top of the kind worn by hospital orderlies in the UK.

'It is time for her lunch,' says a nurse to Sergei. She gives Janina a tall cup filled with some sort of shake, and a straw that is poked into Janina's distorted mouth. 'Slowly,' the nurse

194

says, then explains, 'her oesophagus is badly damaged. If she eats too fast, she will be sick.'

Davy pulls up a chair beside Janina. Her face is intensely shiny, as if varnished.

'Do you know that Lukas — ' he begins.

Janina nods. Either she knows some English or she is reacting to the name. She signs to the nurse, who gives her a notepad and a pen. Janina writes furiously.

'I wish it were me. I wish I could take such an easy way out.' She writes in Lithuanian, which the interpreter translates as he reads out loud.

'Were you threatened before this happened?' Davy asks.

She shakes her head, writes again. Sergei reads, 'They shouted *Something for your boyfriend*. I don't have a boyfriend, do I? I'm not going to have a boyfriend now. They drove away on mopeds. I didn't even see who they were. Helmets. I thought Lukas was a good man, but he was a coward.' She's underlined this word, Sergei explains.

'Lukas was captive,' Davy says, feeling a need to defend the dead man. 'He was being exploited — forced to work in the UK by illegal gangmasters. He had no way out. We think he was murdered. We are investigating who killed him.'

Janina looks out of the window. Then writes again, 'It doesn't matter now, does it? It would have been better if I never met him.'

On their way out, Davy has Sergei ask the nurse how Janina is doing.

'She's in a terrible state. So angry. The anger is

195

worse than the injuries. She is learning sign language,' the nurse says. 'Fastest learner I've had. Very intelligent girl. I think this makes the whole thing harder in some ways.'

'Will her injuries . . . ' he wants to say 'get any better' but feels silly.

'No,' the nurse says. 'This is how she is now.'

★ ★ ★

Davy and Bridget have some extra time before their flight home, so they decide to visit the Curonian Spit — a nature reserve on a strip of land out in the sea off the Klaipeda coast. On the spit is a maritime museum (incomprehensible) and an aquarium (pitch dark). They wander disconsolately around the aquarium, where most of the animals are made of plastic and where the labels are in Lithuanian. They spend a long time staring into a tank of giant turtles, waiting for them to move, before realising they are fibreglass.

In the dark, Bridget takes his hand.

'I can't,' he says.

He is grateful for the terrible lighting.

★ ★ ★

Despite being homesick for most of the trip, he finds himself perturbed about going back to Juliet. He has got used to hotel life with Bridget. Their breakfasts accompanied by Hooked on Manic Classics; their dinners at Forto Dvaras. Sliced beetroot with everything. The quiet

196

beauty of the river inlet where the hotel is situated.

It's flexing in and out of a relationship that's difficult. It's the same after intense jobs — twenty hours at work, then domesticity, the supermarket, Juliet's accusing look with regards to the laundry basket.

Do these feelings mean his relationship is bad, or are all relationships just really hard work?

After a long job or an absence, Juliet is always suspicious of him, hard to thaw out. With reason, so it turns out.

BEFORE

ELISE

They spent time together, Elise and Matis, learning words (him) and facts about each other (her). Neither was aware of the miracle inside her belly, though occasionally she noticed feeling different as she walked down the street — her body alive with voltage, a magical tingling at cell-level. This, she put down to love.

'I borrow this?' he said one day, a hand on her laptop.

She looked at him, her mind racing, wanting as she always did to indulge him in everything (he had that sort of face, she had that sort of heart) but behind this urge, suspicion. Would she ever see it, or him, again?

'No, sorry, I need it for work.'

He nodded, the curl of his lip the only evidence of disappointment.

'Excuse me,' he said, and got up from their table in the Rosmini Centre. She watched him move to the toilets at the side of the hall and felt the symbolism of his gesture: that her refusal of him would lead to his departure. *God*, she thought. *Men are such babies. They want total freedom, but can't stand it in anyone else.*

198

When he came back, he was distant but polite. This only hardened her resolve. She wasn't about to dance to his tune. She was far too experienced in the manipulative ways of her mother to react to his flouncing.

'I must to go,' he said, leaning back and tapping the table.

'OK,' she said.

'Tomorrow?' he said.

She nodded, but in a way that indicated she didn't care either way, gathering the laptop, pad and pens and placing them in her backpack with the panda faces and sequins on it.

★ ★ ★

The next day he tried harder.

'And what is this?' he asked, in a low voice, his hand stroking her shoulder.

Love! She wanted to shout. *Lust!*

Instead, she said, 'Shoulder.'

'Shoolder,' he said.

'This?' he said, palm cupping her cheek.

'Cheek,' she said, turning her head into his touch.

★ ★ ★

She wonders why there is so much emphasis on companionship, things in common, when it comes to relationships. Seems to her that lust, wanting to bang the hell out of the other person, is just as strong an indicator of compatibility. In fact, Elise thinks it's probably the most important thing. She'd watched her parents split up over sex, her mother being more and more brazen in her search for new sexual thrills. Had heard her mother shouting downstairs, 'We never fackin' do it, Dean!' She didn't want a relationship like that.

MATIS

When the pendulum swung him back into the room from sleep, it was generally at the behest of a text message buzzing in his jeans pocket — be at the BP garage in twenty minutes — or being shaken awake by another house resident.

Not the gentle awakening he longed for, the type that began in his groin with the stirrings of his libido, as if he really were of the animal kingdom — a sleepy, horny lion, or a flea-picking horny gorilla, in need of expressing his primal urge. However, he never woke gradually, not these days, and if he did rouse naturally there were never any females on hand eager to address his needs. And so his needs abated. Did lions have this problem?

'She has money,' he whispered to Lina, who was lying on the mattress next to him. He was aware of Lukas awake nearby and so tried to keep his voice very low. Lukas's disapproval was like a low-lying cloud following him everywhere.

'How much?' Lina whispered back. She shifted on her side, her two hands clasped under her cheek.

'Ten thousand English pounds,' he said,

watching Lina, waiting for her to be impressed.

'How will you get it?'

He shrugged.

'You can marry her or you can kill her,' said Lina, smiling. 'Or maybe both.'

Lukas turned over on his mattress noisily.

'Get her to bring it over here, in cash.'

'Why would she?'

'You need to think of a reason. She loves you. You need to use that to make her do what you want.'

★ ★ ★

They were waiting about on mattresses.

Lina came in, carrying a bag from New Look.

How she had money for clothes, he didn't know. A direct line to Vasil was his guess. She was better kept than the other girls.

There were men on various mattresses or propped against the walls, either sleeping or staring at phones. They slept at any opportunity: in the van, during their break at the chicken farm, just lying on the floor in the dust and mud. Sleep swung before Matis like a pendulum, and sometimes he went with it, sometimes he jolted himself out of it, telling himself it wouldn't be too long before he could shut his eyes. When he was upright, he longed to be horizontal.

Lina pulled off her leggings, revealing a perfectly oval bottom, entirely bare because her underwear was a string attached to her vest.

She bent, he almost couldn't believe she was bending because she was directing her buttocks

202

at the room. She shook from the bag a pair of white shorts and pulled them on slowly — *Is she being deliberately slow?* he wondered — over her quite extraordinary bottom. The men watched, open-mouthed.

She had a tiny waist. Enormous breasts. That shapely behind. *Like an underwear model*, Matis thought. *Like an American actress.* The shorts coated her like milk.

'Anyone got a mirror?' she said over her shoulder, as if she could see the back of herself this way.

'I can take a picture,' offered one of the men, holding up his phone.

I bet you can, thought Matis, *and I know what you'll do over that picture, too.*

Lina was looking over her shoulder at the camera, bottom pushed out, one knee bent. She glanced at Matis while the photos were being taken. *If this display is for everyone*, Matis thought, *is it for no one at all?*

'Wouldn't you like a photo?' Lina asked Matis.

He shrugged. He would've liked one. He'd have liked to gaze at it when he was alone with some toilet paper ready. Not that he was ever alone. Perhaps that was what was driving him mad: the lack of privacy, even in sleep.

But he didn't want her doling it out like this, sweeties to obedient boys.

Once, she'd said to him, 'This is only temporary.' And her assurance that she was on her way somewhere better and that therefore the stinking shared house, the filthy bathroom, and the way Edikas came and took her in the night to

Vasil's house, were nothing at all. Matis knew that he, too, was nothing at all; just a diversion on her way to the good life.

* * *

'Lukas, open up!'

He had the bathroom door locked again. Matis could hear him coughing inside. Eventually, the door rattled with unlocking.

Lukas, extremely pale, had some toilet roll to the edge of his mouth. A dark red spot of blood on the paper.

'Is that blood?' asked Matis.

'Yes, I'm coughing up blood.' He gave Matis his most hangdog worried look, the look that said *look at the place you've led me to*, the kind that made Matis turn away.

'I'm sure it's nothing. You'll be fine. You just need rest.'

'How am I going to get that?'

ELISE

He needs a holiday, she thought, looking at his pallor, his hooded eyes and the lilac circles beneath them. Week in Tenerife, lying in the sun sleeping, eating big dinners, sleeping more, getting some vitamin D, eggs for breakfast. *I could give him that*, she thought; *pay for us to go together*. None of this 4 a.m. malarkey.

They were standing in the smoking spot behind the garage.

'Very more trouble,' he told her, looking into her eyes. *Pleading for what*, she wondered. *For help or for her to believe him?*

'What sort of trouble?' she said. 'Can I help?'

He shrugged. 'Men. Men I work. I must to them money give. They will kill me if no.'

'How much?' she asked.

'Thousands.'

'*Thousands?*' she said, wide-eyed. 'And *do* you owe them this money? Is it . . . is it true?'

He shook his head. 'They say I must pay bus from Lithuania, house and food. They no pay me for work. I have scare.'

'You *are* scared,' she said, feeling a bit sick of reiterating this particular element of grammar.

205

We don't have thirst, we don't have scare. That said, this is the most English she's ever heard him speak. She wonders if he's rehearsed this particular speech, had help with it.

'If you give me money, I will pay you back,' he said.

My arse you will, she thought.

'OK,' she said. 'Shouldn't you go to the police? I could help you with that.'

He shook his head. 'They kill me. They hang me in tree. You bring money to my house? We pay them, and then' — he lifted her hand from where it hung by her side — 'we two go. Start new life.'

'Start new life with what?' she asked.

'I work hard, you work hard also.'

She smiled at him. *Scrap the holiday then.*

'What time shall I come to your house?' she asked. 'At 6? 6.30?'

'That doesn't give us much of a chance to go away together,' she said. 'I'll come at lunchtime.'

★ ★ ★

She had an app on her phone that told her when her period was due. She was never late, her menstrual cycle as efficient as her Easy eBay operation. She looked at the app, which said 'period due?' heart starting to knock with the possibilities. *Calm down Elise. Let's deal with the facts.*

Half an hour later, she was looking at the second line on a Clear Blue test. She wasn't sure what she felt. Hadn't she wanted to rough life up a bit, take a chance, make something happen? Well, it'd happened all right. And she wanted *him*. She wanted Matis, after all.

The question was, with her doubts lurking, ought she to take a chance on him? Earlier, when he'd asked her for money, a part of her said, *No way. No way am I handing you my money.* If you felt like that about someone, should you have a baby with them? Or was it all one big risk, life, so why not go with it? There were no guarantees, with anyone. And she had a feeling that the things you would regret in life were the things you *didn't do*, not the things you did. She couldn't possibly be a worse parent than her own mother and father.

Did she love him to the tune of £10,000? Perhaps she loved her money more, after all the time it'd taken her to earn it.

She would take the money to him, she decided. She would take her chance — to run away with him and start a new life with this extra person in tow. It couldn't be worse than being hauled off to the next shit-hole with her dad.

★   ★   ★

It was not Matis who came to the door of the house, but some stranger who walked away without saying anything. Elise was left to peer around doorways to try to locate him. The house was squalid and smelled deeply unclean. Before she could find Matis, Lukas had pulled her into the bathroom and locked the door behind them both.

'You must go,' Lukas whispered. 'He will take your money, him and Lina.'

'Lina?' said Elise.

'Yes, Matis and Lina . . .'

Elise leaned back against the door, blowing out as pressure built in her chest. 'Oh God. Oh God oh God oh God.'

She was struggling to breathe.

'What is wrong?' asked Lukas, examining her face. He was always the better English student, and now his face was searching hers for understanding.

'Panic attack,' she said between pants. 'Panic attack or heart attack. One or the other. I didn't know . . . about Matis and Lina.'

'Ah,' said Lukas gently. 'I sorry.'

'So am I,' said Elise. 'I'm pregnant, you see.'

Lukas put his arms around her.

'I sorry,' he said. 'Matis is fool. Have you told him?'

She shook her head. 'No point now. Will you tell him I've gone? That I had to go. Give me ten minutes to get away.'

She kissed Lukas then, wondering why she'd picked the wrong Lithuanian, and slipped out of the bathroom, down the stairs and onto the road, fast as a streak of light.

★ ★ ★

At home, with the front door safely closed, she checked the money was still in her handbag, in the fat crinkly envelope, unsealed. Then she dragged herself up the stairs, into her bedroom

208

with all its pink blankets and faux fur cushions, its softness always a comfort to her, but not today. All her problems followed her into this haven. The baby, the *for ever* baby, its father who had deceived her and was with someone else, the way all routes were barred to her now, and she being such a go-getter of a person. What was she *thinking*, getting into trouble with someone so unreliable? With *foreigner vermin*?

The worst kind of recrimination was the one against yourself, the way everything at the end of it all, was your own fault.

Elise hated herself. She wanted her mother to say, 'Come on now. No sense crying over spilled milk.' But her mother had never been a comfort to her, so perhaps this was something she needed to say to herself.

Being in her bedroom allowed her to cry and cry and cry, loudly, until she was quite raw and worn out. She seemed to have more tears than usual — was that because of the baby? Every time she thought of the baby, she cried harder. *Saddled*, she thought. For ever. *I'll never make a success of myself with a baby at seventeen.*

When her father came in, searching her face with his concern for her, she felt too exhausted to prevaricate or lie. She confessed everything. Yes, an EE. Yes, pregnant. Yes I know, I'm only seventeen. It was not exhaustion, not really. She knew what she was doing, setting her father on Matis's tail. She knew, and, like a kamikaze pilot, she didn't care.

Far from flying off the handle, he sighed, taking her in his arms.

'Ah, Elise love. You poor, poor thing. My lovely girl.' And he kissed her temples, smoothed her hair. It was not without anxiety, this uncharacteristic gentleness of his. She wondered where it would end, when the steel-capped boots would come out. 'Can't you get rid of it? How far along are you?'

'Not far,' she said. She had already wondered why this wasn't her first thought: an abortion. Her natural inclination to solve via activity would surely have sent her to Google, typing in *Wisbech abortion clinic*. She had the money, after all.

No. Some part of her was enjoying the destructiveness of her predicament. It didn't require much effort, after all. She would go the whole hog, tell her dad his name, where he lived, and let the explosions go off. *Fuck openness, fuck kindness.* She'd been dealt a sorry hand, and it was time to pass the bad luck on. When you are finished, you want to be with other people who are finished, too.

'Right, where does he live, Elise. You tell Dad, and I'll sort it.'

'Prospect Place,' she said.

★ ★ ★

'Give me a placard, I want a placard,' she tells her dad.

'You've changed your tune,' he says.

'Yeah, well, I've realised you're right about them. They're vermin. Absolute vermin. They want destroying.'

210

'Good girl,' he says. 'The apple never falls far from the tree, eh 'Lise?'

She's chain-smoking, doesn't care about the baby or her body. Doesn't care about *him*, or what happens to him. She's in the mood to hurl a grenade.

She's with the right bunch, the exact bunch to fit her psychic mood, gathering outside her father's house with their St George's flags, their Tommy Robinson banners. The anger in the air is just the oxygen she needs.

Singing '*Oh, Tommy Tommy. Oh, Tommy Robinson.*'

T-shirts saying Freedom of Speech. English Defence League skinheads calling everyone 'mate'. Shane Farquharson at the front with a portable microphone that keeps squeaking. Someone has a set of speakers, playing 'Never Forget' by Take That.

Banners saying, 'Not racist, not fascist, not happy.' 'Refugees not welcome. We are FULL.'

They'd be happier if the migrants were Muslims, preferably part of a grooming gang. It's Islam that really floats their boat. Al-Qaeda, paedophilia. 'No more mosques', reads one sign, randomly. Well, it's a random alliance.

'Respect are country. Speak English.' A while ago she would have rolled her eyes at this. Now, she marches behind it. Her own banner reads, 'One Wisbech. English town for English people.'

At the front, in his countryman's coat, Farquharson leads, alongside her father. Letter-box mouthed, grinning at the following. They are almost arm in arm, smiling at each other,

211

coaxing the rabble like a herd of unruly goats. Bleating goats. In truth, it's a small crowd, but they are vocal, in high spirits, full of song. *Oh Tommy Tommy . . .*

But crikey, she becomes tired. Marching, bellowing, chanting. It's all exhausting. She cannot muster the anger of the others, not for any length of time. Perhaps it's the pregnancy, making her long for bed. She's almost falling asleep standing up. She starts to plan when she'll peel off and quietly make for home, without her dad noticing.

They get to Prospect Place and she watches her father go up the path to the migrant house. Some of them come to the door, her father shouts, 'Which one of you is Matis?'

The crowd, at the sight of the migrants, starts shouting 'Vermin! Ver-min! Out! Out! Out!'

No, she thinks, *no, no, no. What have I done?* Everyone so pumped. Is it tiredness that makes her see where she is, all of a sudden? She can see how dangerous it is. She starts to sweat, her heart jittering with anxiety, heartbeats bunching together then missing their rhythm. She doesn't want to see where this ends, what she has set in train.

Yet she doesn't intervene. Easier not to. She stays, shrunk back in the flank of the march, like one of the smaller muscles in the body of a caterpillar. She slinks off down a side road, not wanting to see the end of her father's confrontation with Matis. Not wanting to see Matis at all.

BEFORE

MATIS

The disappearance of Edikas, around four days after Lukas's death, had brought with it a new regime of sorts — a calmer, kinder handler called Dominykas. All the migrants assumed Edikas had done a runner because of heat from the police over Lukas's death. Dominykas was more reliable in doling out petty cash for sundries — toothpaste, shampoo, that kind of thing. It had been sporadic, at best, under Edikas. Also, the dog was not missed.

Matis managed to gather together £16.50 for a litre of Glen's vodka. He sat in a doorway on Norfolk Street, swigging it and hoping the image of Lukas on that awful night would leave him. He passed the evening drinking in the doorway, before staggering back to his mattress in the shared house.

Lying next to him, Lina said, 'You stink of it. You have to stop.'

'I have to get out of here,' said Matis. 'Maybe we should go to the police, there must be a way out,' but Lina shook her head. Slightly too quickly, he thought.

'Too dangerous.'

'What about you, you don't want to get out? Too cosy with the boss? What happens at Vasil's house?'

'Mostly, he talks,' she said. 'About his mother. His younger brother died in childhood. There was a fire in his house. After that, Vasil lost his mother. She said to him, 'I stay alive only for you.' But she was there only in body, not in spirit. Dead eyes, dead soul.'

Like you, Matis thought, *now he sleeps with dead-eyed women like you.* He said, 'You want me to feel sorry for him?'

She shrugged. 'I don't care what you feel. All the money he makes, is to make it up to her. To buy her back into life.'

'He doesn't make it though. He steals it from us. What are you, his therapist?'

'I suppose.'

'If I went to the police, it could blow Vasil's operation wide open.'

'No,' Lina said, hastily. 'You mustn't. I help you. We will find a way to get out. I will get money. I know a place we can go. But only if you stop drinking. You have to stop. This is the Lithuanian disease. It will kill you.'

'When will we go?' he asked, the blur of the vodka wreathing his mind.

'Tomorrow night,' she said. 'You must get a car.'

He closed his eyes, immobilised by the vodka, which has muffled him, slowed his limbs. How the fuck was he supposed to get a car? He couldn't ask Lukas what to do as he normally would have. Lukas would have sighed miserably,

214

shaking his head as if the situation was sadly impossible. Then he would have said, *I'll help you.* And having Lukas on the case would've made everything all right.

This thought made Matis reach for the bottle on the floor beside his pillow, but Lina's hand got there first. She was up and out of the room with that bottle before he could have some.

He heard liquid glugging down a distant plughole.

He rolled onto his back. A window was open. A car whooshed down wet tarmac outside. The clack of a woman's heels on the pavement, growing quieter as she receded.

Elise would have bought him his own car with her money.

Elise would have done anything for him.

Why didn't she come?

The back of his hand was resting on his forehead. He opened an eye. Some of the mattresses were occupied, some were not. People came and went from this house. He didn't know where they went, didn't want to ask what happened to them. It is not as if they were bound by chains. Only by language, threats, and economics. And often by their own chains: mental health problems, blindly working and drinking without questioning who for, or why. The gangmasters didn't need to lock them up.

'Dominykas is not a problem,' said Lina, as if answering his concerns. 'He is too lazy to stop us. He won't notice.'

It was true. The corpulent Dominykas had none of Edikas's blood lust. While Edikas had a thirst for sadism, Dominykas wanted a quiet life. He wanted to clock off.

'We will go in the night, you must get a car, I will work out where we go,' Lina said.

'Vasil will notice if you're gone,' Matis said.

'Maybe he will help me.'

'Really?' Matis felt incredulous. He wondered what Lina was planning to do to Vasil. She had depths of ruthlessness. She could get Matis out, but she could kill him, too. It was as if the nerve endings of her feelings had been cauterised with a soldering iron, or by the things she had endured as Vasil's sex slave. She appeared to feel very little. She was just Matis's type.

Some of the men in the house guarded their possessions closely, though no one had much — mobile phones mostly (they were given cash to top up their phones, because it was the way they were called to work), some food and booze, maybe a nice T-shirt or belt or a clean towel — taking everything with them when they used the bathroom. They had so little, they were in constant fear of something being stolen. Lukas was never like that. Lukas was philosophical about everything. 'If they want it so badly, they should have it,' he'd say. Lukas was the sort to trust first, ask questions later. 'Most people are good,' he told Matis. 'Most people don't mean you any harm.' He was so wrong, Matis's gentle friend.

The thought of Lukas made Matis want another swig, so viscerally it came from the base of him, just below the ribs. As if his lungs wanted the drink, his very organs jangling for it. A swig

216

would calm the shivering feeling he had when he thought of Lukas. Of the sacrifice.

How to get a car?

The only thing he could think of was to steal one. The neighbours had a car. A spotless Nissan Micra that he had been in before. He could hot wire it, pick up Lina from Vasil's when she'd completed her 'business'.

★ ★ ★

The clanking of cranes was the soundtrack of his childhood. He went to sleep and woke to its rhythmic tock in his cot. The seabirds. The fresh smell of the water.

He missed the emptiness of Klaipeda. Its quiet pace. He'd found it boring, its horizons too narrow, but now he longed for its stultifying security. 'I like the misery I know,' Lukas had said to him, in that bar in Rybporte.

He missed Švyturys beer. In England they drank vodka because it was cheap and it got the job done quickly, but in Klaipeda it was always Švyturys. He missed his local bar in Rybporte, where he would always find one or two of his friends. He missed knowing how things work — the pedestrian crossings, his way around the back streets, which bus to catch, where to get off, what was good value and what wasn't. Travel broadened the mind but it could also make you live small, sticking to the few roads you knew. In England, he lived in a house without privacy. This, too, was taking its toll. Only in the bathroom, with the door locked, did his emotions rise to the surface and make him gasp.

He would not choose to live in the UK, where the island mentality had made the people mean. They knew nothing of hardship, these people — had never been invaded by Nazis, then Soviets. His people had been free for such a short time, and though he was too young to know about the transition period of the Nineties, his father was fond of reliving it when drunk. 'No one is interested in democracy when they are hungry,' he would say.

Lukas's father, Jüri, was kind to Matis's father. Kindness was in the Balsys DNA. Jüri tolerated Viktor, though they all acknowledged Viktor was a ranting drunk. Jüri would go to the pub with him, though Viktor could out-drink him quickly.

'Have some sympathy,' Lukas used to say. 'My father has my mother to go home to. Your father has no one.'

'And whose fault is that?' Matis asked.

DAY 9

MANON

'Finger painting with Odette today,' she'd said to Ted, with a spring in her step that denoted her joy at heading to the world of work.

Her mood is soon dampened by a 'chat' in McBain's office.

'So the phone idea,' McBain says, 'was a good hunch.' She looks positively euphoric.

'It was a good idea, yes boss,' says Manon reluctantly. She can see McBain wants to dwell on this. 'Coupled with my on-the-ground intel.'

McBain inevitably brushes over this last remark.

'And what about a trace on Matis's phone?' she asks, clearly wanting a repeat result.

Wants to solve everything with phones, thinks Manon. Though it is true, she concedes grumpily, that phones solve a great deal — most of the population being constantly tracked via GPS is obviously a boon — and that luck plays its part, too.

'If Matis's phone is among the stash taken from Edikas's house, then clearly it's not going to lead us to Matis,' she says, while being aware

219

she had become one of those 'knock it down before we even try' employees. *I like to put the 'no' in innovation.*

'But it might not be,' says McBain.

'It might not be, no,' says Manon. 'We are cross-referencing with what Davy picks up in Klaipeda.'

'Yes, expensive trip.'

'It's normal to do victimology over there. You start with the victim and work out,' she says, then worries she's ventured too far into *teaching her grandmother to suck eggs*. 'As of course you know. It's not an outlandish expense.'

'No, but the cuts, Manon, you would not believe the cuts I'm being asked to make.'

'Oh, I would believe them,' she says. 'Anyway, I better go and calm down Vince Guthrie, who is hopping mad over his driveway.' Despite her euphoria at having found Saulius, what she really doesn't need is a fresh murder investigation on her desk. 'Anyone we can hand the Saulius case on to?' she asks McBain.

''Fraid not. We're cut to the bone. There is literally no one else available. You'll have to run a dual investigation alongside the Balsys case.'

★ ★ ★

'Thank you,' says Derry Mackeith, bringing his autopsy report into MCU with a slight bow like some Poundland Rumpole of the Bailey, 'for delivering to me such a beautifully preserved corpse. If only they all came in concrete . . . '

'Pleasure,' says Manon. 'So?'

220

'Our chap had several broken ribs, which were left untreated. The jagged edge of broken bone caused a rupture and he died from blood loss.'

'And the broken ribs — caused by a person?'

'A fall from a significant height, a punch or a kick. Can't be any more precise than that.'

'A fall fits with what Dimitri told us. Burying him reeks of cover-up. Gross negligent man-slaughter at the least, as well as preventing lawful burial.'

'Well, this is all rather more your department than mine,' says Derry. 'He would have been in unconscionable pain, every breath agony. Nasty way to go. We've sent away toxicology, but I doubt he could have functioned without Trama-dol.'

'And definitely dead before he was laid in concrete?'

'I'd say so, yes.'

* * *

'I want to know who I complain to about all this,' says Vince puce-with-rage Guthrie, to some bewildered PC on reception, who fends him off with some forms to fill in.

Vince Guthrie is a Conservative councillor on Wisbech Town Council with UKIP leanings; a purveyor of dog-whistle politics. If Guthrie wasn't already hopping mad about having his new driveway dug up and Saulius dredged from under it, he is further incensed by today's headline in the *Fenland Citizen*.

221

Tory councillor hired illegal Latvian gangmaster to lay drive

The story, which is bound to be in tomorrow's *Daily Mail*, details the value of his house (£600k) and the savings he made by getting Latvians to do the work. 'Cut price quote' and 'Quite the saving' ran the subheads.

'We all want the Eastern Europeans in when stuff needs doing around the house,' says Manon now, back in McBain's office. *If only one would come to my house,* she thinks, visualising the coat hooks.

'This is no laughing matter,' Glenda says, pacing behind her desk. 'Guthrie wants to know where the leak came from.'

'He can want away,' says Manon.

'He's on the police liaison committee,' announces Glenda, as if this is somehow significant.

'Oh who *cares*? Press could've got it from a neighbour. It's hardly a secret that we've got a great big white tent outside his front door, is it? Neighbour probably sidled up to Vasil's lot while the work was being done and asked for a quote for his own driveway.'

McBain considers this with a lightening of her demeanour. 'Yes, that could've happened. Didn't necessarily come from us.'

'No, it didn't.'

All she wants, Manon can see, is something to feed Guthrie when she has to face him at some deadly evening committee meeting, at which traffic calming measures are discussed at length over stifled yawns. Unusual for a det supt to attend local meetings like this — they commonly send their keenest baby bobby, some twenty-two-year-old, eagerly holding his police hat under his arm and wanting to help with everything — but McBain would go to the opening of an envelope if she thought it would 'raise her profile'.

The whole debacle was unlikely to make Guthrie less vocal on the need for tighter immigration controls, despite his desire for a competitively priced new driveway.

Manon says to McBain, 'Look, I don't know how to get through the workload relating to this new investigation. We have to interview the owner of the farm where Saulius was working when he was injured, re-interview all the migrants about him, try to establish a link with Vasil. But I've got the Balsys investigation on the go.'

'Nigel doesn't seem too busy,' says McBain, and Manon wonders if that's a sly smile with it. She wants to scream *Have you ever worked with Nigel? Have you ever tried to get Nigel to do anything?*

'Yes, great idea. I'll put Nigel on it straight away. Responsibility be good for him.'

★ ★ ★

She marches alongside Nigel down the corridor towards interview room two, notices with irritation how he looks at his mobile phone and laughs, says to her, 'My mate Dave. Legend.' As if she might be gagging to find out what hilarious stunt pea-brained Dave has pulled.

223

She stops, swivels, and blocks Nigel's progress. 'Look, Nigel, this is a big deal, taking the Saulius case. Also, just between you and me, you are *this close*' — she puts her fingers a centimetre apart, a centimetre from his face — 'to being managed off the force. So I would forget your mate Dave, and, well, concentrate, to be honest.'

'Right,' he says. 'Yeah, right.'

Outside interview room two, she says, 'In here, we have Talcy Malc, dealer to the migrant house.'

'Talcy Malc,' Nigel says, with the same half-laugh prompted by Legend Dave. 'Classic.'

Fuck's sake, she thinks. *Manchild*.

Her hopes that Nigel would miraculously step up when given responsibility are fast evaporating. He should be working for some Stag Do or Go-karting firm, where saying 'Legend' and 'Classic', along with 'this could get messy' are part of the job description, as well as having no discernible personality bar a love of booze.

The name Talcy Malc derives from two sources: Malc is the only way to make Malcolm sound 'street'. If she wants to annoy her sometime-informant, Manon only has to bellow MALCOLM MCGINTY YOUR MOTHER WANTS YOU at top volume from her open car window, and watch this flaxen-haired creep with the baseball cap on backwards run for cover. The Talcy part of the name derived from the white powder found about Malcolm's person, especially around the nose area. Talcy Malc once told Manon he had drunk four desperados (pints of beer with tequila shots in them), smoked twelve spliffs, and done four lines of coke, but he was 'fine to drive'. Which put her 'asleep after half a glass of Chardonnay' into perspective.

Talcy Malc leans back in his chair, a languid C-curve, arms forwards on the table and his head down.

'Did you supply opioids to the migrant house on Prospect Place?' she says, after the preliminaries about who is in the room.

'No comment.'

'Come along Malcolm, you're not being charged. You don't need to go no comment. Is our little arrangement come to an end? Because if it has, there are quite a few offences on record I'll need to put before you.'

Talcy Malc shakes his head irritably. 'I don't want this shit. I'll get both my legs broken by my suppliers if they know I talked to you.'

Talcy Malc is surprisingly well-spoken when he's not around his posse. His parents are antique dealers in Hitchin, Hertfordshire. From her days in CID, Manon remembers a geriatric couple, living in a quiet bungalow, who were dumbfounded by their son's lifestyle choice.

'Well,' says Manon. 'I'm not going to tell them, if you're not.'

'Yeah, I supplied the migrants. Chap was in terrible pain, broken ribs it looked like. He needed Tramadol. I gave it to him, then he needed more.'

'Did he get addicted?'

'That *is* the aim,' says Talcy Malc with a hint of wounded professional pride.

'And this was a guy called Saulius?'

225

Talcy Malc nods.

'For the tape.'

'Yes.'

'Did you supply anyone else?'

'I didn't ask who was taking what. They bought various pills, Tramadol mainly. I offered sleeping pills — people on Tramadol usually want help sleeping — but they said they weren't allowed to sleep. Needed to be able to get up at 4 a.m., in which case tranquilisers aren't your best bet. Physically, they were not in a good way. A few of them looked sick to be honest, but . . . I'm not a doctor.'

'Come on now,' says Manon, who is tempted to consult Talcy Malc about her corns. 'Don't do yourself down. You're as good as medically trained by now. So . . . nothing for a guy called Lukas or his friend Matis?'

Talcy Malc shrugs. 'Like I say, I don't know who took what. There was some ketamine purchased. Primarily I was supplying Tramadol to Saulius. More and more of it. Nice little earner. Can I go now? And just so you know, I'm not testifying in court for you or nothing.'

'We'll see about that,' says Manon. 'You'll be amazed at how a summons can focus the mind.'

★ ★ ★

The vulnerability of loving him, the way her happiness is tied to his existence in her life, is hard to tolerate. A feeling of contingency, knowing she is at risk of hurt from anything happening to any one of them. It is hard to

226

acknowledge this. Hard to keep the thought. In large part, she has got around this by burying herself in work, and there is plenty of work to get lost in: the Balsys case, which has stalled over the absence of Matis; and overseeing Nigel's frankly woeful handling of the Saulius case.

She sends Nigel a text. 'Have you interviewed the owner of the farm yet? Where Saulius fell?'

Three dots indicating Nigel is texting back. Or thinking about it.

'Haven't tracked down the name of the farmer yet.'

Oh FFS.

'Get Kim to help you,' she texts back. She longs for Davy to come back to work after his day-owing following Klaipeda.

She and Mark are waiting in oncology for their meeting with the consultant. For the diagnosis to be given.

She has written a list of questions to ask, and shows it to Mark. On it, are:

Diet — effect of

Exercise — lack of, effect of

Mark is writing something on it: 'Nagging — effect of'.

'Oh *har har*,' she says, then looks at him, feeling there is no time for this. 'I'm sorry. I'm so sorry. I'm sorry I'm such a cow to live with, I'm sorry I'm always nagging.'

'You're not,' he says. 'You make me very happy.'

227

Yet he says it mildly, whereas what she feels is hot and cauldron-like. They are not the same people. That's why it works. Also why it doesn't.

'I just . . . please stay. Please don't let anything bad happen.'

'I intend to stay. I'm not going anywhere,' he says, pulling her in, pulling her head into his chest, muffling both the reality that they don't know and can't control the future, and muffling also the eye contact she seeks.

He accepts her in his mild way. He puts up with her, and for this she feels weak with gratitude. His finest attribute is his tolerance — both political and domestic. He is morally good. He is loving. He is kind.

She wants to howl all over again at the thought of losing him.

★ ★ ★

'So there is some tentative good news. Mark's cancer has not metastasised,' the consultant says. 'It is grade 1a, treatable with surgery. The next step is for you to have a meeting with your surgeon.'

'A meeting with our surgeon . . . ' she says, in a daze. She urgently needs to read everything on the Internet about grade one pancreatic cancer. All websites, even the most kooky, self-published blogposts about how to cure yourself with turmeric.

Her face hangs limp, unable to form itself decisively. There is cause for celebration, yet no cause for celebration at all. This is the limbo they will be in for a very long time.

'She's very keen for me to die,' Mark explains, smiling apologetically at the doctor. 'Feels she's been somewhat robbed. She's got her widow's weeds all ready.'

The doctor says, 'I'd say the early outlook is positive. There's no sign of anything elsewhere in the body, no spread. I think we've caught it reasonably early.'

Here is the land of variables that is adulthood. No epiphanies in beautiful Italian churches. Just mixed outcomes: schools that might be all right, but contain a rough element. Scans that are all clear, for now. Teenagers that haven't been arrested, as yet. Partners who might not die, this year. A constant state of telling herself to calm down. What she longs for is the security of childhood, though she didn't have it for long thanks to her mother's death. The feeling of being carried in the back of the car at night, motorway lights like chains of bright pearls, unaware that the driver was fallible. The warmth, the safety. There is no such place in adulthood.

The consultant is talking. 'I would strongly advise you to go home, feed yourself up. Lots of fruit and vegetables. Get plenty of rest, and come back in for your meeting with the surgeon and then have the operation. You might even get away without chemotherapy or radiation.'

★   ★   ★

Mark has his arms around her in the corridor. Cheek to cheek.

229

'I thought I was going to lose you and I couldn't bear it.' She is speaking into his ear.

'He hasn't ruled it out, you know.'

'Also, you really stink.'

'It's never too late to learn how to bed-bath,' he says.

'Also your bum's hanging out of your gown.'

'Calm down ladies,' he says.

'There isn't going to be an end point, is there?' she says.

'To being stuck with me? No.'

'No, to the health thing. There will always be the valley of the shadow of death or whatever. The fear of it.'

Mark pushes her hair from her face, saying, 'Yea, though I walk through the valley of the shadow of death, I will fear no evil: for thou art with me; thy rod and thy staff they comfort me.'

'Haven't got any staff, that's our number one problem.'

She takes him home to his bed. As she hooks her cross-body handbag over her head, she says, 'Right, I'm off to the greengrocers. You are going to be bombarded by freshly cooked vegetables and fruit medleys. I'm thinking cauliflower surprise, aubergine surprise, sprout surprise — '

'The surprise being?'

'That I don't know how to make them.'

'Takeaway night?'

'Dream on, big fella.' She kisses him. '*Pew*, if you could hobble to the bath I'd really appreciate it.'

★ ★ ★

'Davy Walker, you're a sight for sore eyes,' she says, feeling utterly overjoyed to see him when she walks into the office, bags of vegetables weighing down both arms. She'll probably forget to take them home from the office, where they'll rot under her desk until Colin sends out a memo.

'Everything all right?' he asks.

'Don't be kind to me,' she says, 'you know the rule. Anyway, today is a special day. We are going to be all over the One Wisbech lot. Should've got to them sooner, given the route the march took, but we've been somewhat overtaken by events.'

'Righto,' says Davy. 'What about the ANPR putting Mr Tucker's car in Hinchingbrooke?'

'Well, he's dead, so hard to arrest,' she says. 'Hang on, I just have to check in with Nigel about the Saulius case.'

She asks Nigel what the farmer has said in relation to Saulius's injuries.

'Says he thought they were legitimately employed,' Nigel says.

'Yes, but due diligence? Have you got paperwork in relation to his hiring of the Lithuanians?'

'Paperwork,' says Nigel, as if he'd like to kill himself.

DAVY

Driving through the fields outlying Wisbech, on their way to interview Dean Singlehurst, he can see how it's happened. Plant anything in this soil and it shoots up like Jack's magic beans. Impossibly fertile, these former swamps account for half of the most productive agricultural land in England, supplying everything from broccoli to garage forecourt flowers, and modern demands — for crisp apples at 10 p.m. if that's what you fancy — have led to a modern workforce: constantly on hand, disposable, cheap. Enter the Lithuanians, the Latvians, the Romanians. Ten thousand of them in Wisbech alone. Only people without commitments can take on this kind of work; zero hours contracts, back-to-back shifts one week, nothing the next. Texts to be at the BP garage at 4 a.m.

You can't have a mortgage or have to get the kids to school with this kind of work. The English just won't sign up for it, never mind the horrible conditions — no gloves, no health and safety, shifts that stretch beyond legal limits. They're grafters, the people who take on this work.

232

Davy wonders how they put up with the day to day uncertainty of it all. He's at the point in his life where he's wanting to anchor himself with a family, a proper home, maybe a dog and a roof rack and holidays on Brittany Ferries. He's longing to reach a safe harbour, especially after the awful dalliance in Klaipeda, the way he played with extra-marital fire.

How on earth do the migrants put up with going to bed at night not knowing what the next day holds, whether they'll be paid or whether there'll be work?

Manon has turned on Fen Radio (one-oh-seven-point-fiiiive!) for the headlines. A woman in a hijab has been spat at in Ely. Some migrants told to leave Tesco in Wisbech without being served their booze, to a round of applause from the other customers. A local businessman is running as a UKIP candidate in local elections. The same local businessman says the NHS is over-stretched because of immigration.

'Staffed by immigration, more like,' Manon mutters. Turns it off again.

'So the impression the One Wisbech marchers gave,' he says, glancing at her, 'is that Dean Singlehurst was pretty pumped by the time he arrived at the migrant house. Shane Farquharson was on the march with him.'

'How did he know where the migrants were living?'

'No one could answer that, but they said he seemed to know where he was going and who he was after.'

'And did he take Lukas from the house?'

'Ah, at that point, our One Wisbech lot become very hazy. They didn't see or they were not at the front of the march or it was too dark to make out who got into the car with Dean Singlehurst.'

'Ah, but he got in a car. Whose car? Registration?'

'We don't have a registration, but we can ask Dean himself whose car he got into.'

'CCTV around the migrant house?' Manon asks.

Davy shakes his head. 'None. One other thing, social services have had contact with the Singlehurst family. There was concern about the daughter when she was younger. She was on the At Risk Register. Bruises, noticed by the school.'

Manon nods. 'What about Edikas, any vehicles linked to him? Phone work?'

'Also being done.'

'Glenda wants us to get a wriggle on with this one,' she says.

'Right,' says Davy.

'I know you're working your bollocks off, Davy,' Manon says. 'Really. I know.'

''S'OK. It's just . . . things are kind of tricky with Juliet.'

'Pre-wedding jitters?'

'No. It's the job. Things are always difficult when I've been working a lot. She's very possessive, very suspicious.'

'With reason, when it comes to Bridget.'

'I didn't do anything.'

'You thought about it.'

'Yes, and I feel bad about that, but the job

234

— the feast and famine thing. One minute I'm around all the time, going to Homebase and mowing the lawn, and then I'll have a week when I'm in at 2 a.m. and out again at 6 a.m.'

'I know. Join the Force, Get Divorced. Only you have to get married first. It'll be all right, you'll knock the corners off each other. The first few years are the worst, I hear.'

'Oh God.'

'Can you talk to Juliet about it — about the job, the pressure? Because it's not going to change any time soon.'

'I'm not much good at talking about things,' he says. 'I tend to just chug along.'

'That's not going to work with marriage. How did you leave it with Bridget?'

'Awkwardly. Did you know she has two kids as well as a husband?'

'Crikey. Respect to her for cracking on to you. My libido is MIA.'

'Please. That's more than I need to know.'

'Sorry. I bought a new bathrobe by the way.'

'Riveting.'

'And it's all fluffy and posh, like I'm in a spa, or, more realistically, an ad for walk-in baths. But the thing is, it makes the water sort of slide off me in a slimy way. And I realised, I prefer scratchy old towels to fluffy new towels.'

'Is this leading somewhere?'

'Yes, amazingly. Mark is my scratchy old towel.'

'Right,' he says. 'Is that all you've got in the way of marital advice?'

'It's not all I've got, but it's my best

235

linen-related nugget. Fluffy new towels look appealing but they are not actually as good as scratchy old towels.'

'Right,' Davy says. 'Stick with the scratchy old towel. Got it.'

They drive in silence for a time.

Then Davy says, 'These One Wisbech marchers, they were chanting things about purity, and needing to purge the area of foreigners. Vermin, out.'

'That's sounding like incitement to racial hatred to me.'

'Very much so, but Dean Singlehurst was being cheered, everyone getting quite excited by all accounts. Witness said they became emboldened by being in a group of like-minded individuals. She said, 'It was a relief that I wasn't the only one feeling these things and they could be spoken out loud. I mean, who decides what's all right to say and what isn't?''

'Christ,' says Manon. 'The world's gone mad. Stark raving mad.'

After a long silence, in which she looks out across the lush Fenland landscape, she says, 'Still, it's nice to be on the road with you, visiting some racists. I bloody love work. It's the weekends I can't stand. We should've brought Colin with us. He could've infiltrated the other side.'

'They'd smell a lightweight. Colin is only superficially bigoted. Deep down he's sound.'

MANON

'You see? This is nice driving, Davy. This is courteous, beautiful driving.'

'Why thank you,' he says, smiling at her with a sideways glance.

She lays her head back, eyes closed, air rushing in through the open passenger window. 'The open road, eh? I hardly ever get to leave Hinchingbrooke, but on this job I've been out loads. Feel quite giddy.'

'This is quite the day out for you then.'

'It really is. I don't even have to be back for pick-up. I'm willing to spend time with Xenophobes R Us just to be out at 5 p.m. Very nice driving. Have I told you about the Manon Bradshaw School of Motoring Etiquette that I'm planning?'

'You haven't, no.'

No, she thinks. *I told Harriet all about it. Harriet who is now recovering from her mastectomy operation.* Manon hasn't visited yet, despite multiple resolutions.

It must be a month ago now that she'd regaled Harriet about *DI Bradshaw's School of Motoring Etiquette,* while pushing her tray along after

Harriet's in the canteen. This was before the cancer diagnosis. *Or was it?* she thinks now, blanching at her self-absorption.

'We spend millions on murder, right?' Manon had said. 'Every area in the UK has a murder squad. And yet driving in this country is shocking. They don't stop at crossings, they chat on mobile phones, put makeup on, send texts. That's what's really killing people in the UK. What terrifies parents,' and she very much included herself in this, because she has skin in the game, '*sensible* parents, that is, is not paedophiles or gangs. It's *cars*.'

There are times when Manon holds Teddy's tiny hand at crossings and the cars speed past them without stopping, and she cannot imagine ever letting him cross alone. Recently, a car did stop and they crossed, then the driver wound his window down and shouted, 'Don't say thank you or anything!'

Manon was so livid, she picked up Teddy and ran after the car, which slowed along the kerb, probably out of curiosity or in expectation of an apology. The driver buzzed down his electric window. Without putting down her son she whipped out her badge, shoved it in the driver's face and said, 'What did you just say to me, sir?'

'Just that a thank you wouldn't go amiss.'

'Thank you for what?' she asked.

'For letting you cross.'

'*Letting* me? *Letting* me? Are you aware it's a legal requirement to stop at a pedestrian crossing? It's not at your discretion. It's not a matter of whether you're feeling in a generous mood.'

238

'Didn't know you were a copper.'

'Whether I'm a copper is irrelevant,' she said. 'I'm making a note of your number plate, sir, and I'll be recommending a driving refresher course for you, as you've clearly forgotten your Highway Code. Good day to you, and maybe think twice about hollering at pedestrians, OK? Come on, Ted.'

'Was he a naughty mans?' asked Teddy.

'Yes, naughty mans, Ted.'

Harriet, she could see, was barely tolerating her road-safety diatribe, but Manon pressed on, 'If we clean up roads, we clean up life. I'm telling you.'

Harriet walked wearily to a table and Manon sat across from her.

'And how would you clear up our roads then, Genghis?'

'So my department will have the following sanctions: Cars without silencers — driver's ear cut off. Speaking on mobile phone, also loss of an ear. Texting, loss of a hand. Makeup application in rear-view mirror, loss of eyebrows — '

'Seems a bit mild,' said Harriet.

'Racing — loss of testicles. Racing without silencers in super cars — '

'Oh I can't wait to hear this,' said Harriet.

'Loss of testicles *and* penis.'

'What if it's a woman?'

'It's never a woman.'

'So, you're following the Saudi Arabia school of state punishment.'

'I just think we've been too soft for too long.

We're scared to death of murderers and child abusers, but it's drivers who ruin the most lives. Our roads have become lawless.'

'I can see a promotion in the works for you. You're really thinking outside the human rights box.'

'Thank you.'

'You should definitely present this to Glenda McBain. She could tweet about it.'

'Oh, and I nearly forgot: unnecessary blowing of horn.'

'That's an offence?'

'Yes. You're supposed to use a car horn to alert another person of imminent danger. But people blow their horns to say 'Hurry up!' or to say hi to someone on the street. It's out of control.'

'And the punishment?'

'Punch in the face.'

She cannot be bothered to fill Davy in on the Bradshaw School of Motoring Etiquette. He wouldn't approve. Davy is a man to avoid violence at all costs, a lover not a fighter, which isn't true of all coppers. Some of them are cut from the same cloth as the criminals they're chasing. She prefers the cut of Davy's jib.

'So I checked the CCTV around the crime scene for anyone resembling Jim Tucker,' Davy says.

'Yes?'

'And there is a figure, pretty blurry if I'm honest, but it's not impossible that it's him.'

'What if they killed him together, Mr and Mrs Tucker?' she says. 'He makes her bear witness, as a kind of punishment.'

240

'I'm just not buying it though, are you?' Davy says. 'He seemed more . . . pathetic loser than criminal mastermind.'

'I know what you mean,' she says.

In the silence that follows, she thinks about Derry's PM report on Lukas, which has largely confirmed what they already knew. Cause of death: complete hanging, asphyxia and venous congestion. The ligature had blocked both the airways and the jugular veins. Death would have occurred within three to five minutes of hanging, according to Derry, who, in Manon's experience, can be wrong. But he is more chastened these days, less truculent in his opinions. A chastened forensic pathologist is a good thing.

'Lukas's hands weren't tied behind his back,' she says now. 'There were no ligature marks around his wrists. So, why didn't he fight? Why didn't he reach up to his neck, hold the rope, trying to hold himself up?'

'Maybe he lost consciousness immediately,' suggests Davy. 'Or was too weak to fight. His health wasn't good was it?'

'No, it was very bad indeed. He had a chronic chest infection, untreated obviously. He was malnourished. And there was some ketamine use, according to toxicology. We have Talcy Malc to thank for that. I guess it's possible he was a bit out of it, but that only makes it harder to get him into the tree. It's incredibly rare, homicidal hanging. No platform, no wrist ties, no ladder or seeming assistance getting up the tree. Something's not right about it.'

241

'We are living,' she says, as they reach the conurbation of outer Wisbech, 'in the age of stupidity, Davy Walker. Ignorance is the new black. All you need right now is some knee-jerk reactions and a Twitter feed. All you need is to 'feel you're right'.' She is making giant quote marks in the air. 'And then off you go, you can express your half-baked opinions as loudly as you like. Just don't stand near anyone actually knowledgeable.'

'Are you talking about Dean Singlehurst or Glenda McBain?' asks Davy.

'I'm talking about both. The thing about incompetent people is they don't lack confidence. It's the Dunning-Kruger effect, I've just read about it. Truly stupid people are too stupid to realise they are stupid. They don't know what they don't know. And if you're not plagued by a suspicion that you don't know your arse from your elbow — '

'I'm *always* plagued by that,' says Davy.

''Zactly, because actually you're good and not stupid.' Davy starts violently coughing at this, as if he's choking on something. 'Are you done?' she asks him. He takes a swig of water from the plastic bottle between their car seats. 'But if you're stupid,' she continues, 'the vast hinterland of what you don't know is not glimpsed by you, so you can proceed with utter confidence.'

'I see,' he croaks. 'At least, I think I see.'

'Yes, but you're a little bit worried you don't.'

'Always,' says Davy. 'It's like this One Wisbech

242

lot. I think they've got a point. These migrants *do* make life worse in the town. They *do* drink too much and beat each other up. They're hard nuts.'

'They also do all the shit jobs the locals won't do *because* they're hard nuts. Politicians are always wanging on about 'hard-working families' but no one works harder than a migrant. Catching chickens at 4 a.m. without protective gear for below the minimum wage? Only a hard nut will do that. If the migrants don't pick the broccoli, the broccoli will not get picked. And anyway, not like the English are impeccably-behaved teetotallers.'

'True. You see, the minute you give the counter argument, I just don't know the answer.'

'Because you know that you don't know what you don't know.'

'Do I?'

'Yes! Did you hear about the lemon juice robber?'

'Nope. Another thing I don't know.'

'Well, he went around robbing banks with total confidence, with nothing but lemon juice on his face because he was convinced that made him invisible to surveillance cameras. He knew lemon juice was involved in making invisible ink and when he squirted it on his face, it really stung his eyes and prevented him seeing, which all seemed to confirm his theory. So he went into banks, bold as brass, staring straight into the cameras. He was arrested immediately, of course. But he's emblematic: this is the age of stupid. In place of knowledge, people are

243

exalting their gut feeling as if gut feeling is more valuable than being informed. When actually, what gut feeling generally is, is prejudice.'

'Have you finished yet?' Davy asks.

'Barely started mate, but we're here now. Let us alight into the Jaws of Bigotry.'

Davy is squinting at his notebook. 'Jaws of Bigotry is at 62 Tennyson Road,' he says. 'Over there. How are we handling this?'

'Fuck knows. I'm going to go with my gut. My really quite sizeable gut.'

She heaves herself out of the passenger seat, audibly.

★ ★ ★

The Jaws of Bigotry is, to use estate agent parlance, 'in need of updating'.

Dean Singlehurst sits at the kitchen table. His daughter Elise, a very sulky-looking teenager, stands behind him, her back to the wall. Sort of girl Fly would *adore* — voluptuous in the way only the young and firm can carry off.

'Mr Singlehurst, can you tell me about the night of the One Wisbech march, which I believe was organised by you and took place on May 14th?'

'Yeah, well, we wanted our voices heard. No one ever listens to us, the people. We're being overrun. These migrants from Eastern Europe, they come and they turn nice houses into slums. They drink in the parks, on the streets. They're dangerous, they fight. And they take our jobs. There's no jobs for English people. Yet what does

244

the government say? Come in! Stay for free! Have some free health care, some benefits, send your kiddies to our schools, we'll pay. Well, it's got to stop. I'm not racist. There is not a racist bone in my body. Shane Farquharson said so. He said on the radio that we're not racists, we're just making good points.'

'Oh well then . . . ' she mutters. 'And what route did you follow, that night?' Manon eyes Davy to make sure he's taking notes, but of course she doesn't need to. He's all over it.

'Town centre, past the town hall, then down Norfolk Street — '

'Bit provocative wasn't it? Taking it down Norfolk Street?'

''S'a free country. It's *our* country. If we want to walk down an English street in an English town, no one's going to tell us we can't. Shane Far — '

'Yes, never mind Shane Farquharson. And you then went via West Street and Victoria Road to Prospect Place, where Lukas Balsys lived. Did you know Mr Balsys?'

'No,' says Dean.

'Then why did you head there? Prospect Place is a dead end — '

'You can say that again,' interjects Dean, smirking.

'So it's an odd place to take your band of followers, isn't it? Up a cul-de-sac?'

Dean shrugs. 'Just where we ended up.'

'We have witnesses say you knocked on Mr Balsys's door and had words that night. Is that correct?'

245

'What witnesses?'

'Answer the question, Mr Singlehurst.'

'They're lying. I didn't. Who said it, anyway?'

'Did you take Mr Balsys off somewhere in a vehicle?'

'No I did not.'

'Can you explain the posting on your One Wisbech Facebook page. I quote, *It's time — time to get rid of the lawless vermin in our town!* Can you tell me what you meant by this statement?'

'Well, first off, it's true. They are vermin, and we want shot of 'em. Second, I don't know who posted that, might've been one of our supporters. We've got a lot of supporters, 'specially since Shane . . . Lots of people feel the way we do. They're relieved we're saying out loud what they've been feeling for a long time. 'S' freedom of speech. We're standing up to political correctness.'

'Did you talk to Mr Balsys on the night of the One Wisbech march?'

'Dunno, do I? Dunno who he is, do I?'

'Did you talk to any of the migrants living in Prospect Place?'

'Yeah, some of 'em came out to see what the noise was, see what we were doing.'

'Did it get heated, between the two groups?'

'Well, we couldn't understand each other, could we? They came onto the front doorstep, we stopped at the end of the path. Bit of eyeballing. Then we carried on our course.'

'You must've had to turn around though, given Prospect Place is a dead end. Bit embarrassing, wasn't it, marching to a dead end and then having the kerfuffle of turning around and having to march back? Bit emblematic?'

'No, not at all. We made our point to the migrants and the people living near the migrants, who are not a happy bunch, let me tell you. The Tuckers next door, they're having a terrible time.'

'They told you that, did they?' She wonders if Jim Tucker and Dean Singlehurst were in cahoots in some way.

'Everyone knows it. Anyway, it was a peaceful march. We marched back the way we came. Job's a good'un.'

'Sorry, can I just check. Did you know Jerome — Jim — Tucker?'

'I know everyone and everyone knows me. Lived here a long time. Everyone knew the nightmare he was having with the EEs next door. Wiped the value off his house. Not surprised he did himself in, to be honest.'

Manon looks at the teenage girl standing behind her dad. All this while, a silent storm seems to have been taking place on the girl's face. The suppression of great torrents of emotion, if Manon is reading it right, which she might not be. This is what she adores about teenagers, the torrents.

'Elise, did you go on the march?' Manon asks.

The girl shakes her head, biting a lip of skin at the edge of her thumbnail.

'Where were you, back here?'

She nods.

'And what time did your father return home?'

She shrugs. 'I was asleep. So I don't know.'

247

'Leave her out of it,' says Dean. 'She doesn't know anything.'

Davy coughs. Manon makes way for him.

'Some of the One Wisbech marchers state that you didn't, in fact, march back the way you came, but that you got into a vehicle,' Davy says. 'Whose vehicle did you get into that night?'

'Who said that?' asks Dean.

'Can you tell me whose vehicle you got into and the registration number of that vehicle please Mr Singlehurst?' says Davy.

'Don't remember.'

'You don't remember?' says Manon. 'It was ten days ago. Where did you go in the car? Who were you with?'

'There's two questions there, which one d'you want answering?'

'Any one will do.'

Dean shakes his head, gets up from the table. Stands at the French door to the garden and looks out. 'This is harassment,' he says.

'No, these are straightforward questions to eliminate you from our inquiry. Answer them, and then we'll know you're not involved.'

'Yeah, this is harassment. I don't like your tone. You're trying to pin something on me because you don't like my group or what we stand for.'

'What evidence do you have for that?' asks Manon.

'Who's your senior officer? I want to put in a complaint.'

Elise pushes off from the wall she's leaning against and leaves the room. Manon can hear her flumping up the stairs.

DAVY

Outside, they both inhale deeply.

'Well that went well,' Davy says.

'I think we've got enough to arrest him,' says Manon. 'I'm not saying it's the whole picture, but we've got witnesses who put him at the victim's house on the night Lukas Balsys died.'

'One of those witnesses is dead,' Davy points out.

'Still, we've got his statement, and Mrs Tucker. She's not dead. We've got evidence he had words with the migrants outside the house where Lukas was living. Dean was angry, puffed up by Farquharson's endorsement, bit pumped on the march, feeling like a really big player, big man. Volatile group.'

He is shifting foot to foot, hands in his pockets, avoiding her gaze.

'What is it Davy?' she demands.

'I dunno.'

'Come on, out with it.'

'Well, it's your call, obviously. You're SIO. But I don't like it. Without the car, we can't put him in Hinchingbrooke on the night Lukas was killed. I think we're on thin ice without the car.'

'Well,' she says, and he can see the bluster, 'I reckon the custody sergeant will agree with me that it's enough to arrest in order to secure evidence. Then we nail down what car he got into outside Lukas's house, then we forensicate the car, find traces of blue rope and Bob's your — '

But he knows her. She is fiddling with her policy book, uncertainly. She is not so dogmatic that she cannot change course.

DAY 10

MANON

'We've had a complaint. Dean Singlehurst has accused you of harassment.'

She's in good shape, she'll give Glenda that, though since reading *The Beauty Myth* Manon sees this as a mark of oppression. *Don't let the patriarchy deny you your third pork pie, love. Embrace the love handles of emancipation.* She is all over that book, how thinness and youth have become the currency by which free women are kept from happiness and fulfilment. She knows the truth of this because she's addicted to Instagram feeds about emaciated TV presenters' outfits. 'Today's look, from Jigsaw and Very-.co.uk'.

We're allowing ourselves to be enslaved by the idolatry of starved actresses instead of yearning to be, say, a portly chief executive or senior scientist with fuzzy grey hair who can kick serious ass on gene therapy but is also a bit broad about the beam. Manon wants to become one of those older women with *presence* and also really interesting spectacles — women who command the room and who don't succumb to all the appearance bullshit. Women who know that they know what they know but also have a really good time at Christmas, enjoying the mince pies and guffawing over-loudly in a pissed way.

'Right,' Manon says.

'Well?' says McBain. 'Did you?'

'I was going to arrest him. Not sure whether that's harassment. I have grounds. He's our prime suspect.'

'Well, I'd advise you not to arrest him now. Local officers will be picking over absolutely everything we do.'

'Course that would be your advice, Manon thinks, *you spineless —*

'Yes, right. You're probably right,' Manon says. 'Y'know, he probably killed Lukas Balsys, but let's let him go shall we? If we're lucky he'll move house and we'll never locate him again. Oh, and it won't be long before the HMO is requisitioned by the landlord, and the migrants dispersed, so we'll lose track of our witnesses. But yeah, let's lay off Singlehurst.'

★ ★ ★

She's so angry when she leaves McBain's office, she decides to hold a briefing. She might not be able to bear down on Dean Singlehurst, but she can bear down on his cronies. Speaking to the room in a generalised voice-raised way, she says, 'Right everyone. We are going to question every single one of the One Wisbech marchers. Pressure pressure pressure. We are going to rattle some cages. I want them to feel the long arm of

252

the law pressing down on them very heavily indeed. I want you to throw a few fucks into people. You didn't hear me say that, right?'

She senses people looking at her anxiously. They shift in their seats.

But she presses on, 'Starting with Gary Evans and his idiotically named son, Evan Evans. I want digging. Have they got a parking ticket they haven't paid? Bring it up. Have they engaged in some nefarious activity that we couldn't care less about? Bring it up, pretend we care a lot, that we're all over their personal lives, their knock-off fags, their visits to infectious hookers, their welded-together cars. Pressure, pressure, pressure. And if anyone complains?'

Davy is rolling his eyes towards Glenda's office so hard he might detach a retina, but she ignores him.

'If anyone complains, it shows you're doing your job properly. You're meant to make them feel very uncomfortable indeed. Don't. Back. Down.'

She enjoys, for a moment, the stark contrast between herself and McBain, before turning and seeing said boss, arms folded, in the doorway to her office, having heard every word. Scowling wouldn't be too strong a word.

Manon is less sure, should a complaint actually come in, how stark the difference would be. Easy to be strident when the complaint is levelled at you for your own work. She *knows* she didn't put a foot wrong with Dean Singlehurst. With that complaint, she thinks *Bring it on*. But when it's a subordinate, and you weren't in the room when it happened and yet as SIO you're responsible, that's harder to take.

Her confidence starts to drain away. She's about to put in a caveat or two ('look, no physical force, obvs') but the room has broken up. Besides, there's nothing worse than a mixed message from the boss.

★ ★ ★

'How's the paperwork going?' she says to Nigel, stopping by his desk.

'Farmer says he thought the chicken catchers were all legit,' says Nigel with an expression that says *and I'm entirely happy with that.*

'Yeah, well, he would say that wouldn't he?' Manon says.

'Right,' says Nigel, uncertainly.

Has it never occurred to Nigel that people lie to us, like, all the time?

She decides to put this into words.

'Has it occurred to you, Nigel, that people lie to us? All. The. Time. Have you put it to him that he's facing a gross negligent manslaughter charge? That should get him chirruping like a budgie.'

Nigel looks as if he's been slapped. Perhaps she's been brusque. She has a tendency towards that. But so what? He has to hear it. And if she was a male DI, she'd be viewed as powerful and no-nonsense.

★ ★ ★

She doesn't believe the rope leads nowhere. She calls Kim Delaney over to her desk.

'Can you give me the dates and times for purchase of that rope in the Wisbech area?'

'Yup, sure. I've got all that.'

'And have you called in CCTV for the times of all those purchases?'

'Yes.'

'Anyone looked at it?'

'Not exactly. Davy put Nigel on it, but he got pulled off onto the Saulius case, so didn't get round to it.'

'Right, bring me all the CCTV as well.'

'You're going to do it yourself? Bit below your pay grade.'

'If a job's worth doing, Kim . . . '

'Did Davy brief you about the vomit?'

'I'm sorry?' says Manon.

'There was a pile of vomit a few yards from the scene.'

'No he didn't. Send him over here, will you?'

Davy arrives at her desk.

'What's all this about a pile of vomit and why haven't you told me about it?'

'Sorry, I didn't deliberately not tell you. It just slipped my mind.'

'Right, well I'd like a full vomit briefing if you don't mind.'

'Yes, pile of vomit. A few yards from the scene, close to the road. We're having it DNA tested. Could be Lukas's, a fear-puke because of what's about to happen to him.'

'Or the response of someone being made to witness a murder,' says Manon. 'Elspeth Tucker,

255

for example. That's what you do when you love someone, you bear witness to their suffering. Or they could have killed him together, the Tuckers — keep the spark alive.'

'Or,' says Davy, 'someone unrelated to the whole thing was pissed, walked past the scene earlier, and chucked up randomly. Might even be from an animal.'

'Or that, yes. And Davy? Could you not keep me out of the loop please?' she says. She's not sidestepping *that* pile of vomit. Oh no. Although . . . does she sound paranoid?

'Sorry, I didn't mean to,' he says, but his expression is so crestfallen that she feels terrible for raising it. She wants to say, *Oh forget it, I was probably imagining it.*

But doesn't.

★ ★ ★

She quite likes the hermetically sealed warmth of the TV room, especially when she's brought food with her — this time canteen lasagne, so greasy it's slip-slid up the edges of its polystyrene container.

The difficulty, she thinks, yawning and putting in her fifth CD, *is concentrating when the footage is so boring.* Homebase can bring on an existential crisis at the best of times, but black-and-white grainy film of Homebase is enough to make anyone take up narcolepsy.

Focus, focus, focus. So far, the people buying rope are tubby dads rather than criminal masterminds. What she's looking for is a suspect to amble onto her screen.

Could be that Edikas's rope was used, without Edikas being their perp. Manon rests her chin on the heel of one hand and presses play, seeing again the wide aisles of a DIY superstore. Not always Homebase. Sometimes it's the raw thrill of seeing Wickes or Travis Perkins instead.

'Manon?'

She is roused from a deep sleep by Nigel. Marginally-Less-Tired Nigel, it would seem.

Crease in her cheek, dribble down her wrist. Where did she go? Sleep these days is blankly dreamless, offering her no clues. In her twenties, she dreamed like a demon — complex narratives that were Dali-esque in their anxiety. These days, it's like the plug is pulled from its socket. Then when she wakes, everything hurts. Feet, knees. As if her skeleton were made of unoiled chain mail. She has spent a fortune on orthotics. There seems to be a whole industry out there, making a killing out of middle-aged women's aches and pains: physios, orthotics-manufacturers, foot specialists listening to dreary complaints of plantar fasciitis. Herbal tea brands in art deco boxes. Yoga teachers. Purveyors of astronomical leisurewear.

'Yes, sorry, just thinking with my eyes closed. What is it?'

'All right if I head off early? The twins — '

'Yes, yes, you go,' she says, uninterested in what the excuse is this time. *We will not be hampered by the absence of your work ethic, Nigel,* is all she thinks. Perhaps she should take back the Saulius case and do it herself. Handle it at night.

She takes out the playing CD and puts it back in the unplayed pile. She'll have to start again with that one.

258

ELISE

Elise lies in a foetal position on the kitchen floor, her arms shielding her belly where her father repeatedly kicks her with his boots on. His steel-capped boots. He's been made livid by the police officer and she's his nearest punchbag.

Of course it isn't the first time he's kicked her. Of course she's been punched before, when he'd had a few cans of Tennent's.

'Let's get rid of this foreign scum shall we? 'S'not happenin' Elise. Not my blood mixing with their blood.' But as always with her father, rage mixes with tears of self-pity. 'I'm sorry.' Kick. 'I'm sorry 'Lise.' Kick. His abject apologies in the past have led to extravagances like the Jimmy Choo perfume. As if that could make up for it.

'Stop, Dad, please, please . . . ' She has to brace her body against his boot, making speaking difficult. She scooches away from the arc of his foot, curling her body against the kitchen's units. 'Stop. Just listen. Stop kicking me and listen. I'll go and get rid of it properly. Not like this, OK? You'll kill me like this.'

He stops, bent over, saying a high whine:

259

'*Aagh*. I don't want to be like this. You've pushed me too far, girl. You've taken the thing I believe in, and you've pushed it in the mud. How could you think so little of me? And how will I know you've gone and done it, not lied about it?'

'Because I don't want it either. I don't want a baby on my own at seventeen, do I? I'm not stupid. Just leave it with me, all right?'

She crawls to her feet, holding onto the table corner to steady herself.

'Are you sure . . . ' she says, 'its father won't come back? Are you certain?' She wonders if she can take the answer.

She had shuffled away from the march during the confrontation with the migrant house, had peeled off down a side street and back home when she was confident none of her dad's cronies were watching. They were too gripped by the confrontation on the doorstep of the migrant house.

'Dealt with. You don't have to worry about 'im no more, girl.'

In her room she lies on the bed just to give her body the time to calm down, to settle and regroup. She doesn't think there is damage. No lasting abdominal pain, no bleeding, not yet. She's shielded it this time, her forearms blooming with bruises. She falls asleep, dreaming about renovating a remote house with Matis while her bump grows.

A knock on her bedroom door, then her father is standing over her.

'Good news,' he says. 'I've got a mate can do it. Get rid of the baby, I mean. That way, we keep it private. He can come to the house, do it here, which is nicer for you than some clinic, right? No one will know. I can't have my followers knowing about this.'

'Why would we need to keep it private?' she asks. She is groggy from sleep.

'I've got a position. You can't have the leader of One Wisbech having an EE grandkid, can you? Be all over the Internet in seconds. My mate can do it.'

'But abortion clinics keep things confidential. And anyway, how would anyone know whose kid it was?'

'Word gets out, people talk. Gossip. Better to keep it hush hush, get rid of it in private.'

'Is that safe?'

'Yeah, bound to be. He's a good guy. Gary Evans knows him. He fillets fish at the chippy. His daughter got in trouble and he cleared it out himself. Solid chap apparently.'

She is terrified, not just for the baby but for herself. She knows her father would do anything to her, no matter the risk.

'Please let me go to a clinic. It's really dangerous otherwise.'

'I don't trust you, Elise, that's the problem. I don't trust you'll do it. You're like your mother. I couldn't trust her, neither. You've already betrayed me, going with him behind my back.'

'I will do it. I really will. Please don't let your mate touch me. Please.'

When he closes her bedroom door, she hears a key turn in the lock. Her bedroom is right at the top of the house, under its suffocating eaves, facing the back. No chance of calling for help or climbing out of the window.

MATIS

They drive two and a half hours in Mr Tucker's car, he and Lina.

He takes the wheel because she's been up half the night with Vasil. Doing God-knows-what with Vasil.

Dimitri hot-wired the Nissan for him in the end. Dimitri, it turned out, was a sweet, gentle soul. Not the seven-foot gladiatorial hard nut they had all assumed.

'Everyone looks at me and assumes I am violent,' he told Matis before waving him off. 'When in fact, I hate violence.'

Lina made it clear they could not stop — if they cut the engine, they'd have to hot-wire it again in a service station car park, and this, she said, would arouse too much suspicion. Matis was desperate for the toilet, so she agreed to pull in at a service station, but said she would stay in the car with the engine idling. He ran behind a tree, sensing he hadn't enough time to go inside to use the toilet, peed urgently, keeping an eye on the Nissan, wiped his hands on his jeans, fearful that she would drive away.

Frinton-on-Sea seems a spacious seaside

resort, if he could only see it through the rain.

The haze.

The sea spray.

The drops tinkling on the roof, exploding on the windscreen.

A grey fog hangs over the town, persistent through the thrub of Mr Tucker's windscreen wipers.

On the seafront, facing out to the wide expanse of beach, is a café with steamed-up windows where Lina is expected. She has been given keys, and, when they arrive, is shown the deep fat fryer by a taciturn Latvian. They put their paltry possessions in the flat above the shop.

They begin cooking eggs and bacon, chips and beans, occasionally omelettes, and they don't stop. All day, every day. Clean up. Wipe surfaces. They don't change the oil. 6 a.m. to 9 p.m. It is a walk in the park compared to chicken catching.

The scratches on his hands begin to heal. He puts on a little weight. Solid night's sleep every night, after omelette and chips, in a relatively clean bed, off the floor.

Hot showers. Time for a shit. No nits, no bedbugs. This is *living*.

'How did you get this place?' he asks her.

She keeps her back to him, doing something on the counter, wrapping a brick of cheese in cellophane or something. Shrugs. Says, 'I knew someone who needed something.'

'Needed what?'

But she has gone up the stairs to the flat. She is not a confessional sort of person.

264

Nevertheless, Matis's body keeps shaking. He is sweaty. He keeps being sick, having the runs. Lina says she thinks it is the addiction to the drink and will pass through him. He knows it is a physiological reaction to what he saw happen to Lukas and if he can only drink, his symptoms will alleviate. Images of that night haunt him when he closes his eyes. Lina asks him what had happened, but he can't tell her.

★   ★   ★

Their customers are all elderly. Not cute elderly, but mean-spirited, angry elderly. There were two types, in Matis's experience: one delights in the young (old Gregoriev) the other envies the young (his father). One enjoys progress, the other wants to hold it back because he won't be partaking of it himself.

The Frinton oldies sit at Formica tables, waiting for egg and chips. The windows are steamed up, so the froth of the sea isn't visible. But all that is outside, Matis knows, is the pervasive grey smudge of cloud joining land and sky. All he can think is that it isn't the sharp-lit azure sky over the Curonian spit in the Baltic.

The elderly customers talk about littering, about banning shorts at the golf club, about the campaign to stop Network Rail installing an automated barrier at the level crossing, which seems to be their own barrier against modernity. (Matis's ear, attuned to English, has become remarkably good at comprehension, though he had to Google Translate 'level crossing'.) They

265

don't like immigrants, but they keep their voices low to discuss this. Louder, somewhat, when proclaiming they were not racists. 'There's not a racist bone in my body,' is a phrase that crops up a lot.

It is cold in Frinton-on-Sea. Not Lithuania cold, which was dry, minus twenty but nice with it, the kind of northern skies he misses terribly. Frinton is wet-cold, misted up and sea-sprayed. Permanently damp. No long shadows. You can never dry out in Frinton-on-Sea.

'Can we make this place our own?' Matis asks Lina, looking at the cream-coloured greasy walls and wondering about a paint job. A fresh pale blue, clean white woodwork. Thoughts about his baby, whether this might be a home one day.

'Best not to put down roots,' she says.

ELISE

Not just the key turned in the door.

He has taken her mobile phone away.

She has no idea when the fish filleting back-street abortionist will come. When she will be forced to submit to his unsanitary knitting needles, his hands smelling of cod. She is becoming weak with hunger. Her stomach growling. It's too early to feel the baby squirming, but she thinks about it, and it's real to her, and she wonders how long it can survive without nourishment via her blood. Can her body make nourishment out of its own reserves? She's plump enough. But surely she'll need water to drink and something to keep her blood sugar from dipping through the floor?

What if her father doesn't come back?

She spends some time pacing, trying pathetic methods of getting out, like examining the view from her bedroom window — the sky above the trees in the garden. Or rattling the door — it holds fast. She wants to reach that copper. The dishevelled woman who was in their kitchen and who sensed all was not right about her father. The copper seemed like a person who could

267

handle it right, who could get her out of this mess. Marion or something. Bradshaw, she remembers. But without a mobile and with a locked door, how can Elise reach anyone?

After intense psychic troubleshooting of this kind, she lies on her bed and sleeps for a time, until thirst and hunger wake her into her predicament.

MATIS

What have you learned since you came to the UK?

This was one of the questions in the English class he has begun attending in Frinton community centre, run by the British Council.

He has learned he is not wanted here.

He has learned to never want anything again, because his ambition, the restless desire for change, was the root of his destruction. If he had not persuaded Lukas to come to England, he would still be alive, miserably going out with Janina in Klaipeda. They would be having a beer together in the bar in Rybporte, awaiting a very long Lithuanian winter.

Matis would give anything to have Lukas miserably alive in Klaipeda.

He hates the impulse inside that makes him himself.

The way he always craved the alternative — the new country, the new chance, a different life, instead of valuing the life he was living. The good life, as it turned out. And because this is the largest part of him, the striving element, his hatred consumes his whole being. He cannot like

269

the very thing that makes him most himself.

The world appears to confirm this hatred. He and Lina see it on the television they now have access to: the migrants trudging, unwanted, across Europe, described as a 'tide of humanity'; washing up dead on Greek islands, clinging to boats that go down in the Med; desperate for the home that no one wants to give them. Boats full of children being refused entry anywhere. Babies and toddlers taken from their parents in America. People searching for a better life are despised for wanting it, when native strivers are admired. What is the name for this?

Governments fall if they are kind to migrants. Governments are explicit in creating a 'hostile environment' for them. Even little kids in schools in England are being taught the difference between 'refugee' and 'economic migrant', that they might better know who to hate. Dimitri told him this. How he knew, Matis can't guess.

He thinks of the statue in Theatre Square in Klaipeda, of a girl: 'Ann of Tharau'. She had her back to the balcony of the main, ornate building. Rumour has it that when Hitler addressed Klaipeda from that balcony he was outraged that the girl had her back to him. The statue disappeared during World War II. Lithuanians have experience of this kind of juvenile dictatorship. It is nothing new. Ann was reinstated in 1990, the start of transition.

Matis thinks the English don't truly know the fear of war or the dangers of extremism. It is as if they haven't lived it, cannot remember it. Insulated by their seas, which rustle against the stones, back and forth outside the café in Frinton-on-Sea. They can barely tolerate disruption to their living rooms, let alone departing their country with nothing, travelling to a place where they don't speak the language, with no home or possessions. Could the English tolerate that kind of sacrifice? Do they have the will to suffer that much for their children?

He thinks about Elise coming for him, some dinky little car (pink probably) piled high with her things. He has made stupid choices, and giving up on her is one of them.

While Lina is doing the evening shift downstairs, he locates a low cabinet with a bottle of brandy at the back, probably for cooking.

He drinks it. After that, he ransacks the flat for money and goes to the off-licence.

★ ★ ★

The first he knows about it is the feeling of Lina kicking him hard in the side of his body, close to his hip. The same kind of kick Edikas gave to Saulius in the broken ribs. He thinks Lina and Edikas might be cut from the same cloth.

Matis had fallen asleep on the floor, back against the wall.

'What are you doing?' she asks. She sounds disgusted. 'You need to tell me what's going on. You're a dead weight. I can't carry you. I *won't* carry you.'

He starts crying, the loud sobs of a pathetic drunk.

'What the fuck is wrong with you?' she demands.

271

He cannot tell her. He puts his wet face in his hands. He feels as if he might be sick, but then she would be even more angry because of the carpet.

'You have to tell me what this sickness is, Matis. What has happened to you?' she says. 'Did you do something wrong?'

He nods. 'Very wrong,' he says.

MANON

She seems to be in McBain's office more often than not.

'You're quite the complaint magnet,' McBain says.

'Sorry?'

'Nigel has accused you of bullying.'

'Bullying? Me?'

'That's right. I've seen your management style, Manon, and it's unorthodox to say the least. That pep talk you gave the team, about putting pressure on the One Wisbech lot? That was . . . well, it crossed a few boundaries if you ask me.'

No one asked you she wants to bellow, but does not wish to appear out of control or as if she has an aggression problem. But she sees the landscape now: that McBain is going to punish her for *that* briefing.

Manon says, 'Look, not to put too fine a point on it, Nigel is a useless police officer. Worse than useless.'

'Why, then, did you give him the Saulius case?' asks challengey McBain.

'Well, it wasn't really me, was it?' she says, remembering McBain suggesting Nigel for the job.

'I beg your pardon?' says McBain with a directness that says, *That didn't happen.*

'I . . . I don't know . . . '

'And have you established an appraisal system for him, to manage his performance?'

'What, between the Balsys murder investigation and the Saulius murder you mean? With all my spare time while I clean up the Lithuanian problem?'

'If his performance was below par,' says McBain in a robotic tone, 'you should've been managing that. HR would've assisted you with a performance management road map.'

'Road map . . . ' Manon mutters. 'At this rate,' she says, trying to control the wobble in her voice, 'I'll leave the force and you can promote Nigel to DI, see how you like it.'

'You seem a bit overwhelmed,' says McBain. 'Perhaps some leave would do you good . . . '

'Are you suspending me?'

'Let's not jump overboard. A break might do you good. Davy can step up.'

★ ★ ★

Out in the car park, she feels as if she might be having a heart attack but knows it's more likely to be a panic attack. An officer above her in rank, so a DCI, will interview the team about Nigel's bullying complaint. She hasn't much faith in the rest of them leaping to her defence. Not like she'd win a popularity contest any time soon.

Manon bends double, hands on her knees, and takes deep breaths. She is trying to quell the urge to resign. Perhaps if she wrote the letter, she'd feel better.

The force doesn't want all of her, that's the truth of it. It wants a trammelled down version, the corners lobbed off. And despite her belief in the organisation, she's not sure she wants it back. She hears Mark's voice saying, 'only ten years 'til retirement', but ten years seems an awful long time to suffer at the hands of McBain. Is there a place for her in this top heavy, complaint-worried bureaucracy, where everything has a 'flight path' or a 'road map', most of them nothing to do with nailing a perp?

Must she fill in a risk assessment before diving over a hedge in hot pursuit? It's a while since she's been in hot pursuit of anything other than a curry. Her hedge-diving days are surely behind her. Everything hurts before she's dived anywhere. Also, she'd be suffocated by her bosoms at a run.

And what, after all, is the alternative to being DI on the murder squad, given the rent won't pay itself and she has failed to marry an oligarch? Security advisor to some corporate behemoth? Chasing down benefit cheats?

What about all the sides of her that will go unused to her death? Manon the grime artist. Manon the professional dancer. Manon the kick-ass business mogul. Manon the spiritualist. Maybe not that last one.

About to resign. Can I come over? M

Of course. Bit of a situation over here tho. B

Follow-up text from Bryony:

Peter and I are getting a divorce

Yeah right. Did he buy you antifreeze for your birthday again?

Serious

On my way

Bryony's breathing is shallow and she is beginning to pant. 'Oh Bri, it's OK,' Manon says, after Bri has closed her front door. 'Listen, it's OK, it's going to be OK. Tell me everything.'

'Last night . . . last night, he told me he hasn't been happy for a long time.' This causes Bryony to dissolve.

Manon pulls Bri close, wanting very much to kill Peter at this moment. 'Christ, as if that's any reason to leave a relationship.' She is at once shocked and not surprised at all because people were always pulling crap like this in her experience. It is a constant source of surprise that Mark hasn't left her yet.

'Oh God, what's everyone at the kids' school going to say?' says Bri.

'That he's a bellend and poor you. Seriously, that'll be the extent of it.'

'The gossip.'

'Yeah, fuck 'em. People like to gossip, so what?'

'I asked him if there was anyone else,' Bri says.

'And?' Manon says too quickly, because it is

always her first suspicion, usually correct.

'He said not but the way he said it was . . . odd.'

Nodding, like a wise doctor confirming her grave diagnosis, Manon says, 'The language is always the giveaway. Men always speak funny in a break-up. When they talk, it comes out like their first language is German.'

'Yes, that was it, like he'd only just learned English. He kept coming back to the same phrase, *I'm not a perfect person.*'

'Good of him to acknowledge imperfection.'

Bri crumples again at the thought that there is another woman. 'Oh God, he's fallen in love with someone else,' she says, looking at Manon like she's in free fall from a very high bridge and needs catching.

'Hang on, fallen in love is a bit strong. Fallen in sex, quite possibly.'

'That's just as bad.'

'No it's not.'

'I never thought this would happen. I thought we were in it for the long haul.'

Manon puts a mug of tea in front of Bri, who has lowered herself into a chair at the kitchen table, then gets a tissue cube to put alongside it.

'Have you got any biscuits? We definitely need biscuits,' Manon says.

Bri shakes her head. 'I'm trying not to buy them. Weight Watchers. I've got boiled eggs or carrots.'

Sitting next to her, Manon says, 'Bet you haven't had any sleep, have you, my poor darling?'

Bri shakes her head.

'Is it definitely over? I mean, I'm not saying any of it's good, but maybe it's a blip rather than the end?'

'Not up to me is it? He's the one who left.' Bryony looks at Manon very directly, and her eyes fill up with tears in a way that makes Manon notice how much she loves her, and Bri says, 'This will damage the children for ever.'

'No it won't. Absolutely not. Listen, my mum died, that's damage. You're still alive and there for them. This is just a bump in the road.'

Manon has to push down on the urge to do violent things to Peter, whom she has tolerated these last ten years.

'Oh God!' Bryony wails, a fresh wounded cry. 'It's Bobby's birthday party on Saturday. How the fuck am I going to manage that? I can't cancel without telling everyone . . . '

'Me and Mark will come here and do the party,' Manon says. 'You can stand in a corner chain-smoking and eyeing up the dads. We'll enjoy it, jelly and ice cream and the bumps, all that.'

Bryony looks at Manon suspiciously. 'You won't be rude to the children, will you?'

''Course not! I'm all about the maternal instinct these days.'

★   ★   ★

Despite it being May, the day of the party which is intended to take place in Bri's garden is blustery with a sharp wind, the kind of

278

ubiquitous British summer day when a heavy coat and scarf is required.

'You'd think it could've drummed up an extra few degrees,' Manon complains, peering up at the sky out of the passenger-side window as Mark turns onto the Brampton Road. The good news is he feels well enough to participate, though a kids' party will soon have him back in his sick bed. Teddy is strapped in the back, obscured by Bobby's present (on which Manon has spent an obscene and compensatory amount of money) on his tiny lap. To say that Teddy covets said gift is an understatement. He has not let it out of his sight; asked to 'help' wrap it, and clutches it so hard the paper is tearing at the corners.

The trees bordering Brampton Road sway and billow in the high winds. The hedgerows are burgeoning with cow parsley in flower, and ivy glossy with fresh growth. The greenness everywhere is vivid and inner lit.

Manon tried to bribe Fly into coming along, Fly being better with children than any of the rest of them.

'I have to study,' he said.

'Twenty quid.'

'Seriously, Mum' — he calls her Mum consistently these days, *what joy* — 'I've got exams.'

'All right, forty.'

'You'll be fine,' he said, smiling indulgently as if he were the parent and she the child. It often went like that between them. He comforts her frequently.

Under the porridgy sky, the children at Bobby's party run about chaotically, like drunk midgets, being statues, dancing then plopping to the grass, falling over, ducking, crawling and limbo-ing.

Manon is handing out the sandwiches when a very serious-faced boy frowns at her and asks what's in them.

'There's cheese and cucumber, tuna and sweetcorn, or ham.'

'I like cucumber, but I don't eat cheese,' he says, conversationally, while holding his willy.

'Well, you can either eat what's there or you can go hungry,' Manon replies.

She and Mark gear up for a hula-hooping contest. They hand out the plastic hoops until there is one left, a pink sparkly one, which the remaining boy refuses.

'Don't want a pink one,' he says. 'I only want a green one.'

'There isn't a green one,' Manon says. 'Only this one.'

'I only want a green one,' he insists, with intense eye contact, and it strikes her that if women could only employ this level of intransigence, their pay negotiations would go much better.

She squats down so she's level with the child. 'Thing is,' she says, casting a look around her and seeing Mark eyeing her nervously, 'this is a Join in the Fun party. It is not a Gross Sense of Entitlement party.'

She feels Mark lifting her by the elbow, bulging his eyes at her, and saying, 'Can you dial it down a bit?'

280

'What?' she says.

'He's *seven*,' Mark says, nodding at the child.
'You're never too young to learn manners.'

Bryony is smoking and crying behind a tree in the far corner of the garden. Manon approaches her and rubs her shoulder.

'Can I join you in Eeyore's gloomy place?' asks Manon.

'We've ruined their fucking lives,' Bri sobs.

'That's going a bit far. Firstly, everything is Peter's fault, let's not forget that. And secondly, I think the most you've ruined is Bobby's party, but in fact, I'm doing that on your behalf. And truth be told, Bobby doesn't give a shit, he only cares about the presents.'

'Tell me again how your life is worse than mine,' Bri says.

'You mean my mum dying when I was fourteen?'

Bri nods.

'Well, it wasn't all bad. I never had to text with her. It would've all been in capitals . . . '

'Or with my mum it was sexting,' says Bri.

'Yes! I'd forgotten she was a predator. Bet the gentlemen in the care home miss her.'

'Think that's why I'm friends with you,' says Bri.

'You're friends with me because I remind you of your sexually incontinent mother?'

'Kind of.'

'Thanks for the boost.'

Manon takes a cigarette from Bri, checks that Teddy can't see her, then lights it.

'The old geezers don't miss the uninvited

groping,' Bri says. 'I used to apologise to them on a weekly basis.'

'You'd think they'd have enjoyed it.'

Shaking her head and blowing out smoke, Bri says, 'She was too keen on the element of surprise. No one likes that.'

'I'd love someone to grope me,' says Manon. 'No one's hit on me in years.'

Bri has tears in her eyes and Manon realises she's ventured down the wrong Peter-related alley.

'Don't joke about it,' Bri says. 'If you don't keep Mark happy, he might fall in sex with someone else.'

Manon wants to say, 'He's too tired and he's only interested in takeaways.' But a) How can she be sure? And b) wrong time, wrong place, not that this has ever stopped her.

'Look,' Manon says, 'you can't get through this by telling yourself it's all your fault. D'you think if you'd greeted Peter every evening naked but for a home-made casserole, everything would be fine?'

'It'd be more fine.'

'OK, what if you're sixty-five? Are you supposed to be waxing your arsehole and buying lace thongs at sixty-five? Because frankly, I'm seeing a lot of gardening gloves and cream teas up ahead, and it's not a sexy look.'

'I don't know,' says Bri. 'I just want him back. I wish it hadn't happened.'

'D'you want me to go and talk to him?' Manon asks.

Bri shrugs, which Manon knows is the closest

282

she can get to a yes.

'Least you're not about to be fired,' Manon says.

★ ★ ★

Once everyone has left, Bobby, his younger sister Dora, and Teddy are parked in front of the telly watching *Shrek*, while Manon, Bri and Mark hoover up left-over Hula Hoops and crispy sandwiches, while downing a bottle of Cava. She looks at Mark, and though he's holding up OK, he's not shovelling dried party food into his mouth like her and Bri.

'Thank God that's over,' Bri says.

'Cheers to that,' says Manon, trying to chink Bri with her plastic cup. 'Can you put the heating on? I'm not kidding, but I think I've got chilblains from standing out in the garden all day. It's fucking *May*. This country's a disgrace. Now, can we all workshop my career please?'

'I think you should retrain as a massage therapist,' says Bri.

'*Urgh*, all those disgusting bodies,' says Manon. 'At least the dead can't touch you back.'

'It'll blow over, the Nigel thing,' says Mark. 'You just have to hold your nerve.'

★ ★ ★

She's tempted to text Nigel and tell him where to stick his bullying complaint. Or just text him the words *Fuck you, arsehole*. However, she suspects this would not go down well when it's

283

submitted as evidence in a tribunal.

Could she try to pin it on Davy? Sergeants were meant to manage the team, after all. It wasn't *all* on her, having to follow a UPP (Unsatisfactory Performance Procedure, or Utter Pile of Poo as she prefers to call it).

She is tempted to call Davy and go through Main Lines of Inquiry for the Balsys and Saulius cases. But she finds the only way to deal with her exclusion from the office is to disconnect, so she has decided to fix Bri's marriage instead, as if she is marriage SIO, which is wildly ambitious because look at her own relationship.

★   ★   ★

Peter's office is one of those slab-like grey buildings that looks like it took whole minutes to erect.

Inside, there are square light panels in the ceiling and lots of flimsy partitions, as if the workers are in hutches. Acres of grey carpet and pot plants sitting in ashen soil. The lack of natural light creates a sepia tint inside.

The sign on Peter's door says Area Sales Manager, as if this is anything to be proud of. As she has this thought, she recalls Mark saying, 'You can be a real snob sometimes,' after they'd been to a dinner party with some of the parents from Fly's school and she'd held court about being a copper, behaving very much as if she were the only interesting person in the room. She'd spent a sleepless night hating herself and wondering if everyone else hated her, too, after

284

that. In the morning, Mark looked at her sleep-deprived face and hugged her, saying, 'Come on, disappearing up your own arsehole is hardly the crime of the century.'

She knocks while simultaneously pushing the door open, and the vision before her speaks volumes.

Peter is straightening his tie, laughing. To his left, a tiny woman, circa twenty-five, in a tight pencil skirt, titters also. *This* is who he has fallen in sex with.

'Hi!' Manon booms, holding out her hand to the girl. 'I'm a friend of Peter's WIFE, Bryony, who is also the mother of his adorable but very hard work children!'

The girl, who says she's called Shena, backs out of the room. When the door closes, Manon eyeballs Peter with her knuckle on his desk, while he sits behind it looking terrified.

'So, you're knobbing Shanaya.'

'I'm sorry?'

'You've abandoned your long-suffering wife for that twenty-five-year-old flibbertigibbet. Christ, I thought you were better than that.'

'It's complicated.'

'No it isn't. It's the opposite of complicated. If you knew anything about complicated, you'd stay and take part in it, instead of getting your rocks off.'

'Look, Shena and I, we didn't intend — '

'Oh no! You fought it did you? You knew it wasn't right, but the power of your 'connection' was too strong? Is that it?'

'Well, yes, actually.'

'Give me a fucking break, you, you . . . ' She cannot think of an insult strong enough for this lily-livered toad. 'I'll tell you how this is going to pan out for you, shall I? You'll shack up with Shanaya.' Manon starts pacing as she reads Peter's future. 'Sure, you'll have a few mini breaks, you'll be humping away in a Holiday Inn Express thinking 'this is great', and you'll bob down to breakfast without having to wrestle any small people into shoes. But a few years down the line, she'll want kids, and you'll be going through the whole rigmarole again, except this time, you'll be hitting fifty. You're so tired, you can't believe it. Your older kids — the *original* kids — don't talk to you because you destroyed their childhoods, but *my God* they're expensive. You're paying for two households — and don't worry, I'll be encouraging Bri to take you to the cleaners — and you'll be more tired and more skint than you ever thought possible because sodding Shanaya and little baby Chardonnay want the best of everything. And your original friends, the ones you had with Bryony, will be starting to have decent holidays, involving rafting and long haul flights. But not you. Oh no. You'll be hanging out with the most boring baby group on earth, listening to them obsess about baby-led weaning. *That*'s your future. And Shanaya, who used to wake you up with a blowjob every morning, only talks about whether Chardonnay might be lactose intolerant.'

Peter is ashen-faced, staring at Manon.

'It's called revenge of the second wife. You'll be *longing* to settle down in front of *Happy*

286

Valley with someone a bit portly who doesn't want to shag you, but instead you'll be booking some hideous date night or weekend away involving relentless romance and intense 'lovemaking'.' Manon makes extremely large quote marks in the air, with a little knee-bend (monumentally painful, but she styles it out). 'Because Shanaya is nothing if not high maintenance. And then she'll leave you cos you've got a paunch instead of a Porsche and you're not half as sexy as you used to be what with being exhausted the whole time, being skint and having a dodgy prostate. Or, you could reverse fate.'

During her diatribe, Peter has gradually deflated into a slouch. At this, he at least looks up at her, as if searching for hope.

'You could go back to your absolutely lovely wife — and she really is lovely, and God help her she still wants you because there's no accounting for taste — and you could get old together. And yes, her pants are kind of big and there's not much humping in the Holiday Inn Express, but she's kind and good and funny and loving.'

'I can't find a way out,' he blurts, and it's a half-sob, hiding his face in his hands. 'I never thought it would all blow up like this. It happened, and I enjoyed it, but when I think of the kids and the fallout I want to be sick. It's like a bomb going off. I thought I could have both for a bit, the family and the sexy affair, and God it made me feel alive, really . . . I haven't felt alive for a really long time. But Shena insisted I tell Bri. I've never hurt anyone like that before.' And here he does break down into heaving tears.

'Fancy lunch?' Manon says. And at this he looks up hopefully.

Manon looks at Pathetic Peter, wondering if she might be able to deliver the ultimate prize for her best friend.

She adds, 'Only if you pay and we can talk about what a massive dick you are, though.'

'We can,' he says. 'I've had no one to talk to about all of this.'

★ ★ ★

'To be honest,' he says over a lunch that consists of far too much little gem lettuce for one mouth to marshal. 'I don't know how to get out of it without destroying my career.'

'So move firms. Get a new job.'

'It's not that easy.'

'Yes it is. You're a sales guy not a nuclear physicist. Go work somewhere else. You can't remain in close proximity to Shanaya if you're going back to Bri, that'll never work.'

'It's Shena.'

'Don't care. What you have to accept, Peter, is you've broken the heart of an extremely nice person and as a result you'll have to eat shit for a really long time.'

'I don't know if I can. Won't we both be unhappy?'

Manon shrugs. 'For a while, yes. Look, I really don't like many people. Almost none in fact. But Bri, she's just in a different league. In five years' time you'll be better than ever.'

'Five years?' he says, wild-eyed at the thought.

'My God you're flimsy. You've got to start playing the long game.'

She looks at him, seeing that he is persuadable. The way he blows about with the wind, though, she's not sure he's worth having. And why has she suddenly become the great Marriage Advocate, when a large part of her would love to run off with someone extra-marital? Imagine feeling a thrill, any sort of thrill, instead of just tired, heavy, and as if you've eaten too much yet again?

A twitch in some cortex of her brain throws up a worry: *Was it show and tell at nursery today?*

'Can I ask you something?' Peter says.

'Fire away.'

'Are you happy? With Mark I mean?'

'Of course not!' Manon bellows. 'That's not a reason to leave though, is it? Life doesn't owe you happiness, Peter. It's not your God-given right. Anyway, apparently happiness follows a U-bend shape, and I'm not even at the very pit of the U-bend. My dad has to get dementia and become utterly impossible to take care of, for that to happen. But after that, it's all going to get a whole lot better, so I'm told. When I'm in my seventies on my luxury cruise I'm going to be euphoric.'

★ ★ ★

She'd told Davy she prefers scratchy old towels, but the truth was, she was fucking ambivalent at best. Maybe she had a duty to live life to the full and feel 'alive' the way Peter did when he was

289

shagging Shena. Fetching Mark a black cherry yoghurt didn't really satisfy the thrill-seeker within.

She has been the world's most patient nurse for nigh on three days now, but juggling childcare between herself, Fly, the television and Kristine was no picnic, while coming up with veg-laden dinners that Mark pushed away, looking queasy. His hangdog expression seems replete with blame, as if she needs to make it better, and fast. The truth is, ill people are annoying. They don't help much around the house. And staying in touch with her raw feelings about losing him, acknowledging she wouldn't be happy without him and indeed, that the dearth of generalised happiness was not his fault, is hard. Easier, more efficient, to *become* hard.

There are phases of life that are depressing, when it feels as if things are ending — vigour, fertility, excitement, pleasure — and nothing new seems to be coming over the horizon in the way of refreshment. The blame for this can be laid at the door of marriage, but at what gain?

In this sense she has moved: more saddened, less angry. Still, she wants to say, 'If you're feeling a bit better, could you see to the garden?'

He'd taken wan pleasure in the nursery graduation ceremony; rows of four-year-olds in home-made, cardboard mortarboards with the glue showing in darkened fringes. A fight had broken out in the back row, location of the kid who bites. Teddy and one of his little friends had wandered offstage to play with a train set. Tearful parents laughing at the haphazard line-up of kids

290

who hadn't a clue what was going on but were submitting to it in hopes of a snack. She loved the make-do nature of nursery; slightly chaotic, tolerant, the staff aware these tinies would grow out of everything, even their microscopic attention spans. She loved the weary nursery parents, bar the inevitable one or two who were obsessed with flash cards and extracurricular activities.

'Do you think they're making enough progress?' asked a particularly neurotic one.

'Couldn't give a shit mate,' she'd wanted to say, but instead shrugged, thinking *Life is too short for this conversation and for the flash cards you push in your child's face at home.*

She'd held Mark's limp hand, remembering a receptionist at the dentist, who was on her third marriage, saying, 'I shouldn't have bothered. Should've stuck with the first husband. It didn't get any better with each marriage, you know. It stayed the same.' It seemed rather fortunate, in the olden days, that one of you generally died after approx eleven years of marriage.

What madness is it to feel envious of Bri and Peter, and all the fallout of their separation? And yet they have the chance to make something new out of something old and worn out, while she and Mark take a corner of the carpet each, that they may better brush their relationship issues under it.

Marriage is the long haul, the great Put Up or Shut Up of life. Not being *actually* married is irrelevant. She cannot escape the knowledge of how much she could harm Teddy, at his delicate stage. Recently, she'd been absorbed in a particularly knotty case at work, frowning a great deal at home. She had been, in general, anxious and unfree, unable to make jokes. When she emerged from this period and played with Teddy like she used to — very silly and a little bit rude, bottom and fart jokes abounding — he threw his head back and laughed with a joy she hadn't seen in weeks, and at that moment she realised that for him, her emotions were the weather. What he needed was for her to be all right. If she was all right, then he was all right.

His pleasure in her being back to normal shocked her profoundly because she'd been walking around telling herself he didn't notice; telling herself she'd dissembled sufficiently to disguise her inner torments. *Fool!* He felt every cloud in her psychic world, and this brought with it profound pressure. For she couldn't always be OK. Who on earth could? The best she could do was tell the truth about her effect on him — her hugeness for him. The best she could do was accept that her actions had vast consequences.

DAVY

On Manon's doorstep, with Juliet just behind him, he holds aloft three brown paper bags with handles, the grease spots growing at their base, the warmth emanating from them.

'Hurrah!' Manon says. 'Bring those bags in. Fly? Can you lay the table, dinner's arrived!'

Davy is taken aback by how drawn she is. Her eyes are bloodshot and her brow furrowed. She looks positively elderly.

'Teddy in bed?' he asks. He always likes seeing Ted. Charismatic boy.

''Fraid so. So what did you say to McFuckface?' Manon asks, taking out little foil trays and laying them across the table.

'So, Dean Singlehurst claimed we were harassing him — well, you, specifically. Targeting him because we don't like Ukippers.'

'And you said?'

'I said, 'That's not true. We really like them. They're our favourite type of kipper.''

'Good one,' says Manon.

'Yeah, well, she didn't think so.'

Davy notices that Manon isn't interested in the food, whereas normally she would fight him

293

to the death for the last shard of poppadom.

'D'you not like what we ordered?' he asks.

'No, no, it's wonderful. Anything that's not having to cook is wonderful,' she says.

'How's Mark doing?' he asks, scooping dahl onto his bread.

'He's all right, just having a lie down,' she says. 'He's a bit off his food.'

'Oh, I brought you these,' Davy says, leaning to the side of his chair and bringing up a clump of DVDs. 'DIY store CCTV footage.'

'Be still my beating heart,' says Manon, taking them from him and placing them on a sideboard behind her. 'Juliet, how are the wedding preparations going?'

Fly, a taciturn presence at the table, is all ears. Davy suspects it's because being included in adult interaction is relatively new to him. He's generally been shunted off with Teddy and some cartoons in the past.

'Found an amazing venue,' Juliet says, while picking at some chicken tikka pieces. 'Longstowe Hall? It can take 150 in the Rose Ballroom.'

A clump of chilli has become lodged in Davy's throat. He takes a swig of water.

'Do you even *know* 150 people?' Manon asks him. 'I'd be down to some very tenuous acquaintances with that number.'

'They'll do a marquee in the grounds,' Juliet continues, 'dancing to a live band, although you have to pay for that separately. Everything all in one place, which saves people having to get from one venue to another, y'know. Coaches and what not, from ceremony to reception.'

Juliet regales them about party favours, chair ribbons, place settings, all manner of accoutrement that Davy never knew existed. Juliet looks dreamily at him, saying, 'He just wants me to have the most special day ever.' Juliet tilts her head and Davy kisses her on the lips.

Mark appears in the doorway in his dressing gown. 'Anything left?'

'I've got some chickpea surprise for you in the fridge,' says Manon, getting up and pulling out a chair so Mark can sit at the table.

'Damn,' he says, smiling at Davy and Juliet. 'Thought I'd got away with it.'

'What's chickpea surprise?' asks Davy.

'Trust me, you do not want to know,' says Mark.

'Give us a hand with these plates will you DS Walker?' says Manon, rather pointedly.

'She just loves to boss me around,' Davy says.

MANON

Over the dishwasher where they are bent, she hisses, 'That's quite the pricey wedding you're having. How are you affording that?'

'Skanking,' he says. 'Overtime.' But the beads of sweat are gathering around his hair line.

She straightens, a hand on her back.

'Sore back?' Davy asks.

'Listen Davy, if there's one thing this situation with Mark has taught me, it's that life's too short for bullshit. You need to sort this or it'll sink you.'

'I can't,' he hisses. 'Juliet has booked Downton fucking Abbey for the wedding.'

'So she'll have to un-book it and the two of you will have to go to a caravan in Clacton for your honeymoon and you'll have to get through it because marriage is a shit-show and you'd better start learning a way to navigate it. You need to grow a pair and face up to Bridezilla.'

He looks like he's going to cry and she regrets her harshness. 'Dude, you're salt of the earth. Best of the best. There's no one better than you. Now, give your fiancée an After Eight before you shit on her dreams.'

They look at each other across the open dishwasher door.

'That note,' Manon says, 'I've been thinking about it.'

'How have you got room in your head for the case?' he asks.

'I haven't, really. But I'm angry, and sometimes being angry makes you want to solve stuff. So I was thinking about the note, and I think the reason that note said 'the dead can't speak' is because those words — in Lithuanian — are not recognisable to an English person. Whereas if he'd written 'take a long, hard look at Dean Singlehurst' — '

'Then Dean Singlehurst would have torn it off, got rid of it,' says Davy.

'So let's say for the sake of argument that Lukas wrote the note,' says Manon. 'He knew what to write to make it a murder inquiry, to blow the thing open, without anyone removing the note. So we know our perp doesn't speak or read Lithuanian.'

'Could still be a Lithuanian who can't read. Dimitri might not be able to read.'

'But Lukas would've had to know his killer's reading level. More likely it's someone English.'

Davy nods, and they both stare into the middle distance, out of exhaustion, for a moment.

'Anyway, Dean Singlehurst did it. With bells on.'

'Hmm,' he says, and she can see he's wanting to say something.

'What?' she asks.

'Nothing.'

'No, come on. Out with it.'

He walks to the other side of the kitchen, leans against the units, as if he wants to put some distance between them.

'Can I be honest?' he says.

'If you must.'

'I think you're wrong. I just don't buy that it's Dean.'

'Oh right, Judas, and why not?'

'Well, for one, you'd have to be mega stupid to haul Lukas off in front of a crowd.'

'There's grounds for thinking he *is* that stupid.'

'Well, that's an awful lot of people to control, to keep silent, if you've a brain the size of a pea. So you're saying he's stupid enough to do it in front of twenty witnesses but brilliant enough to ensure they all stay silent? You can't have it both ways. So why, if it's Dean, hasn't anyone squealed? Why haven't the migrants told us all about it? It was in Edikas's interests that they pin it on the anti-immigration nutters.'

'Because . . . because they don't talk. They just don't. 'S'a cultural thing,' Manon says. 'They don't trust authority. What if Dean didn't take him there and then, but came back for him later, when no one was about?'

'I think you're on thin ice. I think McBain is right on this. You've been blinded by prejudice. You want it to be Dean because you don't like his type.'

'Let's go and see him, have a little chat. I'll wear a body cam,' Manon says.

298

*   *   *

Next day, they are back at the Jaws of Bigotry, but there is no answer at the door. No answer on Dean's mobile number either. The house has a deserted feel.

'I hope they haven't shipped out,' Manon says, turning off her body cam. 'I thought he didn't have work at the moment.'

'Might be busy organising a far right rally,' Davy suggests.

'Hmmm,' she says, sniffing the air, looking up at the house, scrutinising the windows. She bends to the letter box in the centre of the front door, lifts the flap and hollers into it. 'Police! Anyone home?'

299

DAVY

Deep breath and in we go, he thinks. Juliet is on the sofa, looking at Zoopla on a laptop on her knees. Davy is pacing.

'There's . . . Juliet? Can you listen? There's something — '

'Ooh look, there's a three-bed in Cambridge,' she says.

'We can't afford Cambridge.'

'We ought to stretch ourselves.'

'Can you stop?'

'Come and look at this one. We could view it at the weekend.'

'No, Juliet, I have to tell you something.'

He closes the lid on her laptop gently.

'What did you do that for?' she says.

'So we can talk. I need to tell you something. A few things, actually.'

She is silent, looking up at him.

'The thing is, even with all the overtime, I can't afford it. I can't afford a wedding and a dress and a honeymoon and a house. I can't take the pressure, Juliet.'

'But you earn good money. I don't understand why we can't buy somewhere. Where does it all

300

go? You don't drink. Do you gamble?'

'No.'

'Do you visit prostitutes?'

'No!'

'What then?'

'I pay the rent on my mother's flat.'

He watches Juliet take this in, the flickering on her face as her brain processes, not just his split allegiances, but also the size of the secret he's been keeping.

'Why didn't you tell me?'

'I don't know.'

'Why doesn't your dad pay it?'

'They split up seventeen years ago. Why should he? He hasn't got anything to do with her.'

'Can't she claim housing benefit? Or get a job? She's holding you back.'

'No, she's not. She doesn't believe in taking from the state. Doesn't want to be a burden.'

'Except on us.'

'Look, she looked after me. Brought me up on her own. She didn't abandon me when I was ten like my dad did. It's right that I help her. It matters to me. I'm sorry if you don't like it, but it matters to me.'

She is quiet for a time, looking at her hands. She looks heartbroken.

'Is that all?' she says.

'What d'you mean?'

'Well, is that all you're keeping from me, or are there a couple of kids I don't know about?'

'No! No, there's nothing. I swear.'

'You make me feel stupid,' she says.

'Why?'

'Because by keeping stuff secret, you don't give me the chance to be ... better than I am. You let me look at properties and book a wedding venue like I'm all greed. And I thought the point of this, us, was to try to be our best selves.'

'It won't happen again,' he says.

'Maybe it will, maybe it won't,' she says, ever so sadly. 'But I won't know which it is, will I? You've spoilt it. And it's so soon to be spoiling it, Davy. We're not even married yet.'

'We don't have to get married, you know,' he says, surprising himself. 'It's not that I don't want to, I'm just saying maybe we've put too much pressure on ourselves. You're the one for me Juliet, but maybe we're OK as we are. Maybe we spend the wedding money on a nice holiday.'

He's sitting beside her now on the sofa, ready to take her hand, but she rises, saying, 'Whatever Davy. I'm going to bed.'

ELISE

A night.

A day.

Another night. She wakes to hear the phone ringing and the answer machine click on.

Her watch says 2 p.m. The Evian bottle she keeps on her bedside table is down to its last third and this she has been rationing. She's been peeing into another, empty bottle, which was mercifully in her bin. When she realised she needed a shit, she emptied a drawer in her chest of drawers, did it in there, covered it with tissues, then shut the drawer in the hope of not gagging on the smell, so much stronger than when it's in the water of a toilet bowl. Toilets, what a great invention. She went back to sleep thinking what life would be like without them.

Still no blood. Baby's all right, that's what she's telling herself, finding herself caring about it, her mind always on it, while her stomach growls with hunger. She feels light-headed, keeps drifting into sleep. Perhaps the fasting will do her good, wasn't it supposed to be good for the body? Wasn't it supposed to mimic how we used to hunt on the Serengeti, the long hungry gaps

303

between kills? Perhaps not so good for a pregnant body, however.

About midway through the first day she'd remembered a bag of liquorice she'd bought at the checkout in River Island and which she had in her cupboard because she hadn't liked it. These she devoured like manna from heaven.

The doorbell had rung at one point, but no one had answered it. Perhaps it was Gary Evans's mate with his bag of rusty tools. Cod botherer. Baby murderer.

DAY 16

MANON

There's nothing Ted loves more than being given a job — taking out the recycling, sweeping patio leaves with a broom, mixing ingredients with a spoon. Provided you didn't mind ending up with catastrophically more mess than you started with, Ted was your ideal working partner. He undertook tasks with enormous vim and absolutely no accuracy.

It was important, also, not to focus on time constraints when working with Ted. Or to ask him to do anything contingent to the task, such as putting on his shoes, about which he could become a picture of cast-iron intransigence.

'You can't sweep the garden in your socks,' she'll say.

'Teddy do it,' he'll bellow, sociopathically.

He is wearing his cycling helmet, of course. They bought Teddy this helmet — Spiderman themed — to wear on his scooter or bike. He point-blank refused to wear it on his bike, but donned it for every meal. He also wore it throughout potty training, a dangerous game for all involved.

She recalls Mark coming in from work and

305

saying, 'Hello Ted, safety first I see.'

Ted, nonchalantly helmeted, was at the table.

'You can't be too careful when you're eating sausage rolls,' Manon had said.

She's reminded, sharply, of the uplift she experienced at the sound of Mark coming in at the end of the day. Everyone home. It never got old, the sound of his key in the door. When Teddy was a toddler and fresh from the bath, he'd pelt down the stairs naked and fly into Mark's arms at the front door, like a winged Renaissance putto.

The way, when she was in the bathroom staring disconsolately down at the weighing scales, Mark would make her laugh by shouting, 'One at a time please!'

Sharp intake of breath, back to the screen.

'Looking for naughty mans,' Teddy says, squinting at the laptop screen.

'That's right, naughty mans,' Manon says, taking a sip of coffee and bracing herself. 'Now, d'you want to see pictures of the naughty mans we're looking for?'

'No Mummy. Teddy watch telly.'

'It's not telly, it's CCTV footage and it's potentially crucial evidentially.'

'Be quiet Mummy.'

'Righto.'

He has eaten a biscuit, and the chocolate cream filling has smeared itself all over his fingertips and chin. This he is transferring to Manon's keyboard. 'Shall we just wipe those mitts maybe?' she says, wishing he'd go and read a book for four or five hours while she gets on with stuff. Why couldn't she have had one of those freak

306

Mensa babies with curly hair and bow ties who pore over encyclopaedias all day? She suspects the Mensa babies are home-schooled. She'd rather boil her head in oil than home-school anyone.

'Naughty mans! Naughty mans!' Teddy shouts, bouncing in his chair.

'Let's have a look. No, Ted, that's just another tubby dad.'

His eyes brim with tears. 'I want tub dad,' he says, and she gathers him up out of his chair, because his moments of being in touch with Mark's illness happen suddenly and at the oddest times and she has to be ready for them. They have not, of course, given Teddy chapter and verse about oncology, but he is all too aware of Mark's reduced state and their adult anxiety. Babies pick up on everything in the room, it's delusional to think otherwise.

In the bath or on the walk home from the childminder are his most common break points.

She holds him very tightly while he snots on her neck. She says, 'Dad's upstairs Ted, he's just having a rest.' His helmet is making the cuddle uncomfortable.

When she senses he's indulging in a pity party, she says, 'How about an episode of *Fireman Sam*?' And both are relieved to be no longer 'working together'.

Back at the kitchen table with a fresh coffee and a wiped keyboard, her focus is better than before. Perhaps really boring footage isn't so boring when the alternative is contemplating the abyss.

She goes to sleep every night with a gnawing

fear that she is falling off a precipice. That she won't survive it. That the worst will happen. Not everyone gets through things. This, she feels, is very real. It is like living with a guillotine blade above their heads.

She has just slotted in the last DVD when Ted requests lunch. She fends him off with a banana so she can watch the footage, from the day before Lukas's death.

'Bingo!' she shouts at the screen and the frozen image of Dean Singlehurst pushing a trolley at the B&Q on Elm High Road, simultaneously picking up her mobile and calling Davy.

'Got him,' she says. 'Dean Singlehurst was in B&Q the day before Lukas's death.'

There is momentary silence on the other end of the line. 'Davy?' she says, wondering if the connection has been lost.

'It's not illegal to shop in B&Q,' he says.

'But the same rope.'

'How do you know it's the same rope?' he asks. 'How have you seen blue rope on black-and-white CCTV footage?'

She cannot precisely answer this. Perhaps there was a label on the packaging, but she has a memory of seeing it.

★ ★ ★

'I'm telling you now, you do not want to arrest Dean Singlehurst,' says McBlame Game from behind her desk. Picking up paperclips, laying them in her pedantic pot.

'And I'm telling you I do.' Manon is pacing,

308

barely able to suppress her anger at having to run her work past this miserable mandarin. They have not discussed the fact that Manon is back in the office, nor that she has viewed CCTV footage at home. How many murderers has she arrested? Countless. And here she is asking permission from someone who wouldn't know RIPA (The Regulation of Investigatory Powers Act) if it bit her on the bum. 'He's shopping in the DIY store the day before, he marches past the migrant house on the night of Lukas's death. He's totally pumped, he's got Shane fucking Farquharson backing him to the hilt, who by the way should be charged with conspiracy to murder, that'll get you on the news.' She notices McBain sit up to attention at this. 'Dean reckons he's the Trump of Wisbech. Witnesses say he got in a car.'

'Why haven't you got the car?' asks Challengey McBain. 'And I thought Mr Tucker's car was traced going to Hinchingbrooke on the night of Lukas's death.'

'Well . . . yes, it was, but we don't know who was in it, and seeing as he's dead, it's hard to ask him. Dean, on the other hand, is spewing hate on to Facebook before we even know that Lukas is dead.'

'Yes, but it was fairly generalised hate, wasn't it? Not like it said, 'Lukas Balsys dead.' The Press will say we're mounting a politically correct crusade against One Wisbech.'

'No they won't because a) we're not and b) he did it.'

'Every jot of investigative work will be sifted

309

through after the fact.'

'That's fine, I stand by all of it.'

'It's to protect you, as much as anything, Manon. If the complaint escalates, it goes out of the local force and up to professional standards, and if it escalates again, then it goes up to the IOPC.'

'Look,' says Manon, trying her hardest not to patronise this halfwit. 'This happens *all the time*. People who are under pressure love to complain. It's part of our job not to cave in.' She thinks of Gary Stanton, who wouldn't have batted an eye over Singlehurst's handbag waving. And Harriet, who would've been emboldened by it. 'Fuck 'em!' Harriet would've said, coming over all *Thrones*, 'We're going in.' But Stanton and Harriet had the confidence derived from experience. They knew how it went, had seen it all before.

Manon says, 'Maybe I shouldn't arrest him, but Davy can, or you for that matter. Wear a body cam, that way he can't come back at us over it. Dean Singlehurst murdered a human being. He hung him from a tree. He wants arresting, asap.'

'What's his motive? Just that the boy was foreign? Seems a stretch.'

'It might seem a stretch if you're not a Nazi.'

'You see? There you go again. If you call him a Nazi, you won't come out of this clean. Look, let me take this upstairs, get some advice on it, OK?'

Manon leaves the room without either roaring or kicking the door.

310

Kim greets her on her way out. 'Mrs Tucker's here to see you. I've put her in interview room one.'

* * *

Elspeth Tucker is pacing the room, holding her arm, which is bandaged to the elbow. She looks unkempt and under-slept.

'Hello,' says Manon. 'Are you all right?'

'I need to talk to you,' says Mrs Tucker, urgently.

'Yes, of course, take a seat.'

'I'd rather stand. Look, it's about Jim's car, the Nissan Micra.'

'Yes?'

'I lent it to Lukas. On the day he . . . disappeared, I gave him the car key. I did it so that he could get away. He was being abominably treated.'

'You gave him your husband's car?' Manon says, not wishing to sound too incredulous and failing in this.

'Yes.'

'Not your own car?'

'No. I have a very expensive car. I do see that it was a provocation too far for Jim, what I did. But I just didn't care by that point. I was so sick of him. On the day of the fire, he found out. Well, I told him actually. The car was back by that point. But he was livid. That was why he torched the place.' She starts to cry. 'I wanted rid of him. Jim I mean. That's terrible — a terrible thing to say about someone I used to love.'

'So Lukas had the Nissan on the night of his

311

death. He drove it to Hinchingbrooke.'

'I don't know. He had the key. I gave him the key.'

'How did you get the car back?'

'The key was put through our door, the car was parked back in our street the following day.'

'Do you have anyone with you at the moment? Anyone you could stay with? You seem in a bit of a state,' Manon says.

Elspeth shakes her head. 'I'm fine. I'll be fine.'

'We'll need to forensic the Nissan,' Manon says.

Mrs Tucker digs in her handbag, comes up with a single car key and lays it on the table in front of Manon.

'Where are you staying?' Manon asks. 'The house can't be habitable.'

'No, it isn't. I'm at the Rose and Crown hotel.'

MANON

'Come with me,' Davy says, leading Manon to the video room. 'This,' he says, pointing at a frozen frame on one of the monitors, 'is the CCTV footage you located of Dean Singlehurst in B&Q. Now watch it again. There's no rope.'

She watches Dean Singlehurst, a painter and decorator, more often an odd-job man these days, in B&Q buying *something*. A grey mass in his trolley. In all likelihood, he was probably in B&Q most days.

'Can you see any rope?' he asks.

She shakes her head.

How can she do the job when she fills in the narrative? Is she a fantasist, looking for the perp she wants? Is Holmes there to protect from *her*? She is filled with doubt. An unsure person. Bigots have feelings too. Perhaps Teddy is right, and she is Defective Inspector Bradshaw.

Could McBain be the clear thinker, the one with foresight, the only one to put the brakes on?

'I can't do this any more,' she says to Davy.

'Yes you can. You're just going through a rough patch. Happens to the best of us. 'S'understandable, given the pressure you're under.'

313

'If I can't do my job, I'm not anything,' she says. 'I *am* the job.'

'Well then, that is serious. No one should *be* the job. What would you say to me, in this situation?' he asks.

'Learn from it. I'd say learn from it.'

'Yes, you would. That's exactly what you'd say.'

'It's too much, I *was sure*,' she says. 'I mean I really felt sure.'

'I know.'

'Talk to me about the case,' she says.

'OK.'

'So Lukas had a key to the Nissan,' she tells him, 'which drove to Hinchingbrooke on the night of his death,' she says.

'Oh, right.'

'So we need to forensicate the Nissan to find out who was in the car that night.'

'Right, I'll get onto that.'

'What about the witnesses who said Dean got into a car in Prospect Place?'

'Well, he might have done. Might have got a lift home, or out for a celebratory pint with Farquharson.'

'Then why not tell us that? Would've given him an alibi.'

'He was angry with us by then.'

'Who brings the Nissan back from the crime scene?'

'We don't know. None of the ANPR shots show the full number plate, let alone the driver's face.'

He gets up to leave. 'Boss?' he says. 'You've

314

still got it. Don't worry.'

'I've got something. Not sure it's *it*.'

'There's always security work.'

'You and me Davy Walker, guarding a warehouse full of Lucozade, watching *Cagney and Lacey* all night.'

'What's *Cagney and Lacey*?' he says.

'Christ.'

★ ★ ★

Later the same day, he approaches her desk.

'Slight problem with forensics on the Nissan,' he says.

'Yes?'

'It's disappeared. We can't find it. So I put a new ANPR search on it. It's in Frinton-on-Sea.'

'Any clue who's got it?'

'Nope.'

'I might pop down to the seaside, check it out.'

'Could be totally unrelated to the migrants. Could've just been nicked.'

'Yes, I know. But what else am I gonna do?'

'We could revisit the Jaws of Bigotry,' Davy suggests. 'Talk to the daughter.'

'That can wait,' says Manon.

'You don't want to face Dean Singlehurst?' Davy says.

'Not really, no.'

MANON

If she goes via Cambridge, she's liable to get snarled in traffic but it's a good forty minutes shorter than the alternative route according to Google maps and, given it's two hours each way, it's going to be very tight indeed. She'll have a maximum of a couple of hours there, at best. Fly has offered to not only pick up Teddy, but tend to Mark when he gets home, though he needs less tending these days. He has progressed to getting dressed, and occasional washing (small mercies), though he seldom leaves the house.

She doesn't know what she'd do without Fly.

The Fenland skies are enormous, filled with bulbous cartoonish clouds. She has the heater on because — *what summer?* The country is going to the dogs and the weather is just reflecting this state of affairs. Her family is crippled, but perhaps they'll get better, reach a new status quo involving wellness and intimacy and leisure time (hollow laugh), all reflected in elegant interiors with functional coat hooks and everything. She has resisted saying to Mark, 'If you're home all day, could you get the drill out?' Instead, she says, 'Bye,' while he flicks between breakfast TV channels.

316

Perhaps the world can turn away from nationalist populism, but about this she is even less hopeful. In the past, it has taken a war . . . Perhaps she will leave the police, become a Zumba instructor, be in the best shape ever, in fact be addicted to exercise and its endorphin high (she has NEVER experienced this — the only sensation she experiences during exercise is an intense desire for time to pass more quickly), and run off with a younger lover. Perhaps.

Her little marker in the sand will be to throw Dean Singlehurst into a very secure category A prison, where he can agitate other tattooed meatheads while she throws away the key. Or actually, maybe a Halal prison would suit him better, where he could be comprehensively worked on by the Muslim Brotherhood. Dean Singlehurst blinking into the light at the end of his sentence, wearing Kurta Pajama.

★ ★ ★

Road cameras have put the Nissan on the seafront and this she drives along, leant forward like an eighty-year-old, peering through the sea spray. She has a frozen shoulder, which twinges periodically. Stiffness in her knees. Tension made real.

The sea is like a grey bed sheet recently smoothed, its few wrinkles swelling in to shore in wavelets.

She's not searching for a killer this time, she's searching for Matis, because she suspects that Matis is her most sig wit of all sig wits, her

317

witness to the murder of Lukas Balsys. Matis's testimony, if her hunch is right, can actually put Dean there, with the rope in his hands, and then maybe someone will believe her.

There, in the mist and spray of the front is a small, red car. She parks up behind it. It is stationed in front of The Golden Sands Café, the lettering of which is written in the same 1970s font as 'BBC Television Centre' used to be on telly when she was a child. This café seems as good a place as any to start, seeing as how she's desperate for a pee after two hours in the car. She pushes open the heavy metal door and is greeted by the smell of deep fat frying and the texture of grease on the air and on the surfaces. This place resembles every greasy spoon she's ever been in, as unloved as the bodies that feed here. A few tabloid-reading men are scattered at various tables with their full English breakfasts, their giant mugs of tea, their squeezy ketchup bottles shaped like beef tomatoes. Behind the counter is a hard-faced woman with peroxide hair.

'Hello,' says Manon, keeping her powder dry, badge-wise.

The woman only lifts her chin in response.

'Do you know of a Lithuanian chap called Matis at all?' Manon asks.

'Who wants to know?' says the woman, in an indisputably Eastern European accent that makes Manon whip out her badge.

'Cambridgeshire police,' she says. 'And what's your name?'

The woman appears to freeze momentarily,

gives Manon a queasy forced smile. 'Lina,' she says. 'My name is Lina. Why do you want to know?'

'I'm investigating the murder of Lukas Balsys. Know him?'

'Yes, I did.'

'And Matis?'

'Why don't you come upstairs. We can talk in private.'

'What about the café? You have customers here . . . '

'Everyone out!' Lina shouts, with all the charm of Putin at a military parade. 'We close early!' She flips the closed sign on the glass door, holding it open for the men — complaining yet bovinely compliant — to file out. They had all had their fill, it seems.

'Matis? Is he here?' asks Manon, while Lina turns the key in the lock.

Lina turns to look at her. 'Soon. First you will come upstairs.'

Manon baulks at the imperative, but realises it is only a figure of speech in translation. The Russian-sounding accent makes this woman sound a lot harder than she is. At least, that's what Manon hopes, given she is single crew. She feels for her phone in her handbag.

'D'you think I could use your loo?' she asks, following Lina up the stairs.

'What is loo?'

'Toilet. Could I use your toilet?'

As soon as she is inside the internal front door to the flat, Manon smells bleach. More bleach than is domestically appropriate. Swab-the-decks levels of bleach.

319

'There,' says Lina, pointing at a bathroom directly in front of them.

'Thanks,' says Manon.

On the toilet, ever so relieved to be pissing, she texts Davy:

Golden Sands Café, Frinton on Sea.
Execute warrant and join me ASAP
Urgent backup needed

MATIS

He had watched Lina open the chest freezer to retrieve a moussaka for the café's lunchtime trade. Beneath neat stacks of Tupperware boxes containing pre-cooked meals was the body in a foetal position. Visible in the upper right corner of the freezer is the torn branch of neck, like a splintered pencil with the lead missing. The stem red and frozen solid. The rest of the cadaver, in clothes dusted with ice, was hidden beneath neatly labelled frozen food.

Matis had always wanted to see a brain. He had a scientific kind of interest in what the grey matter might look like — the jelly that contained love and memory, personality and soul, the unconscious and the conscious, creativity and violence. Although in this case he was unlikely to discern love or creativity. What surprised him was how un-squeamish he was about the butchery of Dean Singlehurst. Was it because he hated him? Or because his life since leaving Lithuania had brutalised him? Either way, what would have been unthinkable a few weeks ago was just another thing to get done.

Elise's father had fallen foul of the arsenic

fairly fast, but, while he squirmed and groaned on the floor, Lina held a pillow over his face, telling Matis at the same time, 'I don't want him vomiting and having the squits all over this flat. You never know how long the poison will take. This is quicker.' Her brisk manner and the way she chatted while Dean ebbed away were like someone changing a nappy while conducting a conversation. He was haunted, still, by Lukas telling him about Elise being pregnant, about his baby, somewhere out there. That's what brought about all this trouble.

When Matis was given the task of dealing with the English knucklehead's body, he didn't get to see a brain. There was too much blood. The body, he found, was like an unyielding and very squeezy orange, leaking uncontrollably everywhere.

The neck had been very like meat. Bent over the bathtub, he'd had to saw hard in the way you would have to if you tried to cut through a leg of lamb. Lots of gristle and bone and those truculent nodules of spine. He needed a meat cleaver, and the mess was horrible.

'How does cutting him up help?' he asked Lina, who had told him what to do and how to do it, as if human butchery were her nonchalant sideline. *Cut the head off, would you like cheese in your omelette?*

'We hide bits of him in different places, over time. Bury bits, drive them far and wide so they aren't discovered. Railway lines. There's always bits of human along railway lines. No one worries about it.'

'And where do we keep him while we're separating him up?'

She nodded out towards the back, and they both knew she was indicating the chest freezer in the garage, which they padlocked to protect their stock.

'Only you and I have keys,' she said.

'I worry how relaxed you are about all of this,' Matis said, with a wan smile. 'How long before I'm in the chest freezer?'

'We didn't have a choice. He would've killed us, so we killed him. Don't make a big deal out of it.'

★　★　★

It had been his fault that the knucklehead had found them in Frinton. He'd thought he was texting Elise. Lukas had told him about the pregnancy, had said, 'Make a life for your child.' He still felt bound to obey Lukas, even now.

Texting was better than ringing when you didn't have much English.

'Where are you?' he typed.

His phone told him the text had been delivered and read. But then there was a sizeable gap in time. Perhaps she wasn't sure about him. Fair enough.

'Who is this?' came the reply.

'Matis.'

'What do you want from me?'

'To be together. I know about our child.'

Another gap in time before he saw the . . . that tells him there is a reply coming.

'Where are you?' the text asked.

He gave his address and told her to come and find him.

They had the future to talk about.

★ ★ ★

It wasn't Elise, with a rucksack full of things and a belly full of child, who pushed open the café door the next day. It was her father.

Matis was assaulted by nausea, which reared up like an ocean wave. He turned to Lina, shaking, and told her who this was, this man at the counter with the pockmarked face. Lina, calmly deep fat frying, nodded and said, 'Leave him to me. Maybe I can satisfy him with something else.'

Matis said, 'Be very careful. He is dangerous.'

'I want you to listen to me,' Lina said in Lithuanian, shaking some chips in a frying basket while they frothed the oil, 'I want you to heat a lasagne. Put in half of this powder.' She handed Lukas a tiny plastic bag, the size of a stamp. 'Bring it upstairs, OK? Don't get any of the powder on any other food and don't touch it yourself, is that clear?' She keeps her voice neutral, as if she is giving him a shopping list for the cash'n'carry. 'Wash your hands after.'

She turned to Dean, and in her best English said, 'Why don't we have a nice private chat upstairs?' She could turbo-charge the charm when she wanted to, dissolving the ice.

'I don't want you, I want 'im,' said Dean.

'Yes, yes, we talk about everything upstairs,' she said, showing him the stairs to the flat.

MANON

The flat is immaculate in the way only properties without children can be. No plastic detritus, no pants across the floor, no novelty slippers. Manon feels a stab of envy for its orderliness. Everything just as you left it. Nothing *fiddled with*. Everything she owns is fiddled with by some small person who couldn't give a shit whether she can find her glasses later on. On her way out of the house this morning, she'd tripped over a garishly be-fluffed Furby, which started babbling at the walls in saccharine electro-baby-talk. Insufferable thing. Cost a fortune, cluttered up the house, and Teddy barely gave it a second glance.

In the soullessly tidy living room is a man who closely resembles the images she has seen of Matis via old social media posts.

'Matis?' she asks.

He looks up, looks enquiringly at Lina.

Lina says something to Matis in Lithuanian, and Manon thinks he might actually exit his shoes, so high does he leap from his seat. He puts his back to the wall. Says something back to Lina. There follows an agitated conversation

325

between the two of them, Matis seemingly terrified, Lina calmly delivering responses. Manon would put money on Lina's lines being instructions, but she can't understand any of it of course.

'Can we offer you some lunch while you are here?' asks Lina, with another of her applied smiles. She is Stepford, in the Melania Trump mould, with that slice of ice/hinterland of damage. Or is Manon guilty of anti-Baltic feeling? We are the sum of our prejudices, she reminds herself. 'A lasagne or moussaka perhaps?' presses Lina. She jabs her head towards the door, indicating to Matis that he should get a wriggle on.

'It's Matis I'd like to talk to actually,' says Manon. She is contemplating the lunch. Would it hurt to say yes? Feminism would like her to have that slab of lasagne, to be free enough to embrace the carbs.

Davy and his warrant won't arrive for some time, after all.

MATIS

'You want to put a police officer in the freezer as well?' he says, wildly.

'Calm down,' says Lina. 'She's a detective and we have a body in the garage.'

'I know that! And you want to make it two!'

'Stay calm. You're being hysterical.'

'How are you so calm?'

'We don't know what languages she speaks, so use your brain and shut your mouth,' Lina says. 'All you need to do is get out a lasagne and add the rest of the white powder. We can decide what to do with her body later. She looks like the sort who won't refuse food.'

'You're insane. We cannot kill a police officer.'

'We can and we will. I did not travel halfway across Europe to be put in prison. I did not put up with the things I've put up with, for it to end here.'

'Listen, the Nazi was one thing. But a police officer? You're mad. I can tell her what happened to Lukas.'

'Did you say Lukas?' the police woman interjects. 'Because that's why I'm here, to ask you about the murder of Lukas Balsys.'

327

'This is why you are here?' says Matis, beginning to reassess the situation. She doesn't know about the English guy in the chest freezer. She's here about Lukas.

'Why else would I be here?' she asks.

'No, no. Of course. Lukas, yes. He is best friend.' He can tell the truth. For a while at least. This allows him to exhale, his solar plexus to unclench. Perhaps this is what he needs: to confess.

'Do you know what happened to him?' asks the policewoman.

Matis nods. Lowers himself to the sofa, two hands on the edge of the cushions, holding on.

⋆ ⋆ ⋆

He has some words, more than he used to. Work. Rest. Money. But connecting them is hard. The tense, the *have, did, make, felt*. These he lacks. The 'I', the 'we'. He begins to type sentences into his phone, then shows the policewoman. But this, like everything in his life, feels like failure. He needs to express to her what that night was like.

'English peoples,' he begins, trying to do without the phone, 'no like other country peoples like me and Lukas.'

'Yes,' she says, sitting forward as if she is enthusiastic for this story.

'I cannot . . . my English,' he says.

'You need an interpreter,' she says.

He knows this word, has been told by the other men to say it if police trouble occurs. He nods.

'We will get you one, later,' she says. 'Don't worry.'

Nevertheless, he wants to express to the policewoman the vivid horror of that night, the sorrow it had left within him. The sorrow he feels might never leave him.

'They come to house — '

'Who is they? The One Wisbech marchers?'

He nods. 'Say 'Where is Matis. Who Matis?''

She nods, waiting.

'Lukas say, 'I am Matis.''

He doesn't know how to describe Lukas standing in front of him, facing those nationalists, his hand held behind him to stop Matis from coming forward.

Into his silence, she asks, 'Why were they looking for you?'

'Elise,' he says.

'Dean Singlehurst's daughter?' she says.

He nods.

'The men, they go.'

He thinks of his relief when the skinheads retreated from the house. They threatened Lukas, but they were all bluster. But Lukas, for whom a darkness had descended that was all-encompassing, didn't retreat. He had become his darkness, wedded to it.

'He say me he have car,' Matis says to the policewoman.

'Who said that?'

'Lukas.'

'Mr Tucker's car?' she says.

He nods.

'Where did he want you to go?'

329

She sits forward, listening. He has wanted to unburden himself for the longest time.

Everything is my fault, he types into his phone, for translation.

She tilts her head at him with sympathy and concern.

But language lets him down, and he senses they are both exhausted at the effort of communicating, like being at a very loud party and having to bellow into someone's ear, you can't help thinking it'd be easier not to.

It had been the worst night of his life. He's not sure he can put it into words, even in his mother tongue.

BEFORE

'Where are we going?' Matis asked.

'I have looked it up on a map. Police headquarters, it is only an hour from here,' said Lukas.

There was some rope in the boot, rope that Edikas had brought to the house for a washing line. Matis worked out his plan and wanted to stop him from doing it.

He said, 'You should look after Janina, marry her.'

'I can't,' Lukas said. 'I just can't. This way, I free everyone in that house.'

A negativity had taken over Lukas's whole personality. Sure, he was always pessimistic, but this new depth of sorrow felt deep and contagious.

'You think this is virtuous,' Matis told him. 'But this is cowardly. Why can't we just talk to the police? I wrote down the name, Operation Pheasant. Not this, Lukas, not this.'

'Because if we go to the police, they take their time and Edikas will murder us. I do not want to be killed by him. I want to choose the manner of my death. I have the right to make that choice.'

331

'Don't, please. I can get us out.'

'No you can't. You keep saying you can but you can't. I'm not afraid. I feel liberated by knowing I can make this choice. It is the right of human beings to choose whether to end their lives. They used my body. Now I can use my body. It's my right to do what I want with my body. I feel I am going to die anyway.'

'And never mind your mother, your father, Janina. Never mind me?'

'There are bigger things at stake,' he said. 'My mother is not helped by me being in that house, doing that work. I would rather be dead than a slave.'

'But nothing lasts for ever,' Matis said. 'It will be over some day and life will change, improve. You can be happy again.'

'But I will always know what happened to Janina. That's irreversible. I can't live with it.'

'She has to.'

Matis thought he could persuade Lukas during the long drive, while the satnav on his phone guided them to Hinchingbrooke.

'Why do you need me, then?' Matis asked. He wanted nothing to do with it.

'I don't want to die alone. I think you owe me that.'

And he did. He owed him so much more.

'If we do it near to police headquarters, they will find my body and investigate. It also means Edikas won't find it first or stop us.'

'But they will know it is suicide.'

'I've thought of that.'

'I don't want to watch you do this.'

'You have to.'

'What about me? What do I do?'

'Go back. Watch the police break it open. You will be freed with the others. Return to Klaipeda. Make sure Janina is OK, that she is looked after.'

'You should be doing that.'

'You are in no position to tell me what I should be doing,' he said.

'You have a martyr complex,' Matis said bitterly. 'This is your superior way out, but you leave everyone else in the shit — me, Janina — we have to deal with it. We are forced to live.'

He wondered if Lukas wanted him to watch as a kind of punishment. And when he was dead, Matis was sick on the ground, but then he felt free of Lukas. For the first time, Matis wondered if this had been such a good friendship. Does anyone want to be friends with a Jesus-type? With Lukas, he perpetually felt he was falling short. The guilt was terrible. It still is terrible.

MANON

All this time she has sat silently with Matis, who appears to be in a world of his own.

She says, 'The note, what did it mean?'

He shrugs. This really is beyond his language.

Christ, this is taking an age, and she is flipping starving. Starving equals irritable.

'Do you have a laptop?' she types into Google Translate. Perhaps they could get somewhere with a bigger window for text.

'Lina have,' he says. He brings it to the dining table in the lounge and they move to sit before it.

'I have go out,' Lina says, popping her head around the door to the lounge. 'There is lasagne for you in kitchen.'

Manon is tempted to leap up and say, 'Forget the interview, let's head straight for the carbs!' But realises this would appear indecorous.

While Manon can touch type and then swiftly push the screen towards Matis for reading, when it's his turn — and let's face it, he has more to say — it is an agony of finger typing. Her stomach growls as she watches him hover and peck at the keyboard at glacial speed. It is painful. She could wait until she has him at

334

headquarters with an interpreter, but a) she wants to know, and b) Davy's going to be at least another hour. She wonders if she should haul Matis off, leaving the premises empty, but she doesn't trust Lina not to return with a crack team of evidence removers.

The slowest interview in history reveals two things: the significance of the crime scene (close to police HQ) and how Lukas got into the tree (under his own steam).

'What did the note mean?' she has asked.

After about three hours of finger typing, she reads Matis's response.

'It could not look like a suicide note. Anything more specific . . . it would look like a suicide note. Then, no investigation. I don't know why he chose those words, except it needed to look like a murder. He did not consult with me on it.'

'Why didn't you tell us straight away?' she types, in under a minute. Then leans back in her chair, knowing it'll be a millennium before the reply.

'Because the investigation would be closed down. Because I would be under suspicion. I had to lie low and watch it break open. That is what he told me. That is what I did. Just before he did it, he told me I had a child. That Elise was pregnant and that I should make a life for my child. I do not know how to do that. No one wants me.'

When she looks at him, there are tears in his eyes.

'Shall we take a break?' she says.

ELISE

She left her water bottle out on the window ledge in the rain and some water has gathered in it, not nearly as clean as she thought rainwater would be. Instead of tasting of purity, fresh from the skies, it tasted metallic and was slightly brown. Acid rain, maybe. Still, water is water.

She knows from a school history project on the Irish hunger strikers in the Maze prison that human beings can last up to forty days without food. It's hydration that matters. She sips, carefully rationing what she has. Fortunately, the skies keep on delivering this summer. She empties her urine bottle out of the window and puts that out as a rain catcher. That way she can catch in the wee bottle and drink from the drink bottle at the same time.

Sips, sleeps. Sips, sleeps. No more shits. Nothing to shit. Her father has not returned. Perhaps he has moved house and decided not to take her and her EE baby with him. That'd be fine by her.

Her dreams are solely about food. Mainly egg-based. She visualises fried eggs, hard-boiled eggs, omelettes. Small sideline fantasies about

336

bread and butter, then back to the Spanish omelettes. Even the thought of a raw egg gets her going. When she is awake she feels nothing but depressed. A deep inner hopelessness that she's only previously experienced on a diet. A thick slice of bread and butter would make her un-depressed, she feels sure.

When she gets out. When, not if. She will feast for a whole day on anything her heart desires, never mind the calories. And she will bathe, and she will leave her family home for ever and ever, and she will never have anything to do with her father.

This is her mantra, before she re-descends into the pillowy comfort of Eggland.

DAVY

A warrant on what grounds?

He texts Manon.
Sees the three dots which tell him she's writing.

Over-powering smell of bleach

We're talking crime scene bleach, not the cleaner's just been bleach

Also, woman Matis has shacked up with is shifty

He feels annoyed. She knows the process, the online form to fill in, the Skype call with three magistrates in which he must swear on the Bible and persuade them, and where the word 'shifty' simply won't cut it. They won't grant a search warrant on the basis of 'shifty'. She knows it and he knows it. There would have to be grounds for thinking their body was in there, some piece of evidence that linked the murder victim or perp with that address.

But they have their body. Lukas Balsys's body is in the cold store.

Davy'll have to head up to Frinton-on-Sea, get inside the property with her, see if they can sneak a looksee. Her chatting while he skulks about. He frowns. There must be some way of opening the place up.

Then he has the idea. Googles 'Frinton-on-Sea local authority'.

He picks up the landline and calls Tendring District Council.

MANON

The lasagne is in a white oval pie dish. The minced beef looks plump, its dark grains oozing fat. The cheese on top has bubbled and browned, somewhat crisp but not burned. She can see the beautiful cheesy carb layers. It smells herby, of oregano, its warmth propelling the meat juices towards her nostrils.

The Beauty Myth has it that this lasagne is empowering. That refusing its warm, enriching goodness is giving in to further oppression from the Patriarchy. The lasagne calls to her feminist self, pulling her in with its coiling finger of steam. Refusing the lasagne would be akin to tying an apron (fashioned from kale) around her tiny Fifties' waist and hurrying to get the tea on for her brutish fella.

Oh, and they have even supplied a little side salad, flecked with salty feta. It is past 1 p.m. She generally likes to lunch at 11 a.m. at the latest. In winter, she's been known to have dinner at 4 p.m., then tell Teddy it's time for bed at 5. The joys of him not being able to tell the time.

Matis is looking exceptionally nervy, as if he might bust a blood vessel at any moment.

'D'you want some?' Manon asks him.

'No,' he says, very quickly.

'Sure?'

When she picks up a fork, he yelps.

When her fork tentatively pushes the cheese crust, he puts his hand to his brow.

'Stop!' he shouts. 'Do not! Do not eat!'

She looks at the lasagne, feels the squirming of her empty stomach. He must know what's in it, she reasons. There must be something unsavoury in there. But then, what harm can it do? Even if it's horse meat, it's not as if she's carrying Teddy inside her.

DAVY

He arrives at the Golden Sands Café at the same time as the food safety inspectors.

They bang on the door, in spite of the Closed sign. Then wait, expecting nothing, as the clouds scud over the sea. The tarmac on the coast road is wet. So are the black-painted bollards that line the front. One of the inspectors wears a name badge that says Lindy Worthington.

'Perhaps there's a side entrance,' Davy says, walking a little along the pavement. A door to the left of the café's entrance appears to be residential and has a bell. This he rings.

It is answered by a young man who has the hallmark grey Lithuanian pallor.

Davy, rather than holding up his badge, with which he may be refused entry, steps aside for the food inspectors who can barge their way in anywhere that sells food. *They should have blue lights and battering rams*, he thinks.

Davy follows them in.

He finds Manon in the flat's lounge, staring at a laptop. Matis runs up the stairs behind Davy. Lindy Worthington and her colleague have made their way into the café and are poking around in the kitchen. Davy can smell bleach, industrial levels, just as Manon had described.

'Everything OK?' he says to her.

'First they offer me lasagne, then they tell me not to eat it,' she says and he can tell she's hangry. 'Then he threw it in the bin, the nutter. Matis knows what happened to Lukas by the way. I haven't managed a full interview because we need an interpreter and if I have to watch him finger type for much longer I might kill myself. Anyway, the long and short of it is Lukas hung himself, close to police HQ and left that note to prompt a murder inquiry so we'd break open the slave situation.'

Lindy Worthington has jogged up the stairs and is breathless in the doorway.

'Who's this?' asks Manon.

'Food safety,' says Davy. 'Faster than a warrant.'

'I need the keys to the chest freezer,' Lindy says.

Matis, whose eyes have been darting person to person with a look of confusion on his face, looks to Manon, who is typing into the laptop 'keys for freezer'.

'I no have. Lina have,' Matis says.

'I've got some bolt cutters in my boot,' offers Davy. 'If it would help.'

'Get the bolt cutters and pop off that padlock,' Manon tells Davy.

They all thunder down the stairs and gather in front of the chest freezer in the garage. Manon keeps a close eye on Matis, who looks febrile enough to attempt a runner. She wonders if she

343

should cuff him, but wants to maintain the atmosphere of openness between them for future interview.

They watch Lindy Worthington lift the freezer lid. Inside are row upon row of rectangular ready meals. Lindy lifts a couple of them and the body becomes visible.

'Glad I swerved the lasagne,' says Manon.

'Who is it?' Davy asks.

'He hasn't got a head,' Manon says. 'Hang on though, didn't Dean Singlehurst have a tatt like that across his knuckles?'

'Don't think he'll resist arrest this time,' says Davy.

'Put the call in to SOCO. And let's get Derry out here. I'm assuming the food safety people won't be wild about this on a hygiene level.'

In a corner of the garage, Lindy Worthington is pale and writing furiously on her clipboard.

'Your first body in a chest freezer?' Manon asks, cheerily.

'It is . . . yes,' says Lindy, looking as if she might be sick.

'Stop showing off,' Davy whispers to Manon.

When they return to Matis, he's looking more than a little wild-eyed. 'Where is Lina? Where she?'

★ ★ ★

'Matis, how did Dean find you?' Manon asks.

'I text Elise. She is have baby. He have her phone.'

'Would you ring the number for us please?'

344

says Manon. She mimes making a call.

After a time, a jaunty ringtone emanates from the chest freezer.

'Right, we better get to her,' Manon says to Davy, putting in a call to control and saying, 'I want you to send officers to an address in Wisbech. There's a girl I'm extremely concerned about. An ambulance, too. She's pregnant.'

ELISE

The room is spinning, she's so light-headed. It feels as if her body is levitating from the bed. If this is death, it's quite pleasurable.

The last thing she hears is 'Police! Police!' and a great bang. A fantasy of rescue born of brain malfunction?

She passes out.

MANON

They have captured the plethora of Frinton CCTV and located Lina, aided by her mop of peroxided hair. *Come on Lina*, Manon thinks, *a wig at the very least*.

They watch her meet with a man in a sheepskin coat, very Seventies Martin Shaw in *The Professionals*.

'Who's *that*?' Manon asks Bridget.

'Ah, now, that is Jonas, Vasil's right-hand man.'

'Don't mind if I do,' says Manon.

'You and every other female in Cambridgeshire. Lithuania's answer to Channing Tatum. Jonas is quite the Lothario when he's not laying block paving.'

'Same,' says Davy.

Bridget practically splits her sides laughing, and Davy blushes. *Still in the game*, thinks Manon, admiringly.

'Right, so Jonas has picked up Lina. What's he going to do with her?' she asks Bridget.

'Well, Jonas's success with women is something of a thorn in Vasil's side. A threat to the silverback, if you like. Either Vasil will be setting aside his rivalry with Jonas and joining them,

347

airline tickets in hand, or he will have instructed Jonas to dispose of Lina. And by dispose, I very much mean dispose. Impossible to tell which.'

'Do we have eyes on Vasil?' asks Manon.

'Yup, surveillance outside his house, which he knows about, obviously, and therefore can evade.'

'And do we have a mobile number for Jonas?'

'Yes.'

'Right, let's track that phone and follow them closely. We don't want anything happening to Lina on our watch.'

'Lovely lady that she is,' says Davy, and Bridget smirks.

They track their progress to the Sofitel Heathrow, where they are burning up a tab with gay abandon. Manon and Davy have driven straight there from Frinton. Bridget has met them from Wisbech.

Manon has a quiet word with the manager, who expresses some anxiety about the bill.

'Don't you worry about that,' says Manon, implying mendaciously that the police will cover it.

They must lie in wait for Vasil. If they arrest Lina and Jonas, Vasil would be alerted and hot foot it out of the country to somewhere nice and warm with no extradition treaty.

'I need to arrest Lina on a murder charge,' Manon says.

'Well,' says Bridget testily, '*I* need to arrest Vasil and Jonas on exploitation charges.'

Manon looks at her watch. She also needs to get home to Mark, Teddy and Fly. And pick up some Persil non-bio. Why can't these things happen more within office hours? And they have Matis in custody awaiting interview, the clock's going on that one. *This* is why she's on cold cases, because juggling this much involves dropping something. She pulls Davy aside. 'What do we do?' she asks. 'This could be hours. Matis is in custody with the sand running down. We need to draft in team two, I think. We can't run Lukas, Saulius and Dean Singlehurst all at the same time out of one team.'

'Shall I call McBain?' Davy says.

'I ought to do it,' she says, with a heavy exhalation. 'Yeah, d'you know what? You call her. 'S'better coming from you.'

* * *

McBain, to her credit, swings into action, locating coppers across three counties to swoop in on the Sofitel in a joint op that sees the arrest of Lina, Vasil and Jonas.

Davy stays and oversees, but Manon drives away. She's arrested enough perps in her time to know how it goes, and it's the family she wants to see more. When Davy rings to update her, he says, 'I'm guessing there's quite a bit of paperwork relating to this.'

'It'll bury us until Christmas,' she says.

* * *

'Shall we watch the ten o'clock news?' asks Mark.

349

'D'you know what? I don't think I can bear it.'

There are days when she watches the TV news or reads the newspaper headlines and the feeling of existential despair is too great; the feeling of history forgotten. A re-run of the 1930s, and look how well that turned out. A consistent failure of leadership, so epic it makes McBain look positively presidential. One in twenty people either don't believe the Holocaust happened or think it's been exaggerated. Fly came home from school, and, while doing some history homework, told her Hitler happened because of German poverty after the First World War, and she'd swung around shouting, *You can't explain evil away like that. You can't just . . . therapise it, put it in some nutshell like it's done!* And he was like, 'Whoa, OK, calm down Mum.' She was at a loss to tell him how much it mattered, what kids are taught in school.

She'll have to be in early to get going on the Matis interview, but she has little lust for this collar. There isn't much satisfaction in processing someone who's been exploited. The sense of good overcoming evil, the thread she tries to grasp at in every case, is well and truly buried in this one. In order to feel the beauty of her calling, there needs to be a decent delineation of black and white, but in this case, all is grey. Sadness and loss through all of it. Perhaps cold cases and being home by five isn't such a bad gig. Perhaps Davy can keep the excitement of MCU, given he at least still gets a kick out of it. Perhaps life's satisfactions reside more in a chickpea curry and bathing the baby than uncovering torsos in chest freezers.

'You watch the news,' she says to Mark. 'I'm going to bed.'

LATER

Matis is charged with the murder of Dean Singlehurst and the attempted murder of Manon Bradshaw, after toxicology on the lasagne found it laced with arsenic. Glenda was positively hopping with excitement at this double collar without attendant complaint. Not only can the dead not talk, they cannot escalate up to the IPCC either.

It was Vasil who had gifted Lina the Golden Sands Café, possibly to get Matis out of the picture and prevent him yabbering to Op Pheasant. Under normal circumstances, Edikas would've just beaten Matis up, threatened to kill him, maybe a dog bite or two. But the net had been closing around Vasil, and he knew it, so different tactics were required to ensure Matis's silence.

Lina, it became clear, was more a Mrs Vasil than the *actual* Mrs Vasil, who has taken the children back to Klaipeda along with much of her husband's fortune. As with Edikas, Lithuanian police are unable or can't be arsed to locate Mrs Vasil.

Elise, who recovered in hospital (she'd been hypoglycaemic; some orange juice soon sorted her out) and whose pregnancy survived, told Manon about the back-street abortionist who also filleted fish and whose daughter, it emerged, would never be able to have children thanks to his handiwork. Side prosecution, always satisfying.

Kim took over the Saulius case.

'That woman wants promoting,' Manon told McBain. 'She's fucking brilliant.'

And under Kim's watch, once the words 'gross negligent manslaughter' were mentioned, the farmer became extremely voluble about the hiring of migrants as chicken catchers and the chap called Edikas who was the go-between. 'I didn't pay *them*,' the farmer said, 'I paid Edikas. I was assured the wages would be passed on.'

Matis tried to pin everything on Lina. Lina, he said, killed Dean Singlehurst then butchered the body. Lina put arsenic on Manon's lasagne, just as she had on Dean's. 'I would not know where to get arsenic.'

'To be fair, he did try to stop me eating it,' Manon told the investigating officers, she being recused from investigating her own attempted murder.

Dean's head rolled out of a tipper truck in Mepal Quarry, just off the A142 outside Ely. His features, as they tumbled, looked weirdly at peace — as if he could finally stop hating everyone. Forensics on the Nissan found Dean's blood in the boot. Manon could picture Lina marching out of the café carrying Dean's head by his hair, as if she were taking out the recycling.

Operation Pheasant, armed with box upon box of paperwork from Edikas's attic, plus the farmer's testimony, broke open the Lithuanian hub, freeing everyone and emptying the HMOs in which they were inhumanely housed.

If only Mr Tucker could've seen this, Davy thought sadly, as the front garden was cleared. Most nightmares end if you only give them time. *This too will pass* was a good enough motto to live by.

The builders were in on the Tucker side, repairing the fire damage. Mrs Tucker was in and out, project managing the works, saying 'No, the woodwork in Skimming Stone.'

'I was one cheese topping away from death,' Manon tells Davy, as if this is the primary takeaway from the whole sorry saga.

At the inquest into Lukas Balsys's death, the coroner recorded an open verdict, as sometimes happens in suicides where the deceased's intent cannot be proved beyond reasonable doubt. Matis gave evidence through an interpreter.

'It wasn't just Janina,' he said. 'Lukas was ill. He felt terrible in his body. His situation changed him from being a bit pessimistic to being deeply sorrowful. Deeply lost. I was responsible for this.' At this he broke down crying in the witness box, seeming very like a little boy.

The open verdict denied Ludmilla Balsys the compensation Davy so wanted her to have. Lukas's body was repatriated for a funeral not attended by Janina.

Davy was relieved to see Juliet looking at

beach-side UK destinations for their holidays. 'I've always fancied the Jurassic coast,' he told her. 'Fossil hunting in Lyme Regis.'

'We could read *The French Lieutenant's Woman* to each other, learn about Mary Anning,' Juliet rejoined.

Manon told Bridget that what they needed on their Fenland Exploitation Team (aka Op Pheasant) was a Lithuanian, and that she had just the fella.

'He was known as Demented Dimitri,' she said.

'I'm not liking the sound of this,' said Bridget.

'I'm telling you, he's salt of the earth,' she said, wondering how long it will take Bridget to crack on to Dimitri. Less than half a day, would be her guess.

MANON

She is in McBain's office yet again, like the delinquent pupil always in with the headteacher. Is this where she gets her marching orders or, worse, is told she's on traffic for the foreseeable?

'I had a discussion with Sir Campbell Baxter,' says McBain, with some relish at the name drop. She's all about being upwardly connected, all about the network.

So, it's got to the level of Two Soups, as Campbell Baxter is universally known. Two Soups was made Cambridgeshire commissioner when Sir Brian Peabody went off to have an aneurism or similar.

'He is allocating special resources into an investigation of the One Wisbech march as a whole, including Shane Farquharson, with a view to charging them with incitement to racial hatred. There is quite a lot of enthusiasm . . .'

'Course there is, she thinks. Farquharson is a thorn in the side of Two Soups' political mates. Once you get to commissioner level, you start hobnobbing in Annabel's with the home sec, and who do they hate more than the opposition?

356

UKIP. A criminal charge is just what democracy ordered.

'And,' says McBain, as if procedure were her metier, 'we have all resources, according to Sir Campbell Baxter, to investigate.'

'What about Nigel's complaint?' asks Manon. 'Aren't I *persona non grata* at the moment? Aren't I on gardening leave?' God, she would love a bit of gardening leave. *Coat hooks off the floor, get to the bottom of the laundry basket. Read a book in the bath!* She is so bone tired.

McBain coughs. 'Well, no,' she says. 'DCI Connolly has found, following interviews with the team, that the complaint is without foundation.'

Bloody hell, the team came through for me.

'Actually, Campbell Baxter would like you to lead this one,' says McBain.

Two Soups asking for me personally. I have arrived.

'To that end, I've had a word with Nigel,' McBain continues. 'I've suggested to him a role as school liaison officer would offer reduced hours and a more family-friendly working pattern. Chance for a fresh start. He's taken up the offer.'

Lazy man jumps at chance to work less. How he will inspire young minds!

Manon says, 'Well, I think they met all the tests for incitement to racial hatred. The issue will be witnesses. The migrants have scattered, and it's doubtful whether the One Wisbech lot will dob each other in. We have got Elise Singlehurst, she's a witness. And Mrs Tucker. And their Facebook page is pretty incendiary.'

'I'm sure you'll come up with the right result,'

says McBain. 'We've got the resources, let's use them. Also, prosecution of Farquharson would put us in the spotlight, in a very good way. A high profile team doesn't get cut in the same way, you see.'

★ ★ ★

That summer — the summer of Mark's recovery and Fly acing his GCSEs — turned into a broiling heatwave. The summer when the air was so thick with heat, you could chew on it. Heat of the kind that blasted you on the steps down from an aeroplane in tropical countries. Heat that wrapped itself about your face like wool.

That summer a dragonfly got trapped in Manon's kitchen, frantic papery rustling as it bashed itself against glass. Un-beautiful. And the ennui returned.

Sweat, constant sweat, heavy legs, head struggling through the heat-wool. Movements slow, outside worse than inside. Hot, turbulent nights, wanting the covers for protection but throwing them off. Eyes stuck together, mouth thick. Crispy garden borders, parched grass. Electric fans sold out across the land. It was 29°C by 9 a.m. By 3 p.m. it was 35°C.

The summer of drinking ice, of longing for shade, switching to the other pavement if there was a sliver of it. Of heat beating out from melting tarmac. Of fires across moors and forests and in urban flats. At dusk, of hearing cutlery on plates from neighbouring gardens, of peach skies aflame, of watering systems dripping at twilight, the temperature only marginally lowering. Crying

358

children unable to sleep in the heat. Shorts dried to the texture of cardboard on the line. The summer when sweat ran down the backs of the knees, even when watching TV.

Peter moved firms and went back to Bryony, who took him in with a kind of sad resignation. 'It's not the same,' she told Manon. 'It's broken.'

'Bound to be,' said Manon.

'I'm glad he's back,' said Bri. 'For the children.'

'Oh *love*.'

'We're 'working on it',' she said, drawing quote marks in the air. 'It's fucking exhausting.'

'Give it time.'

'Yeah, I will. But I can see why people plump for something shiny and new and not totally depressing.'

'Maybe you can grow to love the damaged thing,' says Manon. 'Y'know, like an old sweater with holes in it.'

'This is a marriage we're talking about. It's hard to forgive someone. If I'm honest, I'm not even sure I *like* him. How about you?'

Manon exhales. 'Oh, I'm all right.'

She and Mark were back to a kind of normality, punctuated by scans at the hospital. Clear for now. 'You keep thinking, right, we just have to get through the next thing. But there's always something behind that. But anyway, I think I'm about to Ring. The Changes,' Manon says, dramatically.

'Oh yes? What changes are these?'

'Leave the Force. Portfolio career. Home

359

working will mean I can attend Zumba daily, maybe even twice daily, and be in the best shape ever.'

'How often do you attend Zumba now?' Bri asks.

'I haven't found the right class, that's all. The right fit.'

'You can't leave the police. You *are* the police.'

'I'm not though. I've lost my mojo. All the *good guys versus bad guys* that I used to rely on? I don't know who's who any more. There aren't any good guys or bad guys — only the exploiters and the exploited. Makes the job close to impossible. Last year, I arrested a man who had shot his father in the kneecap. His father who had raped him since the age of four. I wanted to hand him my weapon and say, 'Do the other one and we'll call it even.' This is not the right response from law enforcement. Take Matis, right? He's nineteen, for fuck's sake. A child — practically Fly's age. And he's about to spend half his life in prison. I mean what's the point? Yes, he'll get hot meals, but prison is endemically violent, it doesn't offer *anything*. Cuts are so savage, they're incarcerated twenty-three hours a day. Matis won't get a degree, probably won't even learn English. He'll come out at, what, forty, unable to function, of no use to society. What did I achieve there? You need the moral compass of a ten-year-old to be a police officer.'

'Must be why I'm fine then,' says Bri, icily.

'You can't just do the same thing until you die though.'

'Why not? Why can't you trundle into the

same office, have sex with the same person, order the same takeaway, for thirty years? What's wrong with that? Why do we need to keep reinventing ourselves?' There is a sharp edge to Bri's diatribe. 'It never fucking works, anyway.'

'Maybe we're living too long,' Manon says, wanting to be conciliatory. She and Bri, they have to be on the same side. 'So instead of one life, one career, one marriage, we need to parcel off several lives.'

'How will you make money?' Bri asks, sulky now.

Manon shrugs. 'Maybe Mark's ship will come in. Anyway, lots of places need to consult police officers — companies, about security, VIPs, about personal protection.'

'You're not going into personal protection! Can you imagine you, running alongside a limo like some out-of-puff Clint Eastwood?'

'Yes, but I won't be out of puff, will I?'

'Oh yes, Zumba, I forgot.'

'TV cop dramas, crime writers, they need to consult police.'

'Please don't go,' says Bri. 'Who will I meet for pepper-flavoured water in the canteen?'

'Colin. There's always Colin. If he hasn't left to become PPO to Shane Farquharson.' Bri has tears in her eyes, and in response, Manon tries to lighten the mood. 'Thing is, you always want to be growing, changing, developing.'

'*Urgh*,' says Bri, standing with an over-dramatic scrape of her chair backwards along the floor. 'I can't listen to this. It's like being with Peter, who '*grew*' a stiffy and stuck it in Shena. *I* am stasis.' At this she beats a flat palm to her heart. 'Me! I'm the going nowhere option. I'm the soup with Colin scenario. I'm fucking sick of it.' She is full-on crying now.

'Oh Bri, I didn't mean to hurt you.'

'Well, you did, and *he* did. I want everything to stay the fucking same. For ever. Why is that such a bad thing?'

Quietly, Manon embraces Bri. 'I'm not leaving you, you daft girl.'

'It feels like it.'

'Look, this is dry-clean only, so watch the snot. If you feel like this, I won't go. Simple as that. Or . . . you could join Bradshaw Consulting. Attic room. Internet. Fan heater if we can stretch to it. Coffee machine. M&S website. You know you want to.'

'Sounds like a fast track to bankruptcy.'

'It's my only chance to lose the weight. Seriously. My eye-to-face ratio has tipped into full doughball. I am 97 per cent face. Shall we get some bar snacks?'

When the heavenly little bowls of salted almonds and olives arrive, Manon says, 'Of all the things I've lost, it's my mind I miss the most.'

She can *almost* follow a television series, but finds herself often bewildered or asleep, open-mouthed, head back on the sofa cushions. And she is so *forgetful*. It's as if she can feel the Swiss-cheese holes in her brain. She loses things, constantly; roars in impotent fury at the house for swallowing whole her reading glasses, iPhone, notebook, retail receipt, an array of single socks,

362

her favourite top. She's always searching and never finding, always wandering into rooms and not knowing why she's there. Her holiday packing has become incompetent: someone always without pants or socks, usually herself.

'I miss my pelvic floor,' Bri says, 'speaking of which, I've got a cough.'

'Oh no,' says Manon. 'The laundry!'

'Yes. AND. I attempted yoga while under intense pelvic floor pressure.'

'Did you blow off?'

'Worse.'

'Wet yourself?'

She nods, sheepishly. 'And the yoga teacher came over to correct me. Correct my lower regions, to be exact, and I could tell she got a full Whiff of Goat from my undergarments.'

'Nightmare. The scent of the gentleman. She probably thinks you're homeless. You know those ads, the ones for TENA Lady? They are aimed at us.'

'I know. Also, elasticated slacks at the back of the Telegraph magazine.'

'Bring it,' says Manon. 'My targeted advertising is all slippers, walk-in baths and funeral costs. Which is bang on the money.'

ACKNOWLEDGEMENTS

As with all the Manon novels, I am indebted to DI Graham McMillan (known universally as Maca) who advises me on all things procedural. We have worked together for five years now and it's one of the great pleasures of the job. For this book he put me in touch with Sgt Chris Acourt of the Fenland Exploitation team in Wisbech (Operation Pheasant) who talked to me about his work tackling modern-day slavery. The situation facing Matis and Lukas in this book is based on real exploitation cases involving agricultural work in the Wisbech area.

I knew if I flew to Klaipeda, I'd end up wandering in a lacklustre way around the known tourist routes, but these aren't the places Matis and Lukas would have frequented or lived. I needed a Lithuanian guide.

Thanks to Oliver King, at Channel Four News, for putting me in touch with my fixer in Klaipeda, Audrius Lelkaitis.

With Audrius, I really struck gold. I was looking for someone who could be my interpreter, show me around the poorer neighbourhoods of Klaipeda, where tourists don't habitually go. He took me to Rybporte, close to the docks; he chatted to residents and got us invited into a flat — this became Lukas's childhood home. In a bar, he struck up conversations with Russians and translated all for me. This was the basis for Viktor's diatribe.

Thank you Tom Happold for plotting discussions, early reads, ideas and support and for pushing me to go to Lithuania. (I'm blind, so this kind of trip, to somewhere totally new, alone, is particularly challenging for me.)

Above all, thank you Tom for being the best husband possible through my year of horrendous illness.

Thanks George and Ben Happold for finding my glasses (over and over and over again), bringing my slippers, the cuddles and the laughs. You're the best children in the world.

Thank you Susannah Waters for an early edit, way back when. And to Sian Rickett for reading and making excellent suggestions. And lots of sitting by my bedside, and coming to appointments.

★   ★   ★

Those who know me, will know I've faced an extremely frightening illness over the last year, during which I've been hugely supported by family, friends and all the people who publish me.

Thanks to team PRH in America: Andrea Walker, Cindy Murray, the late Susan Kamil, for being Manon fans. I'm so sorry for your loss. And team HC in London: Suzie Dooré, Ore Agbaje-Williams, Ann Bissell, Kate Elton. I can't imagine being published better or enjoying being with my team more.

Thank you Danny van Emden of West End

Lane Books — my favourite book emporium — for cheerleading and lovely chats.

Above all, thank you Sarah Ballard, the greatest agent of all time, for getting me here. And for dealing with all my paperwork while I was in hospital (sorry for that short straw).

We do hope that you have enjoyed reading this large print book.

Did you know that all of our titles are available for purchase?

We publish a wide range of high quality large print books including:
Romances, Mysteries, Classics
General Fiction
Non Fiction and Westerns

Special interest titles available in large print are:
The Little Oxford Dictionary
Music Book
Song Book
Hymn Book
Service Book

Also available from us courtesy of Oxford University Press:
Young Readers' Dictionary
(large print edition)
Young Readers' Thesaurus
(large print edition)

For further information or a free brochure, please contact us at:
Ulverscroft Large Print Books Ltd.,
The Green, Bradgate Road, Anstey,
Leicester, LE7 7FU, England.
Tel: (00 44) 0116 236 4325
Fax: (00 44) 0116 234 0205

Other titles published by Ulverscroft:

PERSONS UNKNOWN

Susie Steiner

As dusk falls, a young man staggers through a park, far from home, bleeding from a stab wound. He dies where he falls, cradled by a stranger, a woman's name on his lips in his last seconds of life. DI Manon Bradshaw can't help but take an interest — these days she only handles cold cases, but the man died just yards from the police station where she works. She's horrified to discover that both the victim and prime suspect are more closely linked to her than she could have imagined. And as the Cambridgeshire police close ranks against her, she is forced to contemplate the unthinkable. How well does she know her loved ones, and are they capable of murder?